Gracie Ayers

# The WEAVER'S GIRL

***About the Author-*** Gracie Ayers has written four books about Furnace Town. She has chosen this locale that she knows so well as the setting for her first novel, ***The Weaver's Girl.***

***About the Book-*** "Think, think," I said to myself. "There has to be a solution to this problem. People don't just disappear into another stratum of time. Or do they?"

Callie Brentwood has lived an uneventful life until she discovers that her fiancé has racked up gambling debts totaling more than $500,000. In anger, she drives to a nearby historic site, hoping to calm down. There something strange happens to her and she is transported back in time to the 19th century. She is swept into the everyday lives of the people around her. She shares their triumphs and tragedies; finds happiness and true love.

Will Callie stay, or return to the 21st century?

"Gracie Ayers creates a sublime Currier and Ives landscape where the reader wants to linger but the adventure makes the reader eager to turn the pages to find out how it ends." Stephen Long, Palm Springs, CA

"*The Weaver's Girl* is a wonderful blend of tranquility and excitement." Eloise Haas, Chicago, IL

# The WEAVER'S GIRL

*Gracie Ayers*

LINDEN HILL PUBLISHING
Princess Anne, Maryland
www.lindenhill.net

# LINDEN HILL PUBLISHING

11923 Somerset Avenue
Princess Anne, MD 21853
www.lindenhill.net

Printed in the United States

Cover art by Jeanne du Nord © 2007

ISBN 978-0-9704754-8-0

Library of Congress Control Number: 2007925642

Dedicated to Lee Davies, sister extraordinaire,
and to Seth Ayers, grandson and friend.
Thank you for your encouragement.

With special thanks to Kathy Fisher
and Linda Davis for so generously
sharing their knowledge of
Furnace Town's history.

# THE WEAVER'S GIRL

## Chapter 1

I stepped closer to the old furnace and ran my hand along the bricks. They felt pleasantly warm to my touch. I was suddenly drained of energy and decided to sit before my knees gave way. Dropping my backpack to the ground I pushed myself up against the bricks. The heat of the bricks seeped through my shirt. I took out a bottle of water and an apple and tried to think through Jack's problem while I ate but I always arrived at the same conclusion. He was in trouble - big time. And his trouble was why I found myself in this little, off-the-beaten-path place called Furnace Town.

I felt fear crawl into my chest with a familiar tightness. *Jack, Jack, how could you do this to us?* I asked myself. I tried to relax but my mind insisted on replaying the nightmare. I gave in and let the events of the last few days scroll by, one after another.

Jack hadn't been truthful with me. I'm a people watcher. Always have been. And that's how I knew he was lying. When you're a people watcher you pick up on all the little characteristics that make a person that person. A certain smile. The casual brushing of hair from the forehead. Crossing the left leg over the right when seated. Tugging an earlobe during a conversation. Tucking a lock of hair behind an ear while talking on the phone.

Take Jack, for instance. He's not a nervous person and under pressure does not bite his nails or chew the skin on his thumbs. He doesn't fidget but can sit for hours in the same position, barely moving. He has the wonderful ability to really focus on the project at hand and doesn't lose his cool if things don't quite work out the way he wants them to the first time around. Jack's

1

recent behavior was a dead giveaway. He was not himself and was definitely hiding something from me.

For one thing, he had begun to pace. Endlessly. For no reason at all. He'd go from one room to another in the suite and then start all over again. Whenever the phone rang, he'd jump and then race to pick up before I did. He hated carryout but for the past two weeks had insisted we have most of our meals at home. I found myself on the highway every evening picking up orders from our favorite restaurants.

But the thing that really triggered my mental alarm was his total inability to concentrate on his new novel. Jack is a writer and a darn good one, too. We had rented an oceanfront suite at the Mermaid in late March. He said the sound of the ocean helped him write and it must have because he had made wonderful progress on the book. He thought he'd be finished before Christmas but in late August something happened.

He couldn't write. This was no ordinary writer's block. I'd lived through those many times. He'd sit at his computer and try to write. Sometimes he'd actually print a page and then crumple it before tossing it into a nearby wastebasket. Before many days had passed, the words would begin to flow again and he'd sit for hours in front of the computer, locked in a fantasy world that would soon become a novel. This time no words had come for several months. He didn't turn the computer on for days at a time. Instead of writing, he spent hours sitting in the chaise on the balcony staring at the waves rolling in on the beach. He began to go for long drives in the afternoon, to clear his head, he said. He needed to be alone to get his thoughts together.

I asked him if he was ill. He told me he felt fine. I asked him if his publisher was unhappy with the book. He told me the publisher loved the new book and was anxious to see the completed manuscript. I asked him if he wanted to go back to Baltimore to finish the book. He shook his head and then gave me a look so strange I felt a shiver of fear run down my spine. It was obvious he didn't want to tell me what was wrong and I decided then and there to ask him no more questions. But that didn't keep me from wondering and, yes, worrying just a little, too.

The worst part of the nightmare began two mornings ago. I'd gone for my regular workout at a little gym on Ocean Highway, not too far from the Mermaid. When I'd left the suite, Jack was still in bed but it was well after 11 a.m. when I got back and I figured he'd be up and about and hopefully busy at the computer. I parked the car in the lot, grabbed my gym bag and made a beeline for the elevator.

I called out to Jack as I opened the door to the suite. No answer. "Jack. Jack," I called again. The silence enveloped me.

Why is it you can step into an unoccupied house and know immediately no one is at home? I knew Jack wasn't here before I called his name the third time.

I wondered how long he'd been gone. A casual look around the living room gave me no answer. Things seemed to be just as I had left them several hours ago. I looked for a note but found none. To be truthful, I didn't expect to find one but I looked anyway. I went to the kitchen and poured myself a large glass of orange juice and sipped it slowly while I checked out the rest of the suite.

The bed had not been made. The coverlet had been thrown back to the bottom of the bed and both pillows were tossed onto the carpet. The bathroom was a mess. Damp towels littered the floor and the shower stall had not been wiped down from Jack's morning shower. His electric razor was on the countertop as was his deodorant and after shave lotion. The room gave the appearance of having been used and then hastily vacated.

When I stepped into the bedroom Jack used for writing, I heard the hum of the computer. *Has he been working*? I wondered. I saw no paper in the wastebasket or on

3

the floor. *Is that a hopeful sign?* I asked myself. I touched the mouse and brought up what was on the screen. Poker! The man had been playing computer games before he left. I turned away from the computer in disgust and that's when I noticed the blinking light on the answering machine.

Three blinks, three messages. I slowly sipped my orange juice and watched the little red light. Blink, blink, blink. Pause. Blink, blink, blink. It was as if the little light was sending me a message, an ominous one, one I didn't want to get. The rational part of me told me to push the play button and hear the messages but a stab of fear kept me from doing so. I don't know how long I stood there mesmerized by the machine, sipping the juice. I drained the glass and set it down gently on the table. And then, I pushed play.

The first message was a sales pitch for storm windows. I thought the woman would never finish her spiel. The second message was from Jack's publisher. His cheery baritone filled the suite. "Jack, Bart here. Hey old buddy, how's the book coming? You haven't sent me a thing since the first fifteen chapters and I'm getting a little worried that we won't meet our deadline. We already have people working on the illustration for the book jacket. Give me a jangle sometime today to bring me up to date. Thanks."

The machine clicked several times and the last message began to play. The caller didn't give his name but the intent of the message was clear. It was spoken in a clear, no nonsense voice. "Jack. Missed seeing you at the last five games. I'm counting on seeing you this week. You have quite a bit of settling up to do and prolonging the payoff will just make things more difficult for both of us. Don't put me in a position where I'll have to do something I don't want to do." I hurriedly hit save and the machine clicked and rewound. I pressed play again and listened to the messages a second time.

4

What games? When had Jack found time to play games and where? I replayed the messages a third time. The fellow meant business. Jack must owe money, a lot of it, to someone. But who? The same questions ran around and around in my head but no matter how hard I tried, I couldn't come up with an answer to a single one of them.

I don't know how long I stood in that room, watching the little red light go blink, blink, blink, and pause. The last two messages kept playing over and over in my head. Jack had more than one problem. Brad was badgering him for the rest of the book. I didn't blame him. Jack had gotten a hefty advance based on his initial outline as well as on his four previous best sellers. If he didn't finish the book, there'd be the devil to pay. And the other character wanted money. From the tone of his voice, he wanted it soon, as in the day before yesterday.

I went to the kitchen and rooted in the refrigerator for something to eat. There wasn't much to my liking. I fingered a yogurt carton and checked out the sliced ham. Neither appealed to me. I finally settled for a couple of chunks of sharp cheddar and a glass of milk. I found a box of crackers to go with the cheese and carried it all out to the deck. I sat in the chaise with my feet propped up on the railing and nibbled away. And thought.

*How much money did Jack owe? And to whom?*

I didn't know how much advance money Brad had given him. My guess was a lot because we had been living very well at the Mermaid. Ocean front two bedroom suites are not exactly cheap, especially during the summer season. Jack had a big nest egg to use for gambling. And obviously, he had used it.

I sat on the deck long after I finished the cheese and crackers. I desperately wanted Jack to pop through the door and tell me this was all a big nightmare but he didn't. I noticed the shadows lengthening on the beach. Was it late afternoon already? And still no sign of Jack.

I decided to go for a run on the beach. I stuffed a power bar and two small bottles of water into my backpack and headed for the elevator barely conscious of what I was doing. I got off the elevator on the mezzanine, walked down the hall and through the indoor pool and bar area. The bartender flashed me a big smile. I smiled back and gave him a little wave of my fingers. I went out the door and down the steps to the beach.

I barely cleared the steps before I began to run. The sand felt fluffy under my feet but when I got down to the water's edge, it was wet and packed hard. I finally settled on a pace and picked my feet up and put them down without thinking much about what I was doing. The beach was almost empty so I didn't have to worry about avoiding people. I noticed several sand castles standing tall and proud while waiting for the first few waves of high tide to reach them. I tried to wipe all thoughts of Jack from my mind but I couldn't.

I usually iron out my problems while I run. I start out with something heavy on my mind and by the time I return, I have a solution worked out. But not today. No solution came to mind. How could it? I needed to talk to Jack. I ran for more than an hour before I opened my backpack and took out the power bar and a bottle of water. While I ate and drank I watched the waves of the Atlantic Ocean wash up onto the beach. I wanted those waves to soothe me, to take away the terrible pain I was feeling but that was not to be. I put the empty bottle in the backpack and headed for the suite.

Jack was not there. I was not surprised. But he had been. The little light on the answering machine was no longer blinking. I wondered when he had been here and for how long. I checked the master bedroom closet. His clothes were still neatly on the hangers. His luggage was untouched. *At least he hasn't left me high and dry,* I thought with relief.

There wasn't much left for me to do but wait. And I do not wait well. I took a hot shower and washed my long, dark hair. I put on a fresh shirt and shorts. I made the bed and straightened up the bathroom. I was not hungry but decided I might as well eat anyway. I fixed a cold cut sandwich and poured a glass of milk. I felt too confined to sit at the kitchen table so I took my meal out onto the deck. I sat in the chaise and slowly ate.

Daylight turned to dusk and finally to night. And still I sat. Stars popped out over the ocean. One second the sky was black and the next it was peppered with tiny pinpoints of light. I looked for constellations but I was never very good with that stuff anyway and I couldn't find a single one. I watched a spot on the horizon grow lighter and lighter and suddenly the moon appeared, a huge yellow ball, almost full. It cast a long, golden beam that seemed to widen as it came to shore. It reminded me of the yellow brick road from the Wizard of Oz and I wanted to follow it and put all my fears behind me.

Because fearful I was. My hands trembled and my pulse was erratic. The sandwich hadn't gone down well and my stomach felt queasy. I clasped my hands tightly and brought them up under my chin. The night was pleasantly cool and the waves beating against the shore lulled me somewhat. There was nothing I could do but wait. I watched the moon lose its yellow glow and turn silvery white. It diminished in size, too, as it slowly ascended into the night sky. Laughter floated up from the beach from time to time. I could see the small figures of people out for a pleasant evening stroll along the water's edge. I dozed off and when I awoke I was chilly. I went inside the suite to grab an afghan from the couch and then returned to the chaise. I wrapped the afghan around me like a cocoon and slept again.

## Chapter 2

A noisy gull woke me just before sunrise. Far down below I saw the water-swept sand, no footprints or dune buggy tracks yet. I scanned the beach for early risers but saw none. The first rosy streaks of dawn appeared in the sky. I huddled in my cocoon while I watched the sky change from rose, to red and then finally to pink just before the sun popped up on the horizon.

I went in to make coffee. That's when I noticed the door to our bedroom was closed. I was sure I had left it open. *Was Jack home?* I approached the door cautiously, not quite sure what I'd find on the other side. Even before I turned the knob, I heard him snoring. I pushed the door open so hard it swung all the way back and hit the wall.

Jack was sprawled spread eagled across the bed, completely dressed - shirt, trousers and shoes. His blond hair was a rumpled mess and a faint five o'clock shadow darkened his chin. I approached the bed for a closer look and saw a large bruise on his left jaw. He stirred a little and I noticed the knuckles on his right hand were raw and bloody. His trousers were filthy and the left sleeve of his shirt was ripped at the shoulder. He'd obviously been in a fight and from the look of things he had not faired well but he was home and he was safe.

Relief flooded my entire body and my legs almost buckled from under me. And then a terrible anger rose within me. I felt like strangling him.

I yelled, "Jack!" and at the same time I shook him. He didn't move so I shook him again. "Jack! Jack! Wake up! Where have you been? Wake up now!" I shook him harder.

He stirred and opened his eyes. For a second or two they remained unfocused and then he saw me. "Callie, I'm glad you're finally home. You weren't here when I got in last night."

"Come on, Jack. Don't try that stuff with me. I've been right here, on the deck, waiting for you to show. Scared out of my mind, I might add."

I'll give Jack a lot of credit. He tried to bluff his way out of this bad dream we were both having. "Scared? Why would you be scared?" He sat up on the side of the bed and ran his hands through his hair. He made an effort to stand but decided against it and slumped back down onto the bed with a groan.

"I listened to the messages on the answering machine, Jack. The ones you erased yesterday afternoon while I was running on the beach. From Brad and that other guy. Think about it Jack, and you'll know why I was scared."

He was not getting pity from me. I went into the bathroom, washed my face, brushed my teeth and combed my hair. I pulled it straight back, twisted it up and used a pink clip to hold it in place. Jack was still sprawled across the bed when I reentered the bedroom.

"I'm going to give you a few minutes to get your explanation together, Jack. Take a shower and get yourself cleaned up while I fix us some coffee. When you come out to the kitchen, be prepared to talk. And Jack, I mean talk. I want to know what kind of mess you've gotten yourself into. Because whatever you're into, I'm into. I've got a lot of questions and you'd better be ready to answer them."

The coffee and juice were ready by the time Jack stumbled into the kitchen. I put everything on a tray and carried it onto the deck. We sat facing each other at the little round table. A heavy silence filled the space between us. He drank his juice in several gulps and then reached for his mug of coffee. He looked terrible. The shower had brought out the vividness of the bruise on his jaw and the area around his left eye looked purple. I noticed a small cut on his chin. He held his coffee in both hands and they shook when he brought the mug to his lips.

9

"I'm waiting, Jack."

"Callie, I-I-I don't know where to start. The past several months have been a nightmare for me."

"Start at the beginning. Spare me no details. I want to know everything."

"Okay, okay." He was silent for a few seconds. "About three months ago, I was invited to a private card game, a daytime thing. A friend of mine asked me to go with him. I had a few bucks and played fairly well. Came out ahead that time and the next several times, too. At first I just went once a week. The guy has a beautiful home bayside and the same men were usually there. And then, things changed. My friend lost heavily a couple of times and decided the stakes were getting too high for him. I noticed a few of the regulars had dropped out, too, and the new players were very good but I seemed to be holding my own so I continued to go."

He took several gulps of his coffee. "I found myself thinking about cards all the time. I thought I'd sharpen my playing skills so I loaded a game on the computer and practiced. I'd wake up in the morning and think, I'm gonna write today but I couldn't. No words seemed to come. All I could think about was poker. And winning. Winning big, Callie. Because I wasn't winning. The games went from once a week to several times a week and for the past month I've played four or five times a week. I've had a bad streak of luck and I've been losing heavily. I mean big time, Callie. I owe that guy so much money I feel sick just thinking about it. I don't know how I'm going to pay him. Between us, we don't have enough. If we sold everything we own, we still wouldn't have enough. Another best seller might not be enough."

"How much, Jack?"

He put the mug on the table and looked at me with tears in his eyes. "A little more than $500,000 dollars."

I stared at him in total disbelief. My heart was pounding so hard it filled my head with a roar. We lived com-

10

fortably but pretty much from book to book supplemented by my income as an editor for a publishing house. We didn't own a home and we did not have that much put aside for a rainy day. "Help me out, Jack. I'm in a tunnel without a flashlight. Didn't you know you were in big trouble before the debt got that high? Who has that kind of money anyway, enough to let a person just keep playing on credit? I thought you said these games were with friends. What kind of friends do that to people?" I could hear my voice getting high and shrill.

"Look Callie, I didn't know this was going to happen. It just did. I knew I owed him money but I kept thinking I'd win enough to pay him off. But I didn't and what's more I didn't keep track of how much I owed. And before I knew it, I owed that much."

Jack got up from the table and began to pace the deck, his bare feet making soft little scuffles on the concrete floor. He wrapped his arms tight around himself. He was shivering in fear. Back and forth, back and forth he went, shaking his head from side to side.

"I didn't play all this week. I was afraid to go, Callie. I couldn't face him. I don't just owe him, either. I owe a couple of the other guys but I owe him the most."

"Who is *him*, Jack? Doesn't this guy have a name?"

"I don't think I ought to tell you. The less you know about this the better off you'll be. I think it'll be safer for you if he stays anonymous."

"Why? Why would he want to harm me? I 'm not the one who racked up the debt."

"I don't think it matters to him who racked up the debt. He just wants his money. After I listened to the message on the machine, I knew I had to face him. So, I drove to his house and tried to explain why I hadn't been playing. I told him I thought the games were just for fun and asked him to erase part of the debt, bring it down to a reasonable amount. He wasn't very receptive, Callie. He roughed me up. Well he didn't do it personally, two other guys did, but I got the message. And now I'm scared, I mean scared."

"Did you go to the police after they beat you up?"

"Are you kidding? They'd probably kill me next time and you, too. Gambling is this man's business and he wants his money or else."

"Be sensible, Jack. The police need to know. They might be able to help y..." The jangle of the phone interrupted my sentence. One look at the pure terror on Jack's face told me I would have to answer.

It was Brad. For Jack. He took the call in the spare bedroom. I stood in the kitchen and listened through the partially open door to the placating murmur of his voice. A panic attack struck me so hard I doubled over. I stepped onto the deck and inhaled and exhaled deeply, trying to calm my nerves.

I had to get out of there, put some distance between Jack and me. I needed to think about the situation without seeing his tormented face. His lying face! How many times had I asked him if something was wrong? Not once had he admitted to anything. Instead, he had just continued to gamble.

I hastily threw two bottles of water and an apple into my little backpack. Then I grabbed my purse and car keys and left the suite on the run. I thought the elevator would never arrive. When it did, I prayed no one would be on it. Luck was with me. It was empty. I felt tears of anger and frustration rising to the surface but managed to keep them under control until the elevator stopped on the first floor. I waved to the desk clerks as I exited the lobby.

Once in my car, the tears came. I let them roll down my cheeks behind my big sunglasses. I drove south on Ocean Highway and took Rte. 90 west. I purposely kept my mind a total blank. I wanted to find someplace where I could stop and think. I crossed both bridges without looking at the water. I took the cutoff for Rte. 113 toward Snow Hill. Once I crossed Rte. 50 I drove through open farmland broken up with clusters of houses. I looked at the scenery but didn't really see it.

I exited Rte. 113 into Snow Hill. It was a charming little town, with lots of old houses and even older churches. I thought I'd like to return when I was in a better mood and could spend time strolling the streets, poking into the many antique shops.

I turned east onto Rte. 12 and in a very few minutes was once again in open countryside. A big harvesting machine was in a cornfield. The stalks were brown and the ears were bent toward the ground. I watched the machine eat everything in its path. I passed numerous chicken houses and remembered someone telling me that this area was big on raising chickens.

A sign for Furnace Town pointed to the left. The name intrigued me and I slowed the car to make the turn onto Old Furnace Road. Very shortly I entered a wooded area and the dappled sunlight on the road soothed my jangled nerves. Several large signs loomed ahead and a quick left and then right took me into an unpaved parking lot in the middle of the forest. I counted ten cars.

I gathered up my backpack and purse and stepped out of the car. The trill of birds greeted me and I could hear a gentle breeze soughing in the trees. The spot was peaceful and serene and I knew I'd come to the right place to think. I stuffed a little money and the keys into the backpack, tossed my purse and cell phone into the trunk, and headed for the entrance gate.

I wandered all over the little historic site. A sign said Furnace Town had produced pig iron in the mid 1800's and had been surrounded by a small village of 300 or so people. A huge brick and stone blast furnace dominated the area. The sole original structure left, it stood proudly as an historic landmark. There were eight very old buildings situated on the grounds as well as a brand new visitor's center. I walked through a lovely little garden laid out with sections for flowers, herbs, and vegetables. The gardener gave me a sprig of camphor and I inhaled its therapeutic aroma as I strolled around. There were many tall trees in the area and the ground was blanketed with a thick covering of pine needles. Birds twittered noisily in the trees and the air was filled with the scent of pine. Numerous squirrels scampered about and I noticed several large tabby cats eyeing them longingly. Artisans including blacksmith, weaver, broom maker and printer, occupied several of the buildings. They were friendly but I wasn't interested in hearing their spiels. I needed to think. And think hard.

Jack and I had been together four years and not once had he shown an inclination to gamble, let alone gamble heavily. He was always too busy working on his next novel to have time for something he considered frivolous. We took vacations but even then he'd be jotting things of interest in the little notebook he always carried with him.

In fact, when I had moved in with him, he'd been worried that he might not be able to spend enough time with me to keep me happy. But we had made the arrangement work. My job kept me pretty busy, too, and somehow we managed to stay out of each other's hair yet still find time to do lots of fun things together.

We weren't married and I doubted the Mystery Man could take what was mine to clear Jack's debt. However, Jack might feel I was duty bound to freely give what was mine to help resolve the problem. And the truth was, I wasn't sure I wanted to do that.

I leaned into the furnace and totally relaxed. I picked up the twig of camphor and inhaled its rich aroma. *This place is so peaceful and serene*, I thought. *It's hard to believe this was once a thriving iron-making community. I wonder if the people living here then had gambling problems.* I chuckled to myself. *They probably did. People are people no matter what century they live in.*

The sun shone hot on my face. My eyelids were heavy and I had difficulty keeping them open. As I tilted my head back against the warm bricks, I was aware of a shrill buzzing in my ears. The noise wasn't painful but slowly spiraled into a soft humming. I was vaguely aware of a tingling in my fingers. I relaxed and fell into a deep sleep.

# Chapter 3

I opened my eyes to total darkness. It took me a few seconds to figure out where I was. The last thing I remembered was sitting against the warm bricks of the furnace. *How long did I sleep?* It was so dark I couldn't see my hands in front of my face. *Don' t they check to make sure all visitors have left the site?* I was annoyed with them and with myself. Places like this are usually protected with security monitors. Hopefully, I wouldn't set off an alarm as I tried to find my way out.

I was chilly, too. *Does it get this cool at the ocean in September?* I wondered. *I wish I had a jacket. My teeth will be chattering by the time I reach the car.* I felt around for my backpack and struggled to my feet. And that's when I heard the water. Running water. Close by, too. That threw me for a loop. The small amount of water I had seen in the little canal by the furnace could not possibly make that much noise.

I was completely disoriented and had no idea which way to go to reach the car. I took a few tentative steps and then I heard the sound of feet crunching on stones. I looked in that direction but couldn't see a thing.

A whisper floated down to me out of the blackness. "Don't move. I'll come to you."

A hand touched my shoulder and I jumped in alarm. The whisperer said, "You have nothing to fear. No one will harm you. Come with me as quietly as you can."

He tossed what felt like a blanket around my shoulders, took my arm and quickly walked me up the hill away from the furnace. "Keep your head bent toward the ground so light doesn't shine on your face," I was told. I sensed the caution in his voice and immediately obeyed. Nor did I try to speak. Somehow I knew he didn't want to engage in a conversation with me at the moment.

I felt like a lamb being led to slaughter. We crested a small hill and I saw lights twinkling a little distance away. I stumbled and he quickly steadied me, the pressure on my arm was both firm and insistent. We walked steadily toward the lights. I caught the scent of wood smoke in the air.

"Step up," the whisperer told me, "two steps."

A door opened and he pushed me gently into a small room filled with lamplight. A fire crackled merrily in an open hearth on one end. He shut the door behind me and pushed me toward the fire.

"Lean in close, Girl. You are shaking like a leaf. Old Mag, is the coffee ready? This girl's frozen with both cold and fright." He took my backpack and set it on a large, wooden table near the fireplace.

The fire felt good. I rubbed my hands together and then clasped them tightly. I could not stop trembling. I had no idea where I was or how I had gotten here. One brief look around the room told me it was something from a history book. *Have I stumbled onto a movie set?* I wondered. *Maybe they're making another movie in the Ocean City area.* I realized I was wearing a long, black cloak and pulled it tighter around my body, grateful for the additional warmth.

An elderly woman appeared from the dark recesses of the room. A small woman, under five feet in height, she was clad in a blouse and gathered skirt that fell to the tops of her stout black shoes. The skirt was covered with a not-too clean apron. A mobcap covered white hair that reached her waist in a long, thick braid. She carried a steaming cup of liquid that she offered to me. It was coffee.

"Thank you," I managed to say before I took several swallows. It was rich and black, just the way I like it.

The man spoke. "I think introductions are in order. My name is Trog and this is my mother, Old Mag. We are the weavers is this little iron furnace community. And you are?"

"I'm Callie, Callie Brentwood." I glanced at Trog as I spoke. He was about fifty years old and was well over six feet tall. Wide shoulders, a very narrow waist and long legs accentuated his height. He was dressed in a loose blouse, dark blue wool trousers that ended at his knees and a brown leather vest. Long stockings and heavy leather shoes completed his outfit. Brown wavy hair, streaked with gray, fell to his shoulders. "The coffee is very good but if you don't mind, I think I'll just go on home now. I'd appreciate it if you'd point me in the direction of the gate." I set the cup down on the table and took off the cloak. I felt foolish standing there in my shorts and T-shirt. I located the keys in the backpack and headed for the door.

"Callie, there is a small problem."

"What?"

"Well, you see, my dear, you can't go home. You arrived here via the furnace and that is the only way you'll be able to leave. It is far too late for us to try to get you back tonight."

"What do you mean, I traveled here via the furnace? I drove a car and parked it in the parking lot."

"No doubt you did, whatever a car is. But you aren't in that century right now. You have traveled through time. Were you leaning against the furnace or rubbing it?"

I stared at him dumbfounded. "I-I-I was doing a little of both. I was tired and I guess I took a little nap. The last thing I remember was thinking about life back---Oh, no! Don't tell me I've traveled back to when the furnace was in operation? Please tell me this is all a bad dream or a movie set or something silly like that!"

Both Trog and Old Mag shook their heads. With trembling hands I lifted the cup to my lips and took several large gulps of coffee. I needed to think but I was so frightened, thinking was impossible. Fear mingled with the fumes from the oil lamps and my head began to throb. I set the cup on the table and dropped my head into my hands. *Think, think,* I said to myself, *there has to be a solution to this problem. People just don't disap-*

*pear into another stratum of time. Or do they? Stop thinking like that! Pinch yourself and you'll wake up.* I pinched myself hard, twice, but I remained in the smoke-filled room with Old Mag and Trog.

Old Mag spoke for the first time. "Sit down, Girl." She pointed to a bench on one side of the table. I obeyed; she sat next to me. Her clear eyes were an odd shade of green. "Stop your fretting. We'll send you back to your century soon enough. You'll have to wait until the time is right. For now, you'll just have to make the best of the situation." She put one arm around my shoulders and gave me a reassuring smile. Her teeth were surprisingly white and rather large for her small face. "Trog, please pour Callie another cup of coffee. Slosh a wee dram in it, too. Maybe that will help settle her nerves long enough for us to explain what we have to do."

"I don't want more coffee. I want to go home."

"Well, to make it plain and simple for you, Girl, that is not possible. Not tonight or the next few nights. In fact, it won't be possible until the furnace shuts down for the winter." Trog spoke emphatically as he placed the refilled cup on the table. His eyes were green like Old Mags but were flecked with brown and gold. They reminded me of a wild cat I had seen in a zoo.

"Shuts down for the winter! When will that be?" I hoped they didn't notice the whine in my voice. "I managed to get here, didn't I? Why can't I travel back the way I came? Tonight."

Old Mag spoke in a gentle tone. "For one thing, Girl, at daybreak, men will be swarming all over the furnace trying to remove a clinker that lodged in the stack during the smelting process. The furnace was shut down to keep the stack from exploding due to the pressure. That's why it was dark at the furnace tonight. You were lucky Trog saw you arrive. Otherwise, you would have had great difficulty explaining how you got here. You probably won't be able to return to your time until early in December."

I pulled the cloak around me once more. *December! I couldn't return until December!* My teeth began to chatter uncontrollably. I wanted to scream and cry at the same time. *I hate you Jack,* I thought. *I wouldn't be in this mess if you hadn't spent the summer racking up a huge gambling debt.*

I tried to pull myself together. Blaming Jack for my situation wasn't going to help. I looked at Trog. "You saw me arrive? Have others arrived here before me?"

Trog put a hand on my arm. "There are a number of us here who are time travelers. We come and go at will. Old Mag and I have been here several times before. We rather like it here. Our favorite place, though, is Paris during the summer of 1810. But enough about us. There is a lot yet to do tonight and we must hurry. There will be plenty of time for talk later."

"No, I want an answer now." I tried to put a little force in my voice. I looked at Trog. "How did you know I had arrived? It's so dark outside I couldn't see my hand in front of my face. Nor could I see you coming down the hill."

"I was drawing the curtains across the window and I saw the little flash of light your arrival generated. It was only the tiniest of flashes but I knew a traveler had arrived. I grabbed a cloak and hurried down the hill to get you."

Old Mag interrupted. "No more questions. We have work to do and we must hurry else the neighbors will be curious as to why we are up so late." She crossed the room to a large blanket chest and picked up a neat pile of clothing that lay on the top. "These garments are for you to wear. We'll worry about shoes tomorrow."

"Do you have a marker with you?" asked Trog. Seeing my puzzled look he added, "Something to write with?" I rummaged in the backpack and found the pen and little notebook I always carried with me. Both he and Old Mag looked admiringly at the slim, gold pen. "Write down today's date, *exactly*. I can't emphasize *exactly* enough. It will be important when the time comes for you to return to your century. Write down where you were sitting at the base of the furnace. That is very important, too. Right now, you think you will remember but you'll be surprised how easy it is to forget small details."

I did as I was told and for a few seconds the only sounds in the room were the sputtering of the flames in the fireplace and the whisper of my pen as it moved across a page.

When I had finished, Old Mag lit another lamp and handed it to me. She pointed to a small ladder leaning against one wall. "Climb the ladder into the sleeping loft. You'll see a number of sleeping pallets up there. Select one that is far away from the opening." She handed the pile of clothing to me and I caught the faint scent of lavender. "Put on the chemise," she pointed to the garment as she spoke, "and put all of your clothing and jewelry in your little bag. It is essential that there be nothing on your person that does not fit in with where we are in time now. Try to get some sleep, Girl. It will be difficult, I know, but try. Trog and I will be up as soon as we think you are settled."

"Won't I be missed? I mean, won't people be looking for me, wondering where I am? What will happen when they find my car in the parking lot?" I looked at both of them with eyes full of tears.

"You won't be missed as long as you get back on the same day you left. No one will be looking for you because they won't know you have been gone. Now go up to the loft, Girl, and stop worrying. There is nothing more to be done tonight."

I slung my pack over my shoulder, tucked the garments under one arm and began to ascend the ladder, trying to be very careful with the lamp. *Stop worrying. That was easy for her to say,* I thought. About halfway

21

up I stopped and looked down at the two of them. "By the way," I asked, "what is the date of today?"

Old Mag smiled broadly. "The twenty-fifth of September, 1840."

## Chapter 4

Old Mag awakened me early the next morning. Holding a lamp aloft in one hand, she shook me gently with the other. "Get up, Girl. In order to explain your presence, we have to make a journey to Snow Hill. Trog has to hide you in the wagon before daybreak. Get dressed and be quick about it. We have to eat before we leave." She put the lamp on the floor near my pallet and disappeared down the ladder.

I lay under the blanket a few more seconds trying to get my thoughts together. I had climbed the ladder to the sleeping loft the night before and had done as Old Mag and Trog had asked. My clothing and jewelry were packed neatly in the backpack; I'd hidden that under an extra blanket that was folded neatly on the floor. I hadn't been given many clothes: a white chemise, a gathered skirt, a bodice and an apron. I used the chemise for a nightgown.

The straw-filled pallet was on the floor and was covered with a coarse fabric that was rough against my skin. I had barely crawled in under the blanket when I heard the other two enter the loft. Before long the gentle snores of one of them filled the room. I had tossed and turned for what seemed like hours before falling into a fitful sleep.

I was tired and didn't want to get up but I tossed the blanket aside and rose from the pallet. I quickly donned the wrinkled black skirt and light blue bodice. Both were held together with string and laces that gave new meaning to the phrase one size fits all. I tied the white apron around my waist, picked up the lamp and descended the ladder. There was no cheery fire blazing in the hearth and the room was chilly. The floor was cold on my bare feet.

Trog was seated at the table and gave me a broad smile. "How did you sleep, lass? I hope bad dreams didn't disturb your rest." He chuckled aloud at his attempt at humor.

I returned his smile but I was thinking, *Hey, Trog, no dream could be as bad as what has really happened to me!*

"Sit down, Girl." He pointed to a bench. "Breakfast this morning is cold because we don't want to leave a fire while we're gone." He pushed a plate of biscuits my way. "Old Mag, open a jar of your grape jelly and bring the girl some coffee." He handed me the knife he'd been using on his biscuits.

Old Mag shuffled in carrying a jar of jelly and a cup. She set both in front of me. "The coffee's left over from last night. We don't throw anything away and if we can't heat it up the next time, we eat it cold."

I took a biscuit from the plate, sliced it open with the knife and covered it with a generous dollop of grape jelly. I was very hungry and wolfed down the first biscuit. "May I have another?" I inquired.

"Help yourself," replied Trog. "You eat while I talk. Old Mag and I have come up with a plan to get you here so's everybody sees you. Otherwise, you'll have to stay hidden for several months and that will be difficult for all of us. We are going into Snow Hill to purchase some yarns for the loom. You'll hide in the bottom of the wagon on the way in and ride up front with us on the way back. We'll tell everybody you're Old Mag's sister's granddaughter come to visit us. Finish eating, Girl, and then wash up a little. The basin is just to the right of the fireplace. I'm going to get the wagon ready. We'll leave as soon as I get back."

I swallowed the last of my second biscuit and washed it down with the cold coffee. I suppressed a shudder after doing so - no need to make Trog think I didn't appreciate his hospitality. To my surprise, the basin held clean water. A clean washrag and towel were on the back of a wooden chair next to it. The water was cold but felt good against my skin. I toweled myself dry and tried to finger comb my hair to get out the tangles. I pulled it back and braided it.

Just as I finished, Old Mag brought me a pair of stout leather shoes and a pair of long, white stockings. "Put these on, Girl. Your feet must be cold." *Don't they remember my name,* I thought, *or will I forever be 'Girl' to them? And why 'Old Mag'? Doesn't it hurt her feelings to be called old?*

I gathered my courage and said, "Doesn't it bother you to be called 'Old'? Old Mag's face creased into a wrinkled smile, "Oh no. In our time, that is a term of great respect. Age is revered and I am honored."

By the time Trog arrived with the wagon and mule, Old Mag and I were at the door, cloaks wrapped around us to keep out the morning chill. I climbed up into the wagon, lay down in the back and Trog threw several blankets over me. The ride to Snow Hill was long and painfully slow. At first, each bone-jarring bump went through my entire body but I soon discovered I was more comfortable when I let myself relax and sway to the rhythm of the wagon.

After a brief while, Old Mag told me I could uncover my face. I lay there quietly, looking up at the twinkling stars in the black sky. The soft clop, clop of the mule's hooves were soothing to my tired and weary brain. I felt disconnected, an eyewitness to what had happened to me. It was strange to find myself in this unknown place, one I had no thought of before yesterday, and one I might never be able to leave. Oddly enough, I was no longer frightened. I would do whatever I had to do and if things didn't work out for me to go home, I'd have to make the best of this life in which I seemed to find myself.

Old Mag and Trog spoke to each other occasionally, but for the most part they were silent. Like me, they were wrapped in their own thoughts. The stars slowly faded as the first streaks of dawn brightened the sky. I began to hear other wagons as well as the sound of voices.

I was more than ready for the wagon to cease moving. When it did, Trog spoke gently. "Okay, Girl, get down out of the wagon and brush yourself off. Then climb up front with us." My body had stiffened from the long ride and from lying in one position for so long. I stretched a little before brushing my skirt and shaking my cloak. *What I need is a good, long run but who knows how long it will be before I get one.* Old Mag and Trog made a space between them and I climbed up front and sat down.

By the time we came to a river, the sun was well up into the sky. We moved slowly across a bridge into the little town. "Here's the plan," said Old Mag. "We're going to have a little something to eat to celebrate your arrival. We'll introduce you when we have to but don't speak unless you are spoken to, just smile and nod your head. After we've eaten, we'll go to the yarn and textile store to look for things we need in the weave house. After that, we'll start for home."

Like the other garments she had given me, the cap smelled faintly of lavender. I put the cap on my head and pulled it down to my ears. Old Mag looked at me and then reached over and adjusted the cap. She gave me a beautiful smile and patted my cheek. "Don't fret, Girl, no one will doubt our story, and by days end you will be part of our little family with no questions asked."

Trog clucked to the mule and we turned onto a dusty street. There were people everywhere and many of them waved and yelled to us as our wagon rolled past. We pulled up in front of a small building that nestled close to the street. Trog hopped down from the wagon, leaned over the side and pulled out a cloth sack. He helped Old Mag alight and then helped me. I followed the two of them onto a sagging porch and into the house.

We were welcomed by a robust woman with greasy tendrils of brown hair curling around her mobcap.

"Trog, Old Mag, what brings you two into town? And into my little inn?" She smiled broadly as she wrapped her beefy arms around Old Mag.

"We are celebrating a little, Miss Pansy. My dear sister's granddaughter has come to stay with us for a while." Old Mag put one arm around my shoulders. "We are so happy to have her, Trog and I, what with the winter coming and all." I nodded to Miss Pansy and smiled.

The wonderful aroma that filled the house sharpened my hunger. I tried to think back to the last real meal I had eaten. Nothing really substantial for two days. What I'd eaten yesterday barely counted and the day before that was not much better. Miss Pansy took our cloaks and led us to a corner table. As we walked toward it, people seated at tables greeted Trog and Old Mag warmly. They were certainly well liked.

I looked around the room while we waited for our food to be brought. It held about twenty tables, some with chairs, others with benches and most of them were filled with people eating and drinking. A large cupboard in one corner held dishes and crockery. A crackling fire blazed in a huge fireplace and its warmth permeated the room.

Miss Pansy and two serving girls brought several large bowls of food to the table. One held a stew; the others were filled with cooked greens and beans. There was a basket of bread on the table. We filled our plates and ate in silence.

The food was delicious. I didn't know what was in the stew and I didn't ask. I just ate. Miss Pansy kept refilling the coffee cups as soon as they were emptied. When I could eat no more, I sat back in my chair with a very satisfied sigh.

Trog looked at me and smiled. "I was wondering how much more you were going to be able to eat. The problem is, Girl, you are much too thin. You need to put some meat on your bones."

27

*Yeah, right,* I thought. *I haven't been running five miles a day and working out at a gym for fun. But what would you know about something like that, Trog? I take that back; if you're a time traveler you may know about working out. I doubt it, though, because you don't know what a car is.*

Trog signaled for Miss Pansy to come to the table. He opened the sack and took out several woven rugs. They were beautiful, with intricate patterns running through them. Miss Pansy handled each one carefully and then selected the one she wanted. She thanked Old Mag and Trog for stopping by and gave me a pat on the back. That was my first experience with trading and in the days to come I was going to learn how important it was for this man and woman who had so kindly taken me in.

We spent the next hour or so in Lapp's, a shop filled with fabrics and yarns. Old Mag fingered dozens of bolts of material before making her final selections. Trog took less time with the yarns but in the end I was amazed at how their choices in both matched. For each bolt of fabric, there was a suitable yarn. I wandered around the store looking at the things on display. One small table held several rag dolls. They were well made, with pretty faces and colorful garments. One wore a pair of dainty shoes. I was surprised to see a display of beautiful hand woven rugs. The detailing was so intricate it was difficult to believe someone had made them. While I was looking at them, the store clerk added five items to the display. I recognized them instantly; they had come from Trog's sack.

The long road home was very tiring. It was almost dark by the time we left Snow Hill and the air had a fall bite. Trog tucked a thick, woolen blanket around our legs and threw another around our shoulders. Our bodies swayed with the rhythm of the wagon as it rolled along the road. Trog held the reins loosely in his hands and dozed a time or two. The mule seemed to know the way home and needed little or no encouragement from we three in the wagon.

It seemed like we had been riding for hours when I noticed a faint tinge of red low in the sky. With each mile, the tinge got brighter and darker red and before long I could see embers flying into the air. They looked like sparks from tiny firecrackers.

"There must be a large fire up ahead," I pointed toward the glow as I spoke to Old Mag.

"No, Girl, that's the fire from the furnace you're seeing. They must have gotten the clinker out and the men are back at work."

Trog chimed in. "Won't be long until you hear the bellows clacking. They make quite a noise and can be heard for miles around. When we hear them we know we're almost home."

He was right. A few minutes later I could hear a rhythmic clack, clack, clack. The sound grew louder the closer we got and by the time Trog drove the wagon to our door, my head was pounding from the racket.

The site was ablaze with lanterns and torches. I could see men working around the base of the furnace. A black smoke hung over everything, a smoke so thick I felt I was suffocating. I was glad when the wagon was unloaded and I could seek comfort behind the cottage door.

# Chapter 5

I'll never forget that first morning I stepped out of Old Mag's cottage to survey the little village nestled around the huge furnace. My heart beat uncontrollably in my chest. I turned back to Old Mag with fright on my face. "I can't possibly live here," I told her. "I want to go home."

She gave me a nudge in the small of my back. "Girl, take it day by day. Do what you have to do and you'll be gone soon enough."

The most dominant feature in the community was the blast furnace. A brick and stone behemoth, it belched smoke that hung thick and heavy over the area. It was 30 or so feet high, wide and square at the bottom and narrow at the top. Three little sheds clung to the furnace. I found out later these covered the work arches. A long, covered ramp rose majestically from the ground on one side of the furnace. It connected to the top. Mules pulling little carts plied their way up and down the ramp. Men scurried about in the furnace area doing all the tasks necessary to produce ingots of pig iron. There were several long warehouses in the furnace area. I found out later these were used for storing bog iron ore, oyster and clam shells, and charcoal, the ingredients used in the making of pig iron.

A broad canal fed by a dam carried water past the furnace. A waterwheel turned endlessly, forcing water up and over and finally down the wheel in a sparkling cascade. The waterwheel powered a huge bellows tucked into one arch of the furnace, and as it pumped in and expelled air the clacking noise was deafening.

The workers and their families lived in little cottages built a short distance away from the furnace. Two stories high like Trog's, they were somewhat smaller in size and clustered together in a wide U shape. Each cottage had a fair sized garden, and even late into September, the women and young children were busy bringing in the last of the summer's crop and getting the land ship-shape for winter. Trog told me the women grew most of the food that sustained the families during the winter. As much as possible was canned and stored on pantry shelves to be supplemented by wild game shot during the winter.

A brick walkway led to the business area in the village. A bank and post office were housed in a good-sized company store. The broom maker, barrel maker, basket weaver, and bakeshop were close by as was Trog's cottage. A large blacksmith shop sat a little apart from the other places of business, as did a woodworker's shop.

There were two large houses in the village. The largest and most beautiful belonged to the iron master and his wife. The other was a boarding house. Trog told me single men lived in the boarding house but there were also rooms to rent to visitors to the village.

The village sprawled over several dozen acres of land that was completely treeless. If there had been trees, they were all gone. The ground was hard, grassless, and quite barren.

I was surprised at how quickly I adjusted to my 'new life.' I learned to live with the smell, smoke, cinders, and constant noise. To help my throbbing headache, Old Mag whipped up a strange concoction of herbs and lard, put it in a cloth sack and had me hold it to my head several times a day. She also brewed some kind of herb tea for me to drink. Maybe the remedies helped but I think I merely adjusted to the noise.

It was easy to be brave during the day but I suffered through the long, dark nights. I usually cried myself to sleep stifling my sobs so as not to disturb Old Mag or Trog. I cried for Jack and the beach, my car, a hot shower and nice smelling shampoo, clean clothing every day, a wonderful dinner in a restaurant and a decent cup of coffee. During one particularly bad bout of crying, I felt a gentle hand upon my back and Old Mag crooned inaudible words of consolation. Knowing she cared made me feel better and after that, my tears at night came less often until eventually they ceased.

I spent the first week or so walking around the village, familiarizing myself with the shops. I was impressed with the company store. It was well stocked with numerous things that were necessary for living but could not be grown in a garden. Here the women shopped for salt, pepper, sugar, molasses, and other similar items. There was even a large, glass jar of penny candy to tempt the young ones who ventured in with their mothers.

The storekeeper was named McQuerrie and he was quite talkative. He told me a lot more about the store than I wanted to know. I did learn that no one in the village was paid in money. Instead, they received credit in the store. McQuerrie kept a large ledger that listed the names of the workers and how much they had earned. When the women made purchases, that amount was deducted in the ledger.

I asked McQuerrie who used the bank if no one had money and he laughed. He pointed to a dirt road that ran through the center of the village. "The stagecoach runs through here several times a week and gentlemen get off to do business with the iron master. The bank handles the transactions."

Old Mag and Trog introduced me to their friends whenever the occasion arose and before long I was known as the 'Weaver's Girl' in the little community nestled around the brick furnace. Very few people used my name; in fact, I doubt they even knew it.

I didn't venture near the furnace on my own. The red brick stack was always surrounded by dozens of workers. What went on inside the three sheds that were attached to the structure remained a mystery to me. Trog did his best to explain the smelting process but I wasn't interested and as a result, most of what he told me went in one ear and out the other. All I knew was that something called pig iron was made on the site from bog iron ore found in a swamp behind the furnace.

Old Mag did not have a vegetable garden. She was one of the lucky ones. Her weaving skills provided a commodity to trade for whatever she and Trog needed and her pantry shelves were well stocked. She did maintain a small herb garden, though, for medicinal purposes, she said.

The weave house was directly behind Trog's cottage. Inside were two huge looms. A large triangular loom hung on pegs. Crude shelves lined one wall; they were filled with colorful balls of fabric strips, skeins of yarn and bundles of fabric. A well-used spinning wheel sat in one corner.

I was fascinated with the weaving process and Old Mag promised to teach me. First, though, she insisted I start at the very basic step of getting ready to weave. I spent hours tearing lengths of fabric into strips and then sewing the strips together into one long strip. She was picky, too, and any number of times I had to pick out stitches and redo them. I often sewed until my fingers bled. When a strip was long enough, I wound it round and round to form a huge ball.

I had other chores, too. I helped with the meals. Old Mag wouldn't let me cook a thing over the fireplace but I set the table and did up the dishes, crockery and pots afterward. I kept the downstairs swept out as best I could and brought in firewood whenever it was needed.

Sometimes I was sent on errands to the company store or to someone's cottage. It was on one such jaunt that I met a little girl named Lily. Eight years old, with long blonde hair and milk chocolate brown eyes, she took to me right away and we became the best of friends. Lily often sought me out in the weave house to keep me company, she said. She brought her own sewing and with chagrin, I realized she was a much better seamstress than I.

One of ten children, she had lots of chores to do at home but she skipped away whenever the opportunity presented itself. She tagged along with me wherever I went. I grew fond of her and found myself looking forward to her company.

The weather was warm for early October and Lily and I began to go for late afternoon walks. One day, we decided to stroll along the canal towpath to the locks. We received many looks and catcalls as we ran down the hill and past the blast furnace. The bottom of the furnace was a beehive of activity with grimy men bustling about. We walked well away from the area and kept a sharp lookout for the flying embers and hot cinders that often shot from the top of the stack.

By the time we reached the towpath we were giggling. We took off our shoes and stockings and padded along the path. Our bare feet threw up tiny puffs of dust. The soft dirt felt good between my toes. There were no barges being towed up or down the canal and we were alone on the path with the canal on our right and a swamp on our left.

The canal met a little creek about a mile down the path and there were locks in that area. Lily and I had visited the spot several times. We sat on the side of the canal and dangled our feet in the cold water, playing a game to see which one of us could keep our feet in the water the longest.

"Hello, there." A voice that seemed to come from nowhere startled me. I looked over my shoulder and was surprised to see a man standing an arm's length from us. "Sorry, I didn't mean to scare you. I heard you laughing and thought I'd join in the fun. That is, if you don't mind."

"Rune!" Lily cried in surprise. She jumped up from the bank, ran to the stranger, and threw her arms around him. "Oh, Rune, I'm ever so glad to see you back. Did you have a nice trip?"

"Hello, Lily, my pet. I should have known you'd be a party to all the giggling I heard as I came through the swamp." The handsome stranger, and very handsome he was, lifted Lily high into the air and wrapped his arms around her. "My trip was fine but I'm glad to be back."

"Rune, this is Callie. She's the Weaver's Girl and she's my best friend in the whole world."

Rune looked at me with the most beautiful deep blue eyes I had ever seen. His hair glistened in the late afternoon sunlight. It was blonde, so blonde it was white and it fell straight to his shoulders. He was dressed in dark blue and carried a wide brimmed black hat in his left hand.

He extended his right hand to me. "Hello, Callie. A friend of Lily's is indeed a friend of mine." I barely touched his hand with mine and was surprised when a small jolt of static electricity passed between us. I could tell by the flicker in his eyes he felt the charge, too.

Lily sat down and Rune sat next to her. "I don't want to put a damper on your outing but I will sit for just a few minutes." He took off his shoes and stockings and dipped his feet into the water. "Ooh, that's cold!" He sloshed his feet in and out of the water to Lily's delight. "I didn't know the weaver's had a girl."

"They don't," said Lily. "She's not really their girl, she's kin of some kind. Aren't you, Callie."

"Yes, Lily," I replied as I looked at Rune. "My grandmother is Old Mag's sister. I'm just here for a visit."

He gave me a strange look and I felt myself shiver under its intensity. *He knows I am not related to Old Mag. I can tell by his eyes.*

Nothing more was said about me or my relationship with Old Mag. Rune and Lily dangled their feet in the water. They had quite a lively conversation, too, with Lily doing most of the talking. I used the time to cast surreptitious looks in his direction.

*He is handsome.* When he smiled, a double dimple appeared in each cheek. His face was smooth shaven and I could see a deep cleft in his chin. Once I caught him looking at me from the corner of his right eye. I wondered if he was assessing me in the same manner, looking for dimples and what not.

We sat for a long while before Rune looked up at the sun and said, "Well, girls, I must be off. You two need to go home, too, because it's getting close to dinnertime and I know Lily's mother will be looking for her. Right, Lily?"

"Oh Rune, do you have to go so soon? Come have dinner with us. Mama won't mind." Lily clutched his arm, reluctant to let him go.

"Can't do that tonight, Lily. I have other things to do. But let me say before we part how much I have enjoyed spending a little time with you and with Callie." He looked at me as he spoke and I felt a shiver of delight run down my spine.

The three of us used our stockings to dry our feet before we put our shoes back on. Lily threw her arms around Rune again. He patted her on the head, smiled at me, took a few quick steps and disappeared into the swamp. He vanished so quickly and quietly it was almost as though he hadn't been there at all. I listened for a few seconds but could not hear him walking through the underbrush.

Lily and I hurried home in the lengthening shadows. She prattled on and on but I heard nothing she said. My knees were weak. My feet seemed weightless. I felt light-headed and dizzy. A myriad of thoughts swirled around in my brain. They were all of Rune.

# Chapter 6

I looked for Rune each day thereafter but did not see him. Nor did anyone speak of him. I began to wonder if I had imagined the encounter after all. Old Mag kept me busy in the weave house. I had gotten quite good with my stitches, so much so that she told me to put the strips aside, she had something else for me to do.

She took down the large, triangular loom, propped it on a table and began to thread it with a deep crimson yarn. Her fingers were nimble and moved up and down from peg to peg without hesitation. She had covered almost half the loom when she told me to take over the project.

"Here, Girl, I want you to finish this. The threads I'm putting on are called the warp. The tension of the warp has to be even on all the pegs so be careful. Take your time, too, and don't skip a peg. If you do, you'll have to start over from the skipped peg."

"What are we going to weave, Old Mag?"

"A shawl, Girl, a beautiful crimson shawl, fit to be worn by a princess."

My fingers didn't fly like Old Mag's. I wound the thread onto the loom slowly and painstakingly. By the end of the day, the loom was not covered.

Old Mag checked my work before we closed the shop. She tested each thread, checking the tension, and she seemed pleased with what she found. "Looks nice, Girl. I'll make a weaver out of you yet." Coming from Old Mag, I knew I had been given a compliment.

The next morning I was eager to resume work on the shawl. By noon, I had finished threading the warp. Old Mag took over the process briefly. She threaded a wooden device called a shuttle and began to pull it through the warp threads, over and under. On the second row she reversed the process and went under and over.

After each row was completed, she used her fingers to push the threads close together. I watched eagerly.

"We are putting on the weft now and we want it to be tight, but not too tight. Do five more rows with the red and stop. I'll show you what to do after that." She passed the shuttle to me.

I worked on the next five rows but when I showed my work to her, she pulled it all out. "Too tight, Girl. Keep it a wee bit looser if you will. Compare your work to mine and try to make it the same."

I tried not to show my disappointment. I took the shuttle from her and began to work. When I had five rows completed, I showed her the loom again. This time, she seemed pleased. "I think you may have a knack for weaving, Girl. Now here's what we're going to do to dress this shawl up a little."

She brought out a soft gold yarn and cut off a length. She overlapped the gold yarn with the end of the crimson and wove it through. The contrast was beautiful. I could see that the gold enhanced the work I had done. "Should we do one row or two," she asked.

I looked at the loom. "Right now it's difficult to tell. I think one might be enough but I'd like to see what two look like."

"All right," she said, "try two rows."

When I had put in the second row of gold, I still was unsure whether I wanted one row or two. "Old Mag, I might have to do several rows of crimson in order to determine how many rows of gold I like. May I add the rows?"

She looked at me with a smile. "Go ahead, Girl, it's your project."

*My project!* Just hearing her say that made me feel wonderful. *My first weaving project!* I put in the extra rows of crimson and decided one gold thread was enough. I ripped out the extra rows without asking for help. *I can do this,* I told myself. *I want to make Old Mag proud of me.*

During the next several days, I made great progress on the shawl. Trog came in to work one afternoon and was very complimentary. "Callie girl, that is going to be beautiful. You are doing well for a beginner." I basked in his warm smile and kind words for the remainder of the afternoon.

Lily dropped by with her sewing. She was excited about what I had done. "You're weaving, Callie. You're weaving. Maybe someday I'll learn to weave. It doesn't look too hard to do. Is it, Callie?"

"No it isn't, Lily, it's not difficult at all. Here, I'm ready to begin a new row. Why don't you move the shuttle up and over for me?" I pulled her over to the loom, handed her the shuttle and let her work her way through a row. She helped me push the threads tight. She wanted to do a second row and I let her.

The remainder of that afternoon was brightened with Lily's busy chatter. Old Mag and I answered her whenever we felt it necessary but for the most part we just let her talk.

"Why don't you and Lily go for a walk?" suggested Old Mag. "You'll have time enough before dinner. It'll do you both good to stretch your legs a little."

We quickly neatened our workspaces and hastened out of doors. The days seemed a lot shorter now but the warm weather had held. We decided to walk on the stagecoach road. It was wide enough for us to walk side by side. We held hands until we were out of sight of the village.

"Shall we take off our shoes?" asked Lily.

I nodded. As I bent to take mine off I had an overwhelming desire to run. To run just as fast and as far as I could. I wanted to feel the wind whip through my hair. I wanted to feel my heart beat faster and faster.

I kicked off my shoes and tossed them to the side of the road. Off, too, came the stockings, the apron and the mobcap. "Come onc, Lily, let's run!"

I left her standing in the road, mouth hanging open, looking at me like I was crazy. I didn't slow down or look back for a long time. I felt free and unfettered, the nagging worries of going home forgotten, all thoughts of Rune pushed aside. I ran until my chest was painful and I had a stitch in my side. I stopped, arms akimbo, slightly bent at the waist, gasping for breath. *How long has it been since I have done that?* I wondered.

I turned around and cried out in fright. Rune was standing in the middle of the road. "You've got to stop that," I cried.

"Stop what?"

"Sneaking up on people. You scared me to death." He began to laugh.

"It's not funny."

"I think the scowl on your face is funny. Didn't anyone ever tell you you'll have the scowl forever if the wind changes suddenly? Oh, but the wind will have to catch you first! Where in the world did you learn to run like that? I thought a bear was after you." I had to laugh. "There, that's better," he said. "You look just like the girl I met down by the canal." *So, he remembers me,* I thought.

"Where have you been? I haven't seen you since that day." *What a dumb thing to say,* I chided myself. *Don't be too interested.*

He didn't seem to mind my questions. "I've been out in the forest looking at trees. The woodcutting season is almost upon us and the cutters need to know the locations of the best trees for charcoaling. I've just returned today and plan to eat supper with Lily and her family. Speaking of Lily, where is she?"

I'd forgotten all about the girl. She had expected to take a walk with me and I had literally run away from her. "She's waiting for me up ahead, I hope. I felt like running and I just took off. I hope she won't be mad with me for leaving her behind."

"Knowing Lily, my guess is she'll think you run like a deer. Mind if I keep you company on the way back?"

"Of course not."

Our conversation died and we walked along in an awkward silence. I tried to think of things to say but my mind came up totally blank. Up ahead I saw Lily sitting patiently by the side of the road. She jumped up immediately when she saw us and ran toward us, waving her arms.

"Lily will be upon us in a couple of minutes so what I have to say must be quick. Will you meet me outside your cottage later tonight? After supper? For a little stroll?"

I was almost speechless. Me, a polished and well-versed, liberated female of the 21$^{st}$ century and I was having difficulty coming up with something to say. I managed to squeeze out a 'yes' before Lily almost collided with us.

"Oh, Rune! I'm so glad to see you. Did you see Callie run? I'll bet she'd win a race with a deer!"

"What did I tell you," said Rune laughing. "Yes, I saw her run. She's very swift." He swung Lily to his shoulders. "Guess what Lily, I'm having supper with you tonight. How does that sound? I sure hope your mother is having something good to eat."

"Well, it's about time, Rune," Lily replied. "Ma has been asking about you everyday since I saw you along the canal. I wish you could eat with us, too, Callie. Do you think you could? Ma wouldn't mind one more."

I tweaked her right foot. "Your ma might not mind but Old Mag will. Believe me, I know. She's expecting me to help her with supper and I'm already late. I'll see you tomorrow." I gave her a big smile. "I-I-hope to see you again – soon, Rune."

He gave me a sly wink as we parted, the two of them heading toward Lily's house.

"Girl, where in the world did you get to?" queried Old Mag when I entered the cottage.

41

"I'd begun to think you'd gotten lost."

"No, nothing like that happened. Lily and I met one of her friends and I think we talked a little too long, that's all. You may know him. His name's Rune."

Old Mag threw her hands into the air in surprise. "Goodness, is Rune back? Did you hear that, Trog? Rune's back!" She picked up her skirts and did a little jig around the table, all the while chanting, "Rune's back, Rune's back."

Mouth open, I stared at her. *Rune made me feel like dancing, but Old Mag?*

"Don't mind her, Girl," said Trog. "Rune's one of her favorite people. He's been gone quite a few months now and we were beginning to worry he might not return. Your news has made her happy." He lit his favorite pipe and blew a wreath of smoke into the air. "Mag, enough's enough. Let's get supper on the table.

In no time at all the three of us were sitting at the table, eating the last meal of the day. I ate heartily; there would be nothing else put out until tomorrow morning. I drank a second cup of coffee while Trog slowly finished the last of the stew on his plate. I thought we'd never start the dishes. As time passed, I grew more and more anxious. I managed to drop several serving utensils and almost dropped a coffee cup.

Old Mag missed nothing. "Girl, what's the matter with you? Are you coming down with something?" she asked anxiously.

"No, no, I don't think so. But I think I would like a little fresh air. Will it be all right if I take a little walk before I go to bed?"

"Go ahead, Girl, but be careful," she cautioned. "Stay away from the furnace. That's an extremely dangerous place at night. The torches don't light the area well enough and it's easy to step on hot cinders or worse, hot iron."

I told them I'd be extra careful, threw my cloak around my shoulders and stepped outside

# Chapter 7

The night air was cool against my hot face. I took a few steps away from the cottage and then stopped to let my eyes adjust to the darkness. I glanced toward the furnace. The area was well lit with torches but the men cast eerie shadows in the flickering light. The lights from the nearby cottage windows were softer and, as my eyes grew accustomed to the darkness, I could distinguish the familiar shapes of the wagons that were kept near the blacksmith shop.

A soft rustle to my left signaled the approach of Rune. Even in the black of night, I could see his white hair, halo-like, framing his face. I sensed rather than saw the big smile on his face. When he was beside me, he touched my arm briefly.

"Let's walk down Stagecoach Road for a few minutes. We'll be able to see where we are going with no problem." He spoke softly but I sensed his quiet strength and his gentleness.

We strolled amiably along in silence at first. But I was not one to stay silent for long. There was so much about him I wanted to know and before many steps had been taken I asked the first question.

"Why haven't you stopped in to see Old Mag? When I told her Lily and I had met you today, she jumped up and down with joy."

"I haven't been here; I've been scouting for trees for the next wood cut. When I do that, I pretty much stay out in the forest."

"You mean you live out there?" I asked.

"I sure do. It's kind of rough let me tell you, but when I'm out there for days at a time I get used to it."

"Where do you sleep? What do you eat?" The questions poured out of my mouth.

"Whoa, one question at a time, please," Rune laughed. "I live off the land. I hunt and fish and eat lots of roots and grasses. I roost in a tree when I can find a good one. If not, I sleep on the ground. When I'm hungry for a hearty meal, I come in to the village and Lily's ma feeds me."

*I wonder why he doesn't come to Old Mag's for a meal*, I thought, and as if he'd read my mind he said, "Lily's ma is my half-sister. Now, enough about me. I want to know where you came from because I don't believe for a minute you are Old Mag's sister's granddaughter. She doesn't have a sister."

I couldn't tell him I came from another time; from a place he couldn't envision in his wildest dreams. He'd think I was completely crazy. I let a variety of answers swirl around in my head for a few seconds and then replied, "For now, I'm Old Mag's sister's granddaughter. That's all I can tell you."

We stopped walking and faced each other. I could make out his face in the faint light. He smiled and said, "Well, that's good enough for me. We'd better head back now before Old Mag comes looking for you. I'll be around for the next few days and I'll stop in to see her. My visit with her is long overdue."

Our conversation was light as we retraced our steps to the cottage. As we said goodbye he reached out with his right hand and lightly touched my cheek. I felt a small jolt of static electricity from his fingertips. We stared into each other's eyes for a long moment before he turned away. I watched him stride off toward Lily's before I went inside.

That night, as I lay on my pallet I thought about Jack for the first time in several weeks. I wondered if he had resolved the gambling mess. I doubted it. I let pleasant thoughts of Jack filter through my mind and then I thought of Rune. Rune, with his white hair and brilliant eyes, his wonderful smile accented with dimples. *Boy, I really know how to pick a fellow. One is a gambler and the other sleeps in trees.* With that thought I drifted off to sleep.

The next few days were spent in the weave house. I worked diligently on the shawl. It seemed to come to life under my fingertips and I was eager to complete it. I could imagine in my mind's eye how I would look with it wrapped around my shoulders.

True to his word Rune stopped by to see Old Mag. She was home alone; Trog and I were at work in the weave house. She was elated by his visit and fed him hot tea and apple pie. He brought her a bouquet of flowers and she proudly displayed them in a jar on the kitchen table. Trog and I heard all about his visit that night at supper.

The October days slipped by, one after another, each just like the one before. Fall was definitely upon us and I reveled in the warm days and cool, brisk nights. The sleeping loft was very chilly and I enjoyed snuggling into the quilt that covered my pallet. I often went to bed right after supper and slept soundly until the stirring of Old Mag and Trog awoke me.

I guess we were into the third week of October when the weather suddenly turned quite warm. The weave house became hot and stuffy and we threw open the windows to let a draft of air in. Had I not known better, I would have thought it was August. The sun shone down unmercifully. My clothes were damp with perspiration and clung uncomfortably to my body. We suffered with the heat for two days before a huge thunderstorm rolled in. The day turned dark under the ominous clouds and we had to light the lamps to see well enough to work.

I stood outside the weave house door and watched the progress of the storm. A stiff breeze began to blow. It felt good against my hot, sticky skin. I heard the rumble of thunder in the distance and caught the sweet scent of rain in the air. The wind kicked up little eddies of dust. Before long, more than dust was being blown about. A neighbor's clothesline broke free and skirts and chemises were flailing on the ground. I saw a straw hat cartwheeling toward the furnace. It was suddenly airborne in the wind and sailed out of sight.

The first bolt of lightning caught us by surprise. Its jagged edges lit the sky followed by a loud crack. "That was close," I said to Trog. We hurriedly closed the windows to the weave house but kept the door open so we could see outside.

The rain came without warning; a thick sheet that dropped like a curtain in front of the open door. The rug near the doorsill was soaked in just a few seconds. The three of us stood looking out, trying to see. It pelted against the sides of the cottage and drummed hard upon the roof. I could hear individual drops pinging against the windowpanes.

Old Mag walked around the room anxiously, looking at the walls, the ceiling, and the floor. "Trog, the rain is beating in under the windowsills," she called out in alarm. "I've never known rain to do that."

He tried to calm her. "Don't worry about that now. The storm will be over very quickly and then we'll look at the damage that's been done. Come here and stand by us." He put his arms around her shoulders and drew her back to the doorway.

Heavy, black clouds were directly overhead and the thunder was deafening. I was more worried about the lightning. The strikes were close to each other, some with single forks but at times three and four forks lit up the sky at once.

To my horror, I saw Lily, head bent against the wind and rain, trying to make her way to the weave house. Without thinking, I hurried outside to reach her. It was all I could do to keep myself from being blown away. I tried to call out to her but the wind shoved the words back into my mouth. It was difficult to breathe. I bent my body into the wind and moved awkwardly toward her.

I don't know how I managed to reach her. I grabbed her and pulled her close. As we turned toward the weave house to retrace my steps, a wild roaring sound seemed to fill the air around us. Looking up, I saw a huge funnel cloud swirling toward the village. Trees and debris from the furnace had been sucked into the funnel and were swirling round and round. My skin crawled with fear and I felt the hair on the back of my neck rise.

"Run, Lily, run! We have to reach the weave house quickly. Hurry, hurry!" I could hear the fright in my voice. I looked toward the house and saw Trog coming out to meet us. Old Mag stood in the doorway, both hands balled into fists held tight to her mouth. Her face wore a mask of fear.

I don't know how we made it. The thing was almost upon us; so close I was afraid to look. And then, we were in the doorway with Old Mag and Trog groping with eager hands to pull us inside.

"It's a tornado," I yelled. "We have to find the safest place in the room." To be honest, there was no safe place. There was a little alcove near the fireplace and the four of us squeezed into that, arms around each other for comfort. We huddled for anxious minutes, listening to the screaming roar of the wind. The little house trembled and groaned but miraculously remained standing.

And then, all was quiet. The storm moved away, leaving intermittent raindrops pattering on the roof. We ventured from our corner and cautiously opened the door.

The scene outside was disastrous. The village grounds were strewn with litter. I saw dead chickens everywhere and one poor cow lying broken on the sidewalk that led to the company store. Several wagons were upended, their contents spilled nearby. Two cottages had lost their roofs and one cottage was down completely, its contents blown who knew where. Women and children began to emerge from their homes. All looked dazed and many were crying.

The furnace was intact; I was surprised to see the smoke still belching from the top of the stack. The charging ramp had not fared as well. The covering had been ripped away, exposing the wooden planks that led to the top of the structure. Frightened men were running from the furnace toward the houses to check on their families. A small group of men was clustered around the inert form of someone lying on the ground. I looked at Trog with questioning eyes. We both knew the answer to my unasked question.

I looked down at Lily. Her face was white and her eyes were full of tears. "Lily, your mother will be frantic with worry about you. Would you like for me to walk you home?"

For once she was speechless. She simply nodded. As we started down the path, Trog pulled me back. "Girl, don't be using the term 'tornado' to anyone else. That's a word from your time and they won't understand it. If the word slips out, you'll have folks asking questions you don't want to have to answer. You do understand?"

I gave him a weak smile and a nod before Lily and I started toward her cottage. Trog set off for the furnace. I looked back at Old Mag. "Do you want to come with us?" I asked.

She hesitated for a moment. "Yes," she said, "yes, I do." She hurried toward us and took one of Lily's hands in her own. "It'll be all right, Lily child, you wait and see. Everything will be all right."

# Chapter 8

The tornado wreaked devastation on the little site. The loss of life was the most painful. One man was critically wounded in the furnace area and died a few hours later. A mother and her three young children were killed when their cottage was blown apart in the wind. Dead animals littered the grounds. Several cottages were destroyed and many lost rooftops. The maintenance and storage buildings fared no better. An entire section of the front porch on the Mansion House was blown away; no part of it was found on the site. Our cottage was miraculously spared; Trog had just a few shingles to replace.

Mr. James Dodd, the Iron Master, shut down the furnace for a week to allow the men time to repair their homes. Community spirit was strong. Families with no place to live were offered shelter with other families. Tearful goodbyes were said to the wife and children of the lone man who died. Men worked together to rebuild and repair the cottages. Women and children pitched in, too, doing whatever they could to get the job done. Older children collected the broken bodies of pets and small livestock and took them somewhere out of sight for burial. Everything that could be salvaged was collected and put to use.

The storm scarred the furnace, too. Two of the three buildings that covered the arches had been blown away. The leather on the large bellows suffered several major tears and a portion of the charging ramp had fallen. The furnace itself was untouched as were the dam and the waterwheel.

Master Dodd spared no expense to help with the rebuilding. Lumber and bricks were provided daily. He brought in a special crew of men to make shingles round the clock. He personally visited every family to inquire about dead livestock. Horses, cows, goats, mules, chickens, and ducks were replaced. Mistress Dodd went about every day offering hot tea and little cakes to the workers. By the end of the week, the community was back on its feet.

Trog busied himself wherever he was needed. Once I spied him on a nearby rooftop, hammering away. Another time I saw him working on a badly damaged wagon. Old Mag and I worked from sunup until sundown, cooking food, taking care of small children while mothers worked with the men and offering comfort to those in great despair over their losses. The feelings of being useful and needed lay warm against my heart.

On the second day, Trog pulled me aside for a quiet conversation. "Girl, with the furnace shut down, you are more than welcome to go home. You can leave tonight. I'll help you." Old Mag looked on anxiously as he spoke.

I was stunned by his proposal. I had not thought about leaving in a long time. I wasn't sure I wanted to go right now. "Do I have to go?" I asked. "Or rather, do you want me to go? Am I in the way?"

"No, no and no," he replied with a smile. "You are more than welcome to stay. Old Mag has enjoyed having your pair of young hands about. So have I. But if you don't go now it will be a month to six weeks before another opportunity will appear. The decision is yours to make. Be sure it's the right one. Let me know if you change your mind and decide to go. You have a few more days yet before the furnace is up and running."

I stayed. I tried to tell myself to go but I couldn't. In some strange way I found myself altered and the distance between who I was and what I had become could not be bridged at this moment in time. I felt bound to Old Mag and Trog in a way I had never been connected to my own parents. There was something between us, a current of some kind that tied me to them. I wasn't ready to return.

Old Mag let me know how happy she was with my decision. With tears in her eyes, she threw her arms around me and gave me a tremendous hug. She kissed me on the cheek. "I want you to stay Girl but I'm not going to ask. You are…you are…" her lips trembled and she was unable to complete the sentence.

I wrapped my arms around her body and hugged her tightly. "I feel the same way too, Old Mag. I feel the same way." Tears suddenly filled my eyes. They spilled down my cheeks and left a trace of salt on my lips.

That night Rune and I met after supper, the first time I had seen him in several weeks. We walked down the little hill past the furnace and out onto the towpath. It was still and very quiet without the clack, clack of the bellows and the constant tumble of water from the wheel. My skirt made a swishing sound against my legs as I walked.

The night was dark without the bright red glow from the furnace. The sky spread over us like a velvet canopy covered with sparkling diamonds. I looked for familiar constellations but saw none. I could sense Rune looking at me but I didn't want to look at him. I was afraid the magic of the evening would be broken.

He followed my gaze upward and we stood together, without touching, for a long moment. A falling star suddenly blazed brightly in the black sky, trailing a sparkle of light as it fell toward the earth's atmosphere.

And then his arms were around me, holding me close to him. I caught the pleasant scent of soap. His shirt felt scratchy against my face. I reached up and touched his white hair; the silky strands slipped easily between my fingers. He bent his face very close to mine and kissed me lightly on the lips.

"I'm glad you've decided to stay a while longer, Callie," he whispered against my ear.

I pulled away from him. "What do you mean?" I asked. "Where would I go?"

"I thought you might go home, to your mother and the rest of your family in light of what has happened here. The last several days have been rough on everyone."

"Oh, I couldn't leave now. I'm needed here. At least, I think I am." We walked hand in hand along the towpath. "Old Mag and Trog asked me if I wanted to leave but I told them no, not just yet."

The silence between us was comfortable. We stopped several more times to steal a few more kisses. And then, it was time to turn back.

"Old Mag will be worried if I don't get you back soon. She cares a lot about you, Callie. She is the happiest I have seen her in a long time and I think you are responsible."

His words warmed my heart all the way back to the cottage. I asked him to come in for a cup of tea. To my surprise, we found two men sitting at the table, chatting with Old Mag and Trog. Both jumped to their feet when I entered the room. They were tall, well over six feet in height and both had very broad shoulders. Rune gave a delighted whoop as soon as he saw them. He leaped across the room and for a few seconds the three of them hugged, slapped each other on the back and danced around. The cottage walls rang with their laughter.

Trog cleared his throat. "Gentlemen, gentlemen. Enough, enough. We have a lady who must be introduced."

The three of them turned toward me with huge grins on their faces. "May I present Callie? Callie, this gentleman is Taw," Trog continued, pointing to one man, "and his brother is Vance. They have been away for several months but have returned. Needless to say, Old Mag, Rune and I are delighted to see them."

Both men acknowledged me with a courtly bow from the waist. Taw was very handsome, with clear blue eyes and light brown, curly hair. He moved gracefully for such a large man. He wore an easy smile, too, that

52

reached his eyes and made them twinkle. Vance had eyes so dark they appeared black. His black hair was pulled back in a ponytail that hung below his collar. While handsome, his bushy black eyebrows gave him a stern look, but then his nice smile softened his face.

"Sit down, Girl. We've been having a bite of cake and there's plenty for you and Rune, too. Will you both have tea?" Old Mag busied herself setting extra plates and cups on the table. I cut slices of cake for Rune and myself while Trog poured us each a cup of the steaming brew.

"Now that introductions are out of the way and everyone has something on his plate, let's get back to our discussion. Trog, I think you ought to tell Callie about these three fine young men."

I stirred the tea in my cup while carefully studying the faces of the others at the table. The light from the oil lamp cast strange shadows as the flame flickered in a slight draft. The faces before me looked surreal, like something from another planet and for a moment I was sure I was dreaming, that this whole adventure had been a long, long dream.

Trog studied his cup of tea for several long, silent minutes. Then he looked at me with a smile. I felt an odd prickling of the skin along my arms. I wasn't sure I wanted to hear what he had to say. I picked up my cup of tea but my hands were shaking too badly for me to take a sip.

"Callie, we are time travelers - Rune, Taw, Vance, Old Mag and I. We've known each other for many years and have all traveled the world several times over. We prefer the 19th century because that is where we can best use the skills and gifts we have to offer. Rune is a natural woodsman; there is no one better. He can ferret out the best trees in the forest. Better yet, he knows just how they should be cut to get the most wood out of each tree. Taw has a way with animals that is unbelievable. He whispers in their ears and they obey. He's been known to tame the wildest horse in just a matter of hours. Vance is a man of medicine. He has a wealth of information about healing using plants and herbs. Folks will be happy to have him around during the winter."

*Time travelers, all of them,* I thought. *"Rune, too."* I felt the blood drain from my face. Their eyes were upon me and I looked at them one by one, trying to read their faces. They were solemn now, all traces of smiles gone. I saw no twinkle in Taw's eyes. Rune was absentmindedly twirling a piece of hair between the thumb and forefinger of his right hand. Vance's black brows settled lower over his dark eyes. Old Mag's look was anxious. I wondered if they could hear my heart throbbing rapidly in my chest. Trog sat with crossed legs, stirring his tea.

I took a deep breath and in a wavering voice said, "I'm a time traveler, too." My voice strengthened as I continued. "But this is the first time I've tried it. I-I--didn't mean to try it. It just happened." I paused, trying to reach for words. "My gift involves the written word but I must say I'd better pick up another gift or two if I'm going to be successful in this century!" With the last sentence, I laughed and the guffaws of the others filled the little cottage.

We sat at the table long into the night, talking. Old Mag confessed her fear that I might change my mind about staying when I realized they were all time travelers. She told the others how well I was doing in the weave house. I shared with them the details of the ride to Snow Hill and how Old Mag insisted I stay hidden on the way into the town. Taw and Vance were full of their recent adventures in England. Trog told them about the freak tornado that had allowed them to return to the community earlier than they had planned. Eventually the fire burned low in the fireplace and Old Mag nodded off in her rocking chair. Rune left but Taw and Vance remained. They planned to spend the night sleeping on the floor near the fireplace. I crept upstairs and crawled onto my pallet.

So much had happened that day, I was fearful I would have difficulty falling asleep. I needn't have worried. I drifted off as soon as my head hit the pillow.

## Chapter 9

By the time the furnace fired up at the end of the week, life was pretty much back to normal. Taw and Vance hung around a day or so and then found other places to live. Old Mag, Trog and I spent many hours in the weave house, working on rugs and other projects. We were so busy I did not always have time to work on the shawl. Lily often joined us in the afternoons; if she didn't bring work Old Mag found something for her to do.

The weather turned cold at last and felt wonderful after an unseasonably long, hot summer and early fall. Old Mag found a beautiful hooded cloak for me to wear. Made of dark navy wool, it was decorated with black frog closures. I felt quite elegant when I put it on to take the few steps from the cottage to the weave house.

My evenings were spent with Rune. We took long walks in the chilly night air to the canal locks or along the stagecoach road. We held hands and strolled along quietly talking about everything and nothing. Sometimes Lily accompanied us and the three of us held hands. Sometimes we raced each other along the path, boisterous and laughing. Our breath hung above us in the frosty air. We'd stay out until we were thoroughly chilled and then would have a mug of something hot at Lily's cottage or at mine.

Late one afternoon Rune unexpectedly visited the weave house. We all greeted him enthusiastically, especially Lily, who jumped immediately into his arms. He chatted for a few minutes and then stood rather awkwardly, shifting from one foot to another.

"What's on your mind, Rune?" Trog asked. "Make yourself comfortable and share it with us."

Rune pulled out a low stool and seated himself. Lily squeezed right up to him and kept one arm around his shoulders. The four of us looked at him expectantly.

"Every night when I return to the woods I hear drums. They beat out a haunting tune that continues for hours. I wrap up in my blanket and try to imagine who is playing those drums and what causes him to tap out such a melody. It stirs me to the soles of my feet." He paused, as though hearing the drums in his mind. "I thought I'd hunt for the drums tonight. Taw and Vance are going with me. We're going to leave as soon as it gets dark, and we'd like to take Callie with us. That is, if it's all right with you and Old Mag."

"Callie can make up her own mind, Rune. You don't need to ask us what she can and can't do." Trog looked from Rune to me and then back to Rune again. "However, it goes without saying, I appreciate your asking."

"Do you want to go, Girl?" asked Old Mag.

"Yes," I answered without hesitation, "yes, I want to go."

As soon as Lily heard my reply, she began to beg. "May I go, too, Callie? May I? Please. I won't be any trouble. I promise. Please, please." She was jumping up and down with excitement. *I don't blame her,* I thought. *I wouldn't miss this adventure for anything short of an earthquake.*

"Lily, I can't give you permission to go with us. You'll have to ask your mother. If it's all right with her and with Rune as well, you may tag along."

"Rune, may I go? Please?"

Rune ruffled her hair. "The walk will be long, Lily and the night air will be chilly, too. But if you think you can manage, I'll ask your mother if you can join us. And another thing; if she agrees to let you go, you'll have to promise you won't say a word about this to anyone."

"I promise, I promise. Cross my heart and hope to die. Can we go talk to Mama now, can we?"

"All right, Lily, let's see what your mother has to say." Rune looked back at me as he and Lily went out the door. "I'll be back around dark."

57

"Come on, Girl. We don't have much time before dark and we have to get you ready for a night out in the cold. Let's go home and see what we can find for you to wear. And Trog, supper will be a little early tonight. We can't send Callie out in the woods with an empty belly."

As we left the weave house, I heard Trog chuckling. "Drums in the woods! What won't that boy think up next in order to spend time with Callie."

The next several hours were busy ones. Old Mag pawed through a blanket chest to find heavy wool stockings, a dark fichu to wear around my neck and an old black wool cloak with a hood. "You can't wear your pretty cloak in the forest, Girl. It might get ripped on briars. It won't matter if this old one gets torn or dirty." She continued to dig in the chest. "Aha! Here it is! I knew I still had it somewhere." She held up a dark red wool muff, trimmed in black ribbons. "This'll keep your hands warm, Girl."

I looked at the muff and knew it was too fine for me to take into the forest. "Old Mag, I can't wear that tonight. It's much too nice. Something might happen to it. I'll keep my hands inside the cloak. They'll be warm enough."

"If you say so, Girl. Don't blame me if your fingers get chilled." She carefully returned the muff to the chest. "Wear an old skirt of mine, too, not one of yours. Look through the things we were going to rip up for weaving. There are several skirts in that pile."

I did as she asked and found a skirt that had been worn so long it was threadbare. It was missing a drawstring at the waist but I quickly pulled one through.

"Now, let's see about supper. We want to have leftovers, too, so we can fix a sack of food for you to take with you." Old Mag busied herself at the pantry shelves, looking for something to cook.

I was overwhelmed with her generosity and caring. I walked over to her and touched her shoulder. "Thanks,

Old Mag. I appreciate all this. I wouldn't have thought of everything like you have."

"Pshaw Girl, it's nothing. Now go on with you and set the table. We'd best be ready when Rune stops by for you." Her voice was brusque but I could read her face. *She's pleased that I thanked her. She's truly pleased.* I felt a warm glow inside and whistled softly while I set the table.

I was ready and waiting by the time Rune and Lily arrived. She was bundled in a hooded cloak that trailed almost to the ground. As I threw my cloak around my shoulders, I caught the faint scent of cedar. Old Mag handed me two cloth sacks full of food. I gave her a quick hug, nodded to Trog and we were off.

Taw and Vance were waiting for us just past the furnace. We all exchanged greetings and then set off single file down the canal towpath with Rune leading the way. We laughed and talked until we left the path and stepped into the forest. Underbrush and briars were thick and I walked cautiously. Lily didn't whimper once but even so, Taw and Vance took turns carrying her through the heaviest thicket growth.

The underbrush thinned as we pressed deeper into the forest and we soon found ourselves in a stand of hardwoods: oaks and maples for the most part. At least, that's what Rune told us. A three-quarter waxing moon had risen; I could see it through the tree branches overhead. It cast a soft light on the forest floor before us. Leaves crunched under our feet as we moved like slim shadows among the trees.

We had walked for quite a length of time when the drums began. The plaintive sound caused the hair to rise along my arms and the nape of my neck. Like Rune, I felt drawn to it. The forest seemed to resound with the steady beat. We stood very still and listened. Lily grabbed my hand and squeezed it tightly. I could barely make out her face in the moonlit darkness.

We let the drums lead us to them and as we drew nearer the beat grew stronger. I could see a flickering light through the trees. *A campfire,* I thought, *someone has a campfire.*

And then we were at the edge of a very wide circle in the center of which was a huge fire. Off to one side of the fire were the drummers, about ten in number. They held drums gourd-like in shape but with flat tops covered with rawhide. The narrow bottoms of the drums extended downward to their feet and the sides of the drums were tightly held between their knees. The drums varied in size and I realized that size was important, the larger the drum, the deeper the tone. The drums were played in several ways, too. Sometimes the drummer used the flat of his hand to produce the sound but he also used the edge of his hand as well. The tones were quite different but blended in a way that was pleasing to the ear. I marveled that all could play with no musical notations to guide them.

The drummers were ringed by thirty or so men, women, and children. All listened intently to the music. Their bodies swayed together as one and as I watched, I felt myself beginning to sway. They were dressed in work clothes and the women and girls had shawls around their shoulders and gaily-patterned bandanas around their heads. The firelight flickered across their ebon faces and I caught an occasional glitter of gold from an earring. Not all the drummers played at one time. Five or so played and when one tired and stopped another picked up the beat and continued.

The music beat through to my soul; I could feel it calling me, lifting me up and taking me away. I let my spirit ride with the pulse of the music. I felt free and wild. I wanted to run like the wind to a far, far land and never return.

I don't know how long we stayed in that one spot, watching and listening. We neither spoke nor moved but were mesmerized by the scene before us.

As if on cue, the drums stopped. There was lots of clapping and laughing from the group within the circle. The people stood and gathered their belongings. Several men doused the fire with water; the sizzle of dying embers filled the night air. People slowly melted into the forest. In a few minutes, it was dark and bare, as if the scene before us had never happened.

Taw broke the silence. "Wow, that was really something else. I'm glad you brought us here, Rune. I needed to see that with my own eyes to believe it."

"Where did those slaves come from?" asked Vance."

*Slaves! How horrible! I had no idea there were slaves close by. No wonder the music is mournful. It speaks of a lost home in a far away land. In a few years they'll be free. I wish I could tell them.*

I choked back my tears before I spoke. "They must have come from neighboring farms," I said. "I wonder how far they had to walk to get here?"

"All I know is they come here every night because I hear their music. It's sad and touching, isn't it?" replied Rune.

"I loved it," Lily chimed in. "I'd like to come again, Rune. Do you think we can?"

Rune rubbed the top of her head with his hand. "No Lily, I don't think we will. What we saw tonight was something special and we were uninvited guests. Once will have to be enough for us." The rest of us murmured agreement.

"Now," said Vance, "I think it's time we started back. We've a long trek ahead of us. You got us in here, Rune. Do you think you can get us out?" He slapped Rune playfully on the back.

"Just for that, I think I'll lead you around in circles for awhile! Of course I can find my way out. I know this forest like the back of my hand."

"You go leading us in circles, boy, and you'll pay," said Taw jokingly. "Come on, let's follow the leader."

61

The walk out of the forest did not seem as long as the hike in. We found a moonlit area and stopped to eat the food Old Mag had sent in the sacks. There were slices of ham, bread, and apples. We sat in a little circle on the ground while we ate. Taw and Vance told silly stories that made us laugh until we cried. We didn't stay long but even so, the chill from the cold earth had crept into my body. I pulled the cloak tighter and snuggled into it.

"Time to go," announced Rune. He helped Lily up and offered me a hand, too. I started to rise but my feet got tangled in the cloak and I fell backward. I put out my arms to catch myself and, as I did so, brushed up against something furry.

"Ooh, what's that!" I cried.

"What's wrong, Callie?" inquired Lily.

I looked down and there, by my left knee, was a tiny kitten. I picked it up gingerly. "A kitten," I said to the others, "look, I've found a kitten. How on earth did a kitten get way out here?"

The little creature was virtually weightless in my hands. I could feel its fragile bones through the black hair that covered its little body. It shivered from cold and fright and mewed pitifully.

"Poor thing, it's half-starved." I held it close to my body, trying to provide warmth to the small creature. As I did so, it began to purr. I felt its paws kneading against my cloak.

"Let me see, let me see," cried Lily. She and the others crowded around me, trying to get a peek at the kitten.

"It wasn't out here alone, Callie. Look." Taw pointed to a spot not far from where we had sat. A closer look revealed the dead bodies of a full-grown cat and three small kittens. "My guess is mama cat had a late litter of kittens out here. She was probably moving them to a safer spot where food was more plentiful. Unfortunately, she and three of her babies didn't make it." He looked at the one I was holding and added, "I don't think his chances are good, either."

"We can't just leave a kitten out here to die," wailed Lily.

"We're not, Lily," I replied quickly, "I'm going to take it home. Maybe I can feed it milk until it is able to eat table scraps. I'm going to try and you can help me." *And I hope Old Mag doesn't mind if I bring a kitten home.*

I tucked the kitten under my cloak. Its purr sent vibrations through my fingers. *You're a lucky one, kitten. I almost didn't see you back there. It was just by chance that you brushed up against me. Chance. That's a fitting name for a lucky cat. Chance you shall be.* A smile stayed on my lips the rest of the way home.

# Chapter 10

The next morning our cottage was a beehive of talk and activity. Old Mag loved the kitten and its needs had to be seen to before Trog and I got breakfast. She crumbled bread and added enough warm milk to make a soft wet paste. Chance ate it down and then licked and licked the plate to make sure it was all gone. I gave him warm milk afterward and his little tummy bulged. He purred his thanks quite loudly and then jumped onto Trog's lap to take a nap.

Old Mag and Trog wanted to hear about the night before, too, and I shared my story with them over breakfast. "It was quite impressive," I added when I had finished my tale, "but I don't think we'll go again. We invaded their privacy and that was not right on our part. The music was both beautiful and sad. I wish you two had gone with us."

"Good heavens, Girl. I'm way past the age where I can tramp through the woods half the night and then do a decent piece of work the next day," exclaimed Old Mag. "Time has a way of catching up with a body."

"That it does," replied Trog, "that it does." The only sound in the room for a few minutes was the scraping of spoons against the pottery bowls that held our oatmeal. "But a good thing came out of the night. We've got Chance." He stroked the kitten's tiny body. "We haven't had a cat in a long time, have we Old Mag? And it feels good to have one again."

After breakfast, Old Mag fixed a basket for Chance. She used several scraps of wool as a cushion and then fashioned a covering out of two larger pieces. She put him in the basket and drew the covering closed. "Now we can carry him to and from the weave house and he won't get cold." We could see Chance squirming in the basket. "He'll get used to riding in this, don't you fret.

Before long, he'll see us get our cloaks and he'll hop right in, ready to go."

Old Mag was right. In no time at all, Chance hopped into the basket whenever I put on my cloak. He loved riding in it and I carried him about the site whenever I had to run errands. He'd stick his head through the covering and observe everything we passed but made no effort to jump out and investigate on his own.

He spent his days with us in the weave house. Lily came every afternoon to play with him. We fashioned several small balls of fabric strips and he loved to bat those around and around the room. Nothing was sacred as far as he was concerned. He hopped onto the weaving in progress on the loom, he knocked things from the shelves to the floor, and he hid behind furniture and jumped out at us. He was always ready to play and play with him we did. Rune, Vance and Taw stopped by once in awhile to check on his progress. It was comical to see those three big men sit on the floor and roll a ball or dangle a string for the kitten. Laughter filled the weave house and Chance had brought it there.

I tried to encourage the kitten to sleep in his basket during the night. But that was not to be. He'd crawl out and burrow under my blankets next to me. Eventually I gave up taking him into the sleeping loft in the basket. I carried him up and after I hopped into bed and got settled, he crawled in, too. His gentle purring was the last thing I heard at night and the first thing I heard every morning.

Late one November afternoon, Old Mag and I were alone in the weave house. Trog had gone to check on a large basket he had ordered and Lily had not dropped by that day. Old Mag was bent over a rug on the big loom and I was working on the crimson and gold shawl. Chance was fast asleep on a rug in front of the crackling fire.

"You know Girl, you remind me so much of my daughter." Old Mag's voice in the silence startled me.

"I didn't know you had a daughter."

"Oh my, yes. A beautiful girl. And every time I look into your blue eyes I think of her."

"Why didn't she come with you, Old Mag? Isn't she a time traveler, too?"

"No, she's in Paris. That's where she lives. I'll see her when I return." A catch in Old Mag's voice caused me to raise my head from my work to look at her. Tears filled her eyes and trickled down her cheeks.

"Old Mag, what's wrong? Have you received bad news about your daughter?"

She shook her head. "There won't be anything wrong with her when I return. Paris is such a beautiful city and my very favorite, too. My husband, daughter, Trog and I lived in a lovely house on a winding street. We had trees in the yard and flowers, too. Oh yes, and herbs. I always have to grow herbs. Belle, that's my daughter's name, was very popular the summer she turned sixteen. There was always a beau or two hanging around. She flirted outrageously with each of them but they didn't seem to mind. They just kept coming back for more. And then, in the fall, a sickness came upon the city. People that were healthy in the morning were dead by nightfall. I kept the windows down and the shutters closed. My husband and I took turns going to the market but Trog and Belle were forbidden to leave the house. We wanted to protect them." She paused to blow her nose.

"Belle was so headstrong. She didn't want to stay behind closed doors. She missed her outings with her beaus. I couldn't make her understand I was doing it for her. One morning, when I came home from the market, she was gone; she'd slipped out. She didn't return for hours and I didn't know whether to hug or beat her when she finally came home."

I knelt down beside Mag and put my arms around her. After a long pause to gather both her thoughts and her strength, she continued.

"Within two days she was very ill. I used every herb imaginable but nothing seemed to work. She lay for hours, eyes open, barely breathing. And then she was gone. The three of us were gathered at her bedside, holding her hands, talking to her when she breathed her last. I was devastated. I think the light went out of my soul for a long time. I wanted to get the sickness, too, so I could be with her. But it was not to be."

Old Mag blew her nose before she continued. "And then Trog found a way for us to see her every year. We travel back in time to Paris in the summer of 1810. My beautiful daughter is well and happy. Beaus come calling and laughter fills the house. The four of us are a family again for a brief while."

Old Mag blew her nose once again and looked up at me with teary eyes. "So you see, Girl, I'm in no hurry to have you fly away from me. You're a special gift, one I didn't expect to get so late in my years."

I felt as close to Old Mag as I had felt to my mother, dead these past fifteen years. I, too, had been bereft; my school grades had slipped, I spent a lot of time alone in my room, staring at the walls and wishing I could bring her back. But life goes on and, as time passed, I got over my loss. I graduated from college with honors and a major in journalism. I had been snapped up immediately by Jenkins Publishing, a small but enterprising firm, and I was on my way. The thought of seeing my mother again was appealing. *Do I want to travel in time to my life before Mom died?* I thought seriously about that for a minute or two. *No, no, I'm positive I don't want to. Growing up was too difficult to want to go through it a second time. The next time I travel, I'm going home.*

Home! The thought of it made my stomach queasy and my heart race.

"Are you all right, Girl?" inquired Old Mag. "You look like you've just seen a ghost."

"I'm--I'm fine. I was just lost in thought for a minute or two." I felt an urgent need to get out of the weave house, to step outside for a breath of fresh air, to cleanse my mind from all painful thoughts. "Do you mind if I step outside for a few minutes? I think a little air will do me good."

"By all means, Girl, do it. I've got plenty to keep me busy." Old Mag's voice was clear and strong once again. I looked at her quickly and saw no trace of tears or anguish left.

I stood quietly so as not to disturb Chance, threw my cloak around my shoulders and stepped outside into the brisk November air. I inhaled deeply. I saw Trog walking toward the weave house carrying a huge basket. I wasn't in the mood for more small talk so I waved to him and began walking toward the stagecoach road.

Thoughts of home swirled through my brain. I wasn't sure where home was. Should I call the condo by the ocean home? Or the fancy apartment in Baltimore? Or was this home, this God-forsaken little spot where men toiled twenty-four hours a day, pitting their strength against that of iron? I had not come here voluntarily. This place had chosen me but now I had chosen it. Why?

It all came down to Rune. I knew it and I was kidding myself if I thought otherwise. I was attracted to his air of confidence, his wonderful sense of humor and his competence at whatever he turned his hand to. He was powerful in his own way and I was drawn to him like a magnet. There was chemistry between us and I knew he felt it too. Why else would he trek in from the forest every evening in order to spend several hours with me?

The furnace would shut down soon for the winter; I'd have to make decision. Would I go or stay? At this moment in time, I couldn't answer my own questions. What a dilemma!

I walked for quite a while, until the afternoon shadows lengthened and the day began to darken. Lights were on in the cottage when I returned. I could see Old

Mag busy at the fireplace and I felt a pang of guilt that I hadn't been here to help her start supper.

"Did you have a nice walk, Girl?" asked Trog when I entered the cottage.

"Yes, yes I did. But I didn't mean to go so far." I hung up my cloak and washed my hands in the washbowl. "What else can I do besides get the table ready?" I asked Old Mag.

"You can carve a few slices of bread from the new loaf on the shelf. And look at our jars, too. See if you can find us a little sweet to have with supper. We're having rabbit stew."

I quickly set the table and sliced the bread. I opened a jar of peaches and put them in a small bowl. "Is that the last loaf of bread?" I asked.

"Yes, I think it is. We'd better make some up to-night."

I looked at Old Mag curiously. "You said we. Does that mean I'm going to help you?"

"It surely doesn't mean me," laughed Trog.

# Chapter 11

After supper, Old Mag and I gathered the things needed to make bread. I had watched her many times but this was to be the first time she had let me help. I put out the flour, salt, sugar, milk and lard. She crumbled dry yeast into a small amount of warm water to let it soften.

Old Mag measured nothing. She sloshed milk into a pot, put it over the fire and heated it to almost the boiling point. She poured the milk into a large bowl and when it had sufficiently cooled, she added sugar, salt, the softened yeast, a generous dollop of lard and handfuls of flour and then beat the mixture with a large wooden spoon until the liquid batter was smooth. She asked me to add more flour, a little at a time, until the batter formed a ball of dough that left the sides of the bowl. She covered the bowl with a clean cloth and put it aside for a few minutes.

We had just finished when Rune knocked on the door of the cottage. Trog let him in. "You'll have to wait a bit for your walk, boy. Callie is getting a lesson in bread making. Sit down and have a cup."

Rune sat at one end of the table and Trog set a cup of hot coffee in front of him. "Would you care for a little slosh of something stronger?" he asked.

"No thanks, the coffee is plenty. It's chilly outside and this will go a long way toward warming me up." Rune held the steaming cup between his hands and took a cautious sip.

"I can't believe I let the bread get down to one loaf," said Old Mag. "That's why we have to set it to rise tonight. Now's as good a time as any for a girl to learn how to do it. Roll up your sleeves because this part gets a little messy." I pushed the sleeves of my chemise above my elbows. "Sprinkle a little flour on one end of the table, Girl, because the dough's just about ready to begin kneading."

I did as she requested while Old Mag whisked the cloth off the bowl of dough. She turned the ball out onto the floured table and flattened it with the palms of her hands. She picked up an edge of the dough, folded it toward herself and pushed gently with the heels of her hands. "Okay, Girl, that's what I want you to do. Just keep working the dough with your fingers, just like I'm doing now. If it sticks to your hands, sprinkle a little flour on it."

"How will I know when to stop?" I asked.

"You'll know, Girl, you'll know. I won't even have to tell you."

She was right. I picked up the rhythm of kneading quickly and the rocking-rolling motion was soothing. The dough felt good in my hands. A faint aroma of yeast wafted upward each time I folded an edge back. At first, blisters had formed in the dough, but within ten minutes or so, it was smooth and elastic and no longer sticky.

"I think it's ready, Old Mag." She stepped to the table and looked at the dough.

"Sure is, Girl. You did a good job. Shape the dough into a ball and put it in this greased bowl." I did as she asked. "Now roll the dough around in the bowl so the grease gets on the top of the ball as well as the bottom." When I had done that, she covered the bowl with a clean cloth, took it over to the hearth and set it down. "We'll let the heat from the fireplace do the rest. You and Rune go on out for your walk. The dough will be ready for the next step when you return."

The night air was cold and brisk. I caught the heavy scents of dried grass and earth and inhaled deeply. Rune put his arm around my shoulders and we set off down the stagecoach road, retracing my walk from earlier in the day. We walked in a comfortable silence before Rune spoke.

"If you aren't careful, Old Mag will turn you into a homemaker for sure, Callie."

71

"I don't mind. I've always wanted to learn how to make bread. Actually, it was very therapeutic. I hope I get to help again."

"Thera-p-u-what? What does that mean?"

I laughed. "Therapeutic. Remember I told you my gift was words. Sometimes I use special words without thinking. Therapeutic means curative, a remedy for a disease or a feeling one may have."

"Therapeutic." He rolled the word around on his tongue. "I don't think I'll ever need to use that word. Just being in the forest is a remedy for me." He paused slightly before he added, "And being with you. You're like a tin cup of water from a very cold stream on a hot summer day."

"I feel the same way about you, Rune. I look forward to the evenings when we walk and talk. I feel like I've known you forever. You're easy to be with and I like that very much."

"Are you my sweetheart, Callie?" He stopped walking and looked into my eyes.

I put my arms around his neck and pulled him close to me. "Yes, Rune, I'm your sweetheart. That makes you my beau and don't you forget it."

We laughed and kissed and then kissed a whole lot more before Rune suggested we return to the cottage. "Old Mag will send Trog out looking for us if we don't get back soon. You have to finish the bread." We giggled all the way home at the thought of Trog hunting us down.

The chilly night air swirled into the cottage with us. I was surprised to see Vance and Taw sitting at the table with Old Mag and Trog. The four of them greeted us with huge smiles.

"Sit you two," said Old Mag. "This will warm your bones." She set steaming cups of tea before us.

I took a little sip of the hot brew. Laced with cinnamon and rum, it was delicious. "This is wonderful," I told her. Rune nodded his approval. Chance hopped into my lap and purred in agreement.

Rune looked at Taw and Vance. "I haven't seen you two in several days. Where have you been?"

"Oh, I've just been taking care of the horses and mules," replied Taw. "There are new mules down on the tow path and they are giving the men a fit. Seems they don't want to walk up and down all day long. Can't say as I blame them, either." We all laughed. "But I think they are coming around; at least, I hope they are.'

"How do you get them to walk up and down if they don't want too?" I inquired.

"I whisper sweet nothings in their ears." More laughter. Taw scratched his chin. "Well, I do whisper in their ears to calm them and to give them confidence. I say different things to different animals because no two are alike. Words that calm one beast will not soothe another."

"How do you know which words to say?"

"Oh, the right words seem to come out of my mouth. It's a gift. I've been able to calm animals as far back as I can remember. My friends were always envious. Vance wanted to be able to do it, too, but he could never find the correct words to say. Right Vance? Remember the horse Mr. Paulson brought home that time. He wanted to train it to pull the carriage for his wife and daughters." Vance and Taw looked at each other and roared with laughter.

"Yeah, I whispered in his ear all right. Whatever I said upset him, too. He pranced and kicked and finally broke the traces. Next thing I knew he was running across the pasture as fast as he could go. Took us two days to find him and another to coax him anywhere near the carriage. After that I left the whispering up to Taw."

"Because no one else would let you whisper in an animal's ear!" laughed Taw. "But enough about that, Vance. Tell Callie and Rune what you were telling us just before they came in."

Vance stared thoughtfully at the fire before answering. "I walked into the forest near the swamp looking for feverwort. My supply is getting pretty low and I don't want to run out. I found a patch that contained quite a few roots of the plant and was busy digging when I heard a snuffling behind me. Glancing over my shoulder, I saw a black bear so close I could almost touch him."

"Did you shoot him?" I asked.

"With what? I don't carry a gun when I go into the forest and there was nothing around to use as a weapon. So, I did the only thing I could. I lay down on the ground and pretended to be dead. That bear came right up to me. He sniffed me up and down several times. Darn thing even licked my face. He snuffled all the little sacks I carried to put the roots and plants in. I thought he would never leave. I ached all over from lying so still and quiet."

"He must have liked how you smelled, Vance. He didn't take a bite out of you," laughed Trog.

"Well, I hope I smell a lot better than he did. Whew! It was all I could do to keep from gagging. His odor was really powerful." At that we all had a good laugh.

"What is feverwort, Vance? What's it used for?" I was curious about the medicines he used.

"It's a plant with a hairy stem and flowers that grows in the woods. I use the root of the plant so I try to remember where I've seen them during the summer and in the fall, I return to that spot to dig. The roots are helpful in the treatment of painful swellings. I bruise the roots, add a little water and apply the mixture to the swelling. The throbbing and pain will gradually disappear. Boiling the roots provides a liquid that can be applied to sores or drunk like tea to bring down a fever. It's a handy medicine to have around."

"How do you know so much about medicines, Taw? Did someone teach you?"

"My mother was handy with herbs and things. Whenever someone in our village got sick, she was sent for. I often went out into the woods with her to look for the plants and barks she used in her treatments. Before long, I began to go with her whenever she was summoned to a sick bed. Her knowledge rubbed off on me. By the time I was ten years old, I was able to ease simple illnesses."

"He's good," said Rune, "but I always worry that he won't use the right bark or root on me."

"I've been tempted a few times, friend. To pay you back for the jokes you play." Vance tapped Rune playfully on the shoulder.

"It's getting late," interrupted Old Mag. "Excuse us gents, but we have to work out some bread dough." She brought the bowl from the hearth to the table.

"Roll up your sleeves, Girl. Here's what you have to do. Punch the dough with your fist." I did as she asked and the dough collapsed. "Good. Now fold the edges of the dough into the center. That's right, Girl. Turn the dough over and around in the bowl." I followed her instructions carefully. "All right, now cover it with the cloth, put it back on the hearth and we'll let the yeast go to work. Tomorrow we'll shape the loaves."

"That was easy, Old Mag," I said. "And fun, too."

"And don't forget, Callie. Making bread is thera-p-u-tic," chimed in Rune.

Trog shot me a dark look, one that Rune couldn't see. I knew he was displeased that I had used the word. As soon as the three men were gone, Trog spoke his mind.

"Callie, I can't warn you enough to be careful what you say. No harm was done tonight because you spoke to Rune. But others will be more questioning and let me remind you again that you do not want to have to answer the questions some of these people will ask. Please, for your sake and ours, mind your tongue."

I assured him that in the future I would, but for me the evening was ruined. I went to bed with a heavy heart and lay sleepless for a long time on my pallet. My body was tired but my brain raced along at full speed. *Why can't I be more careful when I speak? I knew better than to use the word therapeutic but it just slipped out. Trog shouldn't have had to remind me again. And another thing, Rune is your beau? What about Jack? Or aren't you planning to return to Jack? Think about it. You fit into Rune's world but will he fit into yours?*

I tossed and turned so much Trog left his pallet and came to mine. "Don't let me worry you, Girl. I like the words that come out of your mouth. Besides, most people don't pay much attention to what a body says anyway. Go to sleep. Everything will be fine in the morning." He gave me an awkward pat on the shoulder before returning to his bed.

Chance's purring filled my ears. *Thera-p-u-tic* I said to myself as I drifted off to sleep.

# Chapter 12

Trog was right. I awakened early after a good night's sleep. Old Mag was stirring about getting breakfast and Trog winked at me as he carried in an armload of firewood. After breakfast, he hurried off to the weave house while Old Mag and I dealt with the bread.

I followed her instructions to the letter. The risen dough was turned onto the table and divided into eight pieces. I flattened one piece of dough with my hands and shaped it into a rectangle using a rolling pin. I then shaped the rectangle into a tight roll to form a loaf. I pressed the long seam in the roll with my hands to seal it and did the same on the ends of the loaf. I plopped the loaf, seam side down in a greased pan and brushed the top with a little butter. When all eight loaves were ready, I covered them with a cloth and let the dough rise again.

While we waited for the bread to rise the third and final time, Old Mag and I spent time in the weaving house. Several women came in to see about rugs. Old Mag put me to work taking names and the rug sizes requested.

I overheard one woman speaking in a hushed tone. "How's the girl working out, Old Mag? Is she a help or a hindrance?"

Old Mag spoke too softly for me to hear her reply but the other woman said, "Well, I'm glad. Sometimes an unknowing pair of hands can be more trouble than they're worth."

I chuckled to myself. *When had I stopped being annoyed that people referred to me as Girl? A few weeks ago I was insulted that no one used my name but now it didn't matter. What does matter is acceptance by the people I care about.*

In an hour or so, we returned to the cottage to check on the bread. The loaves had doubled in size and were ready for the oven. The cottages in the little community had nice fireplaces but not one was equipped for baking. Ours was no exception. The bread had to be taken to the community oven. And that was my job.

I liked Mr. Jacobs, the baker. He was appropriately nicknamed Dusty because he was usually covered with flour. He was bald with a rotund body that suggested he ate as much as he baked. He was jolly, too, and always had a funny story to tell.

There were several women in the little bakeshop behind the huge, brick oven. I sensed that Dusty was in the middle of one of his tall tales and I stood outside for a few minutes admiring the oven.

The structure fascinated me. It was about four feet wide at the bottom and gradually assumed a mound-like shape as it rose to about six feet in height. There was a wide door on one side that opened into a large cavity over a baking pit. Here Dusty built a hefty fire each morning. When the fire died to embers, he raked them aside, placed the goods to be baked on racks and lowered them into the pit. Each time I visited the oven, I marveled that nothing came out burned black; he seemed to know just how long each item needed to bake.

The bakeshop was tiny, one small room with two windows. Shelves lined the walls and these were covered with loaves of bread, cakes, and pies. Most of the baked items belonged to someone but others had been made by Dusty and were for sale.

I stepped into the little shop and inhaled the delicious aroma of baked goods. Two women finished their bartering and left, acknowledging me with smiles and nods. "Well, if it isn't the weaver's girl," exclaimed Dusty. "Let me help you with those loaves." His shirtsleeves were rolled up past his elbows and his arms were covered with flour.

I had managed to get the eight loaves into two large baskets and handed one gratefully to Dusty. "I didn't realize the bread would be this heavy. I guess I wasn't figuring on the weight of the tins, too. We were down to

78

one loaf last night. That's why I have so many this time."

Dusty carefully removed the tins from the baskets. "There's quite a bit to be baked ahead of you, Girl. But I'll squeeze one loaf in for you before time for supper. While you're here, take a look at these." He pointed to several large apple pies. "Don't they look nice? Do you think Old Mag might want one for supper?"

I bent my nose toward the pies. "Hm-m-m. She might not want one but I certainly do! I'll tell her you have them."

"Tell Old Mag I'll take one of those small, thick cotton towels Trog weaves. I burned up two last week removing tins from the oven. And I'll try to save a pie."

We chatted a few minutes more and then I scurried to the weave house. I wanted to work on the shawl. It was almost finished and I was anxious to get it off the loom. But that was not to be. Old Mag had other errands for me to run and by the time I finished those, it was too late to start weaving.

"Girl, you'd best check on the bread," Old Mag told me when I reentered the weave house. "What does Dusty want for the baking?"

"He'd like one of the thick little towels Trog weaves. He uses them to remove baked goods from the oven and managed to burn up two this week." We both laughed at the image of plump Dusty trying to manage a hot pan of bread held by a burning towel. "Oh, he has beautiful apple pies, too. If they taste as good as they smell, they are delicious."

"Apple pie! He knows that's my very favorite. He has a secret ingredient that makes his better than anyone else's, even Miss Pansy's. Well, get one of those, too, if he still has them. Pick out a nice towel for him and be off with you."

I picked up the two baskets and returned to the bakeshop. To my surprise, Dusty had baked all the bread. He helped me stack the loaves in one basket and the baking tins in the other. I looked around for the pie but saw none on the shelves.

"You sold all the pies?"

"Don't see any, do you? You sure look disappointed, Girl. Did you have your heart set on a pie?" He laughed at my solemn face, then reached into a basket on a shelf and produced a pie. "Fooled you, didn't I? I put one aside, just like I promised."

Carrying two loaded baskets and a pie was an impossible task. No matter how I tried to arrange everything, I still came up one hand short.

"I'll carry the pie for you, Girl. I'm ready to shut down and go home."

The late afternoon sky was dark with clouds and it began to rain just as we reached the cottage door. Dusty knocked once and then pushed it open. Old Mag was busy at the fireplace; Trog was seated at the table smoking his pipe. Both looked at us, big smiles on their faces. I took the baskets to the shelf where we stored bread. Dusty chatted briefly with Trog before heading for home.

Old Mag and Trog admired the apple pie that Dusty had placed on the table. I envisioned a large slab on a plate to be washed down with a hot cup of Old Mag's coffee. I smiled to myself at the tantalizing thought.

Thoughts of pie had to be pushed aside. I had plenty to do to help Old Mag get supper on the table. I had been busy with the bread and hadn't brought in firewood; that had to be done first. After that I set the table and put the extras on the table; salt, pepper, butter that Lily's mother had sent and the remainder of the bread from last night's supper along with a fresh loaf.

We were all quiet during the meal, each of us locked tight in our own thoughts. The crackling of the fire, the flickering of the oil lamps and the pattering of the rain on the rooftop seemed to lull us into silence. The stew was delicious, too. It contained meat but I didn't ask what. I had learned not to. It was best just to eat what was put in front of me without question. I looked at Old Mag and Trog and knew how fortunate I was that they had taken me in. They had given me shelter, food, clothing and were in the process of teaching me a valuable skill. I felt tears well up in my eyes.

"What's wrong, Girl? You look like you're ready to weep." Old Mag interrupted my thoughts.

I rose from the table in search of a handkerchief. "I think the smoke from the lamps got into my eyes," I told her. "I don't know why; it hasn't bothered me in a long time." I made a big show of blowing my nose and wiping my eyes. I adjusted the wick in one lamp before I returned to my seat.

I had not finished washing the pots when Rune arrived. He stomped his feet on the rug and shook raindrops off his hat and coat before laying them across the back of a chair. He and Trog conversed quietly while I completed my chores under Old Mag's watchful eyes.

By now the rain was coming down hard and I knew there would be no walk tonight. I was feeling a little let down because I relished my evening strolls with Rune. I picked up some fabric strips and brought them to the table. If I couldn't walk, I'd work. Old Mag frowned on idle hands.

Several sharp knocks on the door announced another guest. Before I could reach it, the door popped open; Taw and Vance stood framed in the doorway. The scent of rain swirled in with them. They, too, shook out their wet outer garments and draped them over the back of a chair before joining the rest of us at the table.

"You fellows must have smelled the apple pie there on the shelf," laughed Old Mag.

"Is that the smell we followed, Vance?" asked Taw laughing

The two men engaged in a little game of mock fisticuffs; Rune joined in the fun. I realized they were just boys at heart in huge, overgrown bodies. I envied their ability to enjoy themselves so much while they scratched out their meager livelihoods. They had everything they needed; food, friends, a place to sleep and they were content.

The pie was delicious, as I knew it would be. Old Mag cut generous slices for each of us and served it with hot coffee splashed with a dash of rum. It went down easily and spread warmth throughout my body.

The conversation flowed and at times, the room was filled with laughter. The aroma of pipe tobacco mingled with that of the fire and the oil lamps. The small room took on a rosy glow. As I sat there, next to Rune sipping my coffee, a feeling of peace enveloped me. I, too, had everything I needed - food, wonderful friends and a place to lay my head. I couldn't think of anywhere else I'd rather be.

# Chapter 13

Heavy rain fell for the next three days. I was house bound for the most part; weave house by day and the cottage during the evening. Rune did not pay a call nor did Vance or Taw. The air was raw and cold and even the hottest of fires did not dispel the damp and chill. My fingers were too numb at times to work efficiently and I found myself arising frequently from my work area to stand in front of the fireplace.

The sleeping loft was cold. I put the extra blanket on my pallet and snuggled deep inside with Chance beside me. His little body generated a lot of warmth and I was grateful for it. I wished he'd sleep near my feet. Even extra socks didn't warm them much.

The rain stopped midmorning on the fourth day and the sun peeked out. But it didn't do much toward warming the earth. The wind was cold and seemed to creep in from hidden places in the cottage. Lily ventured into the weave house for the first time in several days and I was glad to have her company.

At some point during that day, Old Mag began to cough, at first every now and then but continuously by the time darkness fell. When she spoke her voice was a croak. As we gathered our things to go home to prepare supper, I accidentally brushed her arm. It felt very hot to my touch.

I took a good look at her face. It was flushed and her eyes were watery. She had wrapped herself in a shawl earlier and I noticed she was shivering in spite of the extra layer of clothing.

"Old Mag, you feel feverish to me. Do you feel well?" I asked her anxiously.

"I think I'm coming down with some kind of complaint, Girl. I'll be better as soon as I get home and take a tonic." Her raspy voice encouraged me to hurry.

Lily and I quickly straightened our work areas and gathered our cloaks. Old Mag continued to sit on the stool in front of her loom and I realized she could not stand up. Lily and I helped her to her feet, one on each side supporting her frail body. As we struggled to the door, Lily looked at me with huge eyes that mirrored my concern.

Old Mag was breathless by the time we reached the cottage. The room was dark and cold; no fire was blazing and, with dismay, I saw that the wood was also very low. *Where is Trog?* I wondered.

Lily and I seated Old Mag in her rocking chair. We swaddled her in a blanket from the sleeping loft. Lily lit the lamps while I brought in firewood and attempted to build a fire. Nothing I did seemed to work; all I got was thick smoke. Soon Lily and I were coughing as often as Old Mag.

"Callie, let me help," urged Lily pushing me aside. "I know what to do."

That she did. Her tiny hands maneuvered the kindling quickly and in no time at all she had a small blaze to which she added larger logs. Welcome warmth began to seep into the room. I gave her a big hug.

"You're a godsend, child. I'd still be working on that fire"

To my surprise, Lily began to giggle. "You look funny, Callie, with soot all over your face and hands."

I looked down at my soot-blackened hands. Lily's didn't have a smudge on them.

"Girl, Girl," Old Mag croaked. "Get some water boiling. I'm going to need a tonic for this cough."

"Okay, first order of business is to get some water boiling. Lily, do you mind bringing in a little more firewood while I do that?"

I put water in a pot and hung it on the hook over the logs. After that, I splashed cold water in a bowl and washed my face and hands with soapy water. The water turned black. I tossed that out, refilled the bowl and repeated the procedure.

"Let's move Old Mag closer to the fire, Lily. We need to get her warm."

We helped her from the chair and she leaned into me while Lily moved the heavy chair. We had just finished reseating her when Trog entered the cottage. A look of concern crossed his face when he saw his mother huddled in the chair.

"What's happened to Old Mag?" he asked as he crossed the room to the fireplace.

"She began to cough this afternoon and by the time we were ready to come home, she had developed a fever. She was so weak, Lily and I had to help her."

Trog knelt beside Old Mag and put his hand on her forehead. "Her fever's high," he said. "Mag, what do you want us to do for you." He gently stroked her hair.

"I need a tonic, Trog. The girl's getting water ready." Her words were barely audible. I leaned over Old Mag's chair to hear. "She'll need the leaves of hedge mustard. They're in a sack on the herb shelf. Put a few of the leaves in hot water and let them boil for a few minutes. Strain the water." She was suddenly wracked with a coughing spell that left her gasping.

Trog patted her shoulders. "Take your time, Mag, take your time."

While I waited for her to regain her voice, I looked for the sack of hedge mustard leaves. I stared in dismay at what I saw when I opened the sack. *Weeds,* I thought, *I'm going to boil a handful of weeds for this dreadful cough and high fever? What she needs is a good shot of penicillin.*

I dumped a handful of the hedge mustard into the pot of now boiling water. The dried, brown pieces swirled wildly and before long, a strange, but not unpleasant aroma filled the air.

Lily tugged on my arm. I had forgotten all about her. "Lily, you need to go home. Your mother will be very worried about you."

"That's what I want to talk to you about, Callie. I'm going to ask Mama if I can stay here and help you get supper. Will you need my help?"

Trog replied before I could open my mouth. "I think that is a splendid idea, Lily. Callie doesn't know much about cooking over a fireplace. We'll appreciate your help very much."

With a huge smile, Lily put on her cloak and left the cottage. I turned my attention to the boiling hedge mustard. *Thank God Lily is going to help me get supper on the table. I don't know any more about that than I did about starting the fire. I've watched Old Mag many times but watching is not the same as doing. What else is that child going to teach me?*

Trog interrupted my thoughts. "She says the leaves have boiled long enough. Remove the pot from the heat. Put a straining rag over a large bowl and pour the water through it."

I did as he instructed. As I poured, the leaves remained on the rag and a light brown liquid filtered through to the bowl.

"Sweeten the juice with a little honey and sugar, Girl," croaked Old Mag, "not too much. Then pour some in a cup to cool a bit."

I spooned honey and sugar into the liquid and stirred it with a spoon. I hoped neither of them noticed me take a small taste of the brown mixture. It tasted like I imagined sweetened boiled weeds should taste. I wanted to scream. How was this going to make Old Mag better?

When the cup was cool enough to be handled, I held it to Old Mag's lips. She took several tentative sips and then drained the entire cup in just a few gulps. "Leave the rest to sit, Girl. I'll need all you made and maybe more." Her feverish hands grabbed mine as I moved

86

away. "Thanks, child." She closed her eyes and leaned back in her chair.

I had just begun to think about supper when Lily returned accompanied by two of her brothers. All three of them carried pots, crocks and bowls.

"Mama sent something for supper, Callie. And broth for Old Mag. And if it's all right, I can stay and help you get it on the table. And there's enough for me to eat, too, if you'll let me stay. But not the boys. They're to return right away, Mama says." Lily talked so rapidly her sentences seemed to run together. The boys heeded her message. They set down their pots and left for home barely pausing long enough for me to thank them.

I couldn't decide whether to laugh or cry as the aroma of a wonderful stew filled the room. Lily and I quickly set the table. The food in the containers was still hot and didn't have to be reheated. The three of us ate heartily. I was grateful for Lily's chatter; it helped keep my mind off the seriousness of Old Mag's illness.

By the time we finished eating, Old Mag was awake. I heated the broth Lily had brought and managed to get a few spoonfuls in her. She also drank another dose of hedge mustard.

"I don't think Old Mag should sleep in the loft tonight, Trog. It's much too cold up there. Let's bring her pallet down here where it's warmer."

"Good idea, Callie. I was thinking the same thing myself. Why don't we do that before you girls clean up the kitchen? She'll be more comfortable lying down." He cast an anxious look toward his mother. "At least her coughing seems to have eased. She swears by hedge mustard. Says it's the best thing for a cough."

A tap on the door interrupted us. Lily skipped across the room and opened it. "Rune," she cried in delight, "I'm so glad to see you."

"And I you, missy." He looked at me and smiled. "Vance sent this for Old Mag." He held out a crock filled with a lard-like mixture. The odor of camphor assailed my nostrils. "He says this is the best thing for a heavy cold. Warm this up a little and put a generous dollop in this little sack." He produced a cloth bag from one of his pockets. "Put the sack on her chest tonight and hopefully, she'll be better in the morning."

"Oh, Rune, thank you so much." I threw my arms around him and gave him a quick kiss on the cheek.

"I'll go back out and return if you'll give me the same greeting," he laughed. "I'm glad to see you, too. Sorry Old Mag is ailing. She's seldom ill. Kind of worrisome to see her down." He looked at Old Mag dozing fitfully in the chair.

"You're just in time to help, Rune," said Trog. We're going to bring Old Mag's pallet down here. It's warmer and she'll be easier to care for. Give me a hand."

The two men disappeared into the sleeping loft. They had no difficulty bringing Old Mag's bedding down the ladder. Trog selected a spot near the fireplace to lay the pallet. In no time at all, we had her settled comfortably in her bed, wrapped warmly in her blankets and a quilt. I heated a brick at the hearth, wrapped it in a cloth and placed it carefully at her feet. She needed all the warmth possible. I warmed the camphor mixture, put it in the sack and placed it on Old Mag's bony chest. For the time being, there was nothing else to be done for her.

# Chapter 14

Lily and I did up the plates and pots from supper while Rune put a pot of coffee on to boil. Trog fixed dessert; blackberry jam slathered on thick slabs of fresh bread. We ate and drank in silence.

Rune finally spoke. "Lily, I think it's time for you to go home. There's nothing more here for you to do. Get a good night's sleep and come back tomorrow. Callie will need you then."

"Will you, Callie?" she asked anxiously.

I nodded. She put on her cloak and then ran to me for a kiss. "Thank you, Lily. We couldn't have done all this without your help."

"I know that, silly. That's what friends are for," and she was out the door with Rune behind her. He looked over his shoulder and mouthed, "I'll be back."

"I think I'll stay down here tonight, too, Trog. Someone has to keep the fire going and Old Mag will need more of her cough medicine. Will that be all right with you?"

"Of course that will be all right. Would you like for me to stay up with you?" His voice matched his tired and drawn face.

"No, you get some sleep. I'll be fine. I'll settle myself in the rocking chair. If I need help, I'll wake you."

I climbed into the loft to get my blankets and when I climbed back down, Rune entered the door, carrying an armful of logs.

"I'll bring in several more loads, Callie. The wood needs to dry out a little after all the rain we've had the past few days."

He busied himself with that while I reheated the hedge mustard tonic. Trog knelt by Old Mag and gently roused her. He elevated her head just enough to let her sip the tonic from the cup I held to her lips.

"That will hold her for a few hours, Girl. Now I'm going to get some sleep. If you two can, catch a few winks yourselves." He ascended the ladder.

I pushed the rocking chair close to the fire once more and draped a blanket over it. Then I sat down and pulled the blanket around me. Rune placed a straight back chair next to the rocker. He wrapped a blanket around himself before sitting down. Then the two of us tugged a quilt over both chairs. We snuggled together as best we could, giggling like school children. I reached for his hand under the blanket; it was calloused from hard work but warm.

"I have a better idea, Callie."

"What?"

"Stand up and I'll show you."

I removed the quilt and blankets and did as he asked. He sat in the rocking chair and motioned for me to sit in his lap. We pulled the blankets around us and then added the quilt. Snug and warm in our cocoon, I nestled my head against his shoulder and nuzzled his neck.

The fire crackled and danced. I watched the flames just as my ancient ancestors must have done thousands of years ago. The fire in the cottage was as fascinating to me as theirs must have been in their cold, dark cave. I looked at Rune and could see the flicker of the fire in his eyes. We sat that way for long minutes before he spoke.

"Callie?"

"Yes."

"Do you find the fire to be thera-p-u-tic?"

"You're wretched," I replied, slapping him on the shoulder. "Now, this is therapeutic," I said as I kissed him gently on the lips.

"Hm-m, I agree. I think I'll need a lot more of that medicine, if you please."

For the next hour, I did my best to cure his illness.

Old Mag did not sleep through the night. Twice she became restless and tossed and turned on her pallet. I heated the tonic. Rune raised her head gently while I held the cup to her lips. She was still hot and feverish. I dipped a cloth in cold water and placed it against her forehead to cool her somewhat. I also reheated the brick at her feet in hopes of providing her more comfort.

Rune kept the fire blazing throughout the night. Its heat permeated the room and we had to move the rocker away from the fireplace. Two blankets and a quilt proved to be too many and sometime during the hours of darkness, we discarded the quilt. I dozed intermittently, asleep yet very much aware of both Rune and Old Mag.

It was almost daybreak when Rune roused me. "Callie, I have to go to the forest today to mark a stand of trees but I'll return around suppertime. Do you think Old Mag will mind if you pack me a little food in a sack?"

I assured him she wouldn't and scurried about gathering bread, cheese and an apple. I didn't want to send him off with an empty stomach either.

"If you'll help me Rune, I'll try to cook oatmeal for breakfast. You need something to eat and Trog will, too, when he gets up."

"What will I need?" asked Trog as he descended the ladder. "My goodness! It is certainly warm down here. You two did a wonderful job of keeping the fire blazing." He glanced at his mother. Her raspy breathing was audible in the room. "How's Mag?"

"About the same, maybe somewhat worse. The tonic eased her cough but she has a high fever. Is that what the camphor salve is for? Because if it is, it didn't work on her."

"No, the salve relieves chest ailments, not fevers." He touched Old Mag's forehead. "You are right, Girl. She is very warm to the touch. How long has it been since you last administered the tonic?"

"Several hours ago. There's a little left in the pot but I'll need to make more as soon as we get something to eat. Breakfast, Trog, that's what you need. And Rune, too. We don't need something cold, either, but something hot."

"Well, Callie, cooking over the fireplace is easy," Trog said. "Let's fill this pot with some water and hang it on the hook. When it comes to a boil, we'll add some oatmeal. Then just keep stirring it until the water boils away and the oatmeal thickens. But you have to keep stirring because if you stop, the meal will burn."

"I'll put water on for tea and set the table for you while you take care of the oatmeal." Rune busied himself putting things on the table.

The oatmeal boiled vigorously; I stirred until I thought my arm would break. The lumpy, gray mess I ladled into the bowls did not look at all like the oatmeal Old Mag often served. I hoped a little honey or sugar would compensate.

Rune and Trog stared unhappily at their bowls. Neither of them said a word. They spooned in honey, added a small amount of milk and ate. I did the same. To my surprise, it did not taste as awful as it looked. I washed it down with hot tea.

Rune was off as soon as he finished eating. He slipped out into the early dawn light and walked quickly toward the furnace, swinging his sack lunch. I fetched the remainder of last night's broth to reheat for Old Mag. She needed to get nourishment to keep her strength up.

Trog knelt anxiously beside her pallet and shook her gently. "Mag, Mag, wake up." She lay still as death with just the rise and fall of her chest indicating life. He shook her again, a little harder.

Responding with a moan, she tried to rise from her bed, unfocussed eyes glancing about the room. "Belle, Belle, is that you?"

*This is not good,* I thought. *She's calling for her daughter.* I looked at Trog. He handled his alarm and concern well. He spoke to Old Mag in a velvety voice.

"No Mag. It's Trog. Take it easy. You need rest. The girl is warming hot broth and the tonic, too. You'll feel better if you eat a little something."

"I don't want anything. I don't feel like eating. Just let me stay here awhile and then I'll go to the weave house."

"No Mag, you have to eat. Here, the girl has it ready. Sit up now and take a sip."

Between the two of us we managed to get the broth and tonic down her throat. I was alarmed at how fragile she seemed. Just yesterday she was bouncing with energy; now she lay limp as a rag. She closed her eyes once again and dozed.

Trog left for the weave house promising to return shortly. He had to make several deliveries. I turned my attention to clearing the remnants of breakfast from the table and was almost finished when Lily arrived.

Like the night before, she came carrying pots. "Mama sent more broth for Old Mag. The vegetable stew is ready to cook. All we have to do is hang it close to the fire and it'll be ready to eat for the noon meal."

She set the pots down, gave me a big hug and then walked to Old Mag's pallet. "She doesn't look much better than she did last night, Callie. Didn't the salve work?"

"I think it worked, Lily but she has a fever and Trog told me the salve didn't help much with fevers. But she drank all of the tonic and most of the broth you sent last night. That's a good sign."

Lily knelt down and stroked Old Mag's face. "Sick people don't look like themselves, do they, Callie? See how little Old Mag looks, like she's shrunk up overnight. She barely makes a lump under the blankets."

I marveled at the child's insight and wondered how much sickness she had seen. She was wise beyond her years. I put my arms around her and pulled her close to me, grateful to have her with me in the cottage. Both Old Mag and I were in very capable hands.

The two of us found plenty of work to keep us busy. There were dishes to be washed, firewood to bring in and the floor to be swept. Lily folded the blankets that Rune and I had bundled in the night before and returned them to the loft. Chance joined in the activity. He wrapped himself around our legs and grabbed at our skirts.

Just before noon, Vance stopped by. He felt Old Mag's head and listened to her cough. I didn't like the grave look on his face.

"What?" I asked, "What?"

"I'm going to have to bring her stronger medicines. She has more than a chest complaint. Someone should have come for me last night."

Last night! Not one of us had thought of sending for Vance. I was in the same room with her, snuggled next to Rune while Old Mag's condition worsened. Why didn't I send Rune or Trog for him? Vance looked into my guilt stricken eyes.

"Not to worry, Girl, not to worry. I have things for fevers. We'll have Old Mag up on her feet in no time at all."

# Chapter 15

During the next three days, Vance supplied Old Mag with a variety of medicines. Some he brought ready to use, others I had to make under his supervision. I chopped, boiled or soaked dried roots, bark and leaves to make teas, infusions and poultices. There was a steady procession of women to our cottage and all of the women agreed that Vance was the best medicine man around. They regaled me with stories of how he had made them or some member of their families well after a near-death illness. I didn't have much faith in his power but he was all I had and I followed his directions carefully.

Under his watchful eyes, Old Mag slowly recovered. She was able to sit in her rocker by the third night and ate oatmeal the next morning. Her face was no longer flushed nor were her eyes glazed. By the end of that week, she was able to walk around the cottage without assistance and insisted that she be allowed to sleep in the loft. With regret, I realized that my night vigils had come to an end and with them, the precious hours I spent with Rune, cuddled in front of the fireplace.

I knew Old Mag had fully recovered when she came down from the loft one morning and said, "Girl, I appreciate all you have done for me, I really do, but I can't stomach your oatmeal one more morning. I just can't."

Trog and I laughed hilariously at that. I'm sure he was thinking the same thing.

Life returned to normal. The three of us, and Chance, too, returned to the weave house. After a week's absence, we had a lot of catching up to do. I wanted to finish my shawl and was glad that neither Old Mag nor Trog found other chores for me to do.

I wove diligently for two days and finally ran the last row of weft. I nearly burst with pride each time I looked at it. I was anxious to have that shawl around my shoulders.

Old Mag suggested I wait until the next morning to begin removing the shawl from the loom. "You're going to need a lot patience, Girl, and it will be easy for a thread to get away from you. It's best if you feel fresh and ready to work on it."

I agreed reluctantly. I decided to sew strips of cloth together and had barely begun to do so when she interrupted me.

"Come over here, Girl, to this loom. I'm going to teach you how to set up the loom for weaving. To do that we start with the warp."

I put my sewing away and did as she asked. She had heavy navy blue thread measured out in a long hank, tied in places with string to keep the thread from becoming tangled.

"See the wooden drum at the back of the loom, near the floor? We need to wrap the blue thread around that. To do that, we have to pass the threads through the heddle."

I looked at her blankly. "Don't worry, Girl, I'm going to explain it to you. See this wire contraption." I nodded. That's the heddle. Each wire has a small eye. See them?" Again, I nodded. "We need to pass each warp thread through an eye in the heddle, take it back to the drum and wrap it around. The heddle is attached to this wooden frame called a harness. Are you ready to begin?"

I nodded.

"Cat got your tongue, Girl?"

"Yes, yes, I'm ready whenever you are, Old Mag."

The two of us worked the rest of the day threading the warp onto the loom. I did most of the work; she handed me the threads and I put them through the heddle and wrapped them around the drum. Old Mag constantly checked the tension of the threads.

"Don't skip an eye, Girl. If you do we'll have to take the threads off back to the mistake. After you've done that two or three times, you learn to be very careful."

When we were finished, the loom was covered with a surface of closely spaced, parallel threads. I was exhausted. My back and shoulders ached from bending over. Old Mag was pleased with what we had accomplished.

"You and I are going to weave a table runner. We'll start on it tomorrow just as soon as we get your shawl off the loom. Be thinking about the color yarn you'll want for the weft."

"I'm going to weave on the big loom, Old Mag? Do you think I'm ready?"

"Girl, if you aren't ready now, you never will be. You've done a good job with your shawl. All the women will be wanting one like it, just you wait and see. You'll be so busy weaving shawls you won't have time to do anything else."

"You'd let me weave a shawl for someone else?" I asked incredulously.

"Well, I won't be weaving them nor will Trog. We're partial to our looms. But first, we have to get yours off the loom and then I want you to weave on my loom. After that, we'll worry about shawls. Come on, let's go home and get supper started."

I held Old Mag's compliment next to my heart for the rest of the evening. That night as I lay in my pallet listening to Chance purr, I thought about weaving a shawl for someone else. *I will not make another shawl like mine; I don't care who wants one. Mine is special, one of a kind and if I have anything to say about it, one of a kind it will stay.*

Just before I drifted off to sleep, I decided on the color for the table runner.

I was eager to get to the weave house the next morning. Trog went early to get the fire going while Old Mag and I stayed in the cottage to do the usual clean-up. I

97

brought in extra armfuls of wood to pass the time and made several trips to the community woodpile for more. On one of those trips, I bumped into Vance.

"How's Old Mag, Callie? I've been meaning to stop by but a number of people have come down with the same complaint and I've been very busy."

"She's fine, Vance. She put in a full day of work yesterday. I don't know how she does it."

"I've got to run now, Callie but tell Old Mag I'll stop by soon." He paused for a second or two and then continued hesitantly. "You seemed awfully interested in my medicines. Would you like to see what I have and where I keep them? Taw and I share a little cottage in the forest. The medicines he uses on his animals are stored there, too."

"Oh, Vance, I'd love to. But not today and probably not tomorrow. I'll be too busy. Give us time to catch up in the weave house and then stop by for me. How does that sound?"

"Sounds great. I'll see you in a few days." With a wave, he continued on his way.

True to her word, Old Mag and I worked on taking the crimson shawl from the loom. It was tedious work. The end of each warp thread had to be worked carefully and the threads pulled through, one over the other. Old Mag kept a watchful eye on me. I refused her offer to help. This was my shawl and I wanted to do it. She sat next to me in silence sewing fabric strips and allowing me to concentrate solely on the work before me.

As I did the final stitch, I breathed a long sigh of relief. "Here it is, Old Mag." I held it up for her to see. "Isn't it beautiful?"

"Put it around your shoulders, Girl. Let me see how it looks on you."

I stood and did as she asked. "Oh, crimson is your color, Girl. It makes your eyes brighter and your cheeks a little rosier." She stood next to me and rubbed her hands across the crimson fabric. "This is extra nice weaving for a beginner. Don't you think so, too, Trog?"

He looked up and nodded his approval. "I well remember my first piece of work. It did not turn out nearly as nice as yours. You have done well, Callie."

With a smile, he returned to his work. He was weaving an intricately patterned rug that required his deepest concentration.

"If the sun is out tomorrow, we'll wash your shawl in cold water to set the color. Then we'll shape it and set it out to dry. In a day or two, you'll be able to wear it." She patted me on the shoulder. "Now, let's think about the table runner I want the two of us to weave."

She had barely spoken the words when the door opened and in stepped Mistress Dodd. She was a beautiful woman with dark hair done up on her head and topped with a saucy hat with a little feather. Her black cloak was trimmed with fur and under it, she wore a bright blue silk jacket and skirt, nipped in tight at the waist. The long sleeves were lace trimmed as were the front of the bodice and the hem of the skirt. The faint scent of violets filled the air each time she moved.

Trog was the first to recover from the surprise of her entrance. He rose from his stool and bent his body slightly at the waist. "Mistress Dodd, how nice to see you this morning. How may we help you?"

She smiled graciously as she looked about the weave house. "I need a few rugs now that the weather is turning colder. I want a variety of colors because they will not all go in the same room. You and Old Mag do such fine work."

At last her eyes came to rest on me. "And who might this be. Have we met?"

"Oh no, Mistress Dodd, I don't think you have met Callie. She is my sister's granddaughter come to stay with us for a while."

"Oh, yes. I may have heard of you. Aren't you called *The Weaver's Girl*?"

Mistress Dodd looked me up and down from head to toe. Her dark green eyes missed no detail of my appearance. I smiled as best I could but frankly felt somewhat intimidated by both her posture and her appearance of wealth.

Trog led her around the small room, showing her the rugs we had on hand. She selected several and then returned to stand in front of me.

"This is a beautiful shawl you are wearing, dear. May I see it?" Even as she spoke, her hands were removing the garment from my shoulders. She rubbed it gently before draping it around her body.

"I think I'll take this, too, Trog. Write up a list of items you wish me to send as payment for my purchases. Or I will give you script to be used in the company store. Whichever you prefer." She gathered up her cloak.

"I'm sorry but the shawl is not for sale." I didn't realize my lips had moved until I heard my voice. I held out my hands for the shawl. "It-it's mine and I'm going to keep it."

There was silence in the weave house. Trog finally spoke.

"I'm sure we can make you a similar shawl, Mistress Dodd. Here, take a look at the yarns we have. Select any color you like." He moved toward the yarn shelf.

Mistress Dodd did not follow. She stood looking at me with slightly narrowed eyes. "And who will weave the shawl?" she asked.

"The girl does that weaving," replied Old Mag. "Her work is excellent."

"Then weave me one just like yours," she said with a forced smile that did not reach her eyes.

My look was unwavering. "I'm sorry but I can't do that. My shawl is one of a kind."

We stood like that for several long seconds. She dropped her eyes first. "Very well then. Forget the shawl. I'll pick one up in Lappe's the next time I go to Snow Hill. I'll send someone for the rugs later."

She tossed her cloak around her shoulders and, with a swish of silk, went out the door.

Trog and Old Mag stared at me incredulously. My knees were shaking. Had I really refused to sell my shawl to the Iron Master's wife? I waited for one of them to scream at me or worse, strike me. Whatever they did to me I knew I deserved it.

The enormity of the situation hit me. *Suppose she goes home and complains to her husband. He might decide he doesn't need the weavers. They'll be out of a home and a job. What will they do? They'll have to leave here, too. Where will they go? If they leave, I'll have to leave. How will I ever get home?*

I was filled with despair. *What have I done?* I thought. *What have I done?*

My reverie was broken by a sudden whoop from Trog. He bent double with laughter. And then he danced. He danced all around the room. Soon Old Mag joined him, the two of them holding hands, laughing, tears streaming down their cheeks.

"Good for you, Girl, good for you! I'm proud of you, so proud of you." Trog gave me a huge bear hug. "You made the shawl, it's yours and I'm proud that you kept it. If she wants one like it, let her weave it."

The thought of the haughty Iron Mistress struggling over a loom kept the three of us laughing for hours.

## Chapter 16

The larger part of the afternoon was spent helping Old Mag with the table runner. I selected red and white yarns to compliment the navy blue warp. Both Trog and Old Mag were pleased with my selection.

"It'll be a patriotic runner, won't it?" he asked.

"Yes," replied Old Mag, "but it can also be used during yuletide. Good thinking, Girl. It will be bright and cheery, too."

I was quite nervous when I perched on Old Mag's stool and faced her loom. I needn't have been. She was a wonderful teacher and before many minutes had passed, I had the hang of it.

Under my feet were two wooden pedals. When I pressed the right pedal, every other warp thread raised. This formed a space between the raised and unraised warp threads called the shed. I passed the weft thread through the shed using a long wooden device called a shuttle. Next I pulled a reed called the beater against the weft threads to push them together tightly. Finally, I pressed the left pedal to lower the raised warp threads and raise a new set. That was all there was to it.

Old Mag and I began with red, did a number of rows in that color and then used white. I didn't get the tension just right and had to rip out a row or two but soon each row was woven perfectly and the pattern began to emerge. The runner was going to be beautiful.

"You're weaving on Old Mag's loom," exclaimed Lily suddenly. I had not heard the child enter the cottage so intent was I on my work. "I've never seen anyone else sit at Old Mag's loom before." She placed her small hand on my shoulder. "You know what you're doing, too. Doesn't she, Old Mag?"

"Yes, child, she does. Trog and I are right proud of her." With that, she began to chuckle and I knew she was thinking of the incident with the Iron Mistress this morning.

"What's so funny?" asked Lily.

"Nothing, Lily." I stopped weaving and looked at her. "I'm finished on this loom for a while. Old Mag and I are doing this runner together and now it's her turn to weave. I'm going to get the triangular loom set up. Would you like to help me?"

"Is your shawl finished, Callie!" exclaimed Lily. "Oh, it is, it is," she cried, clapping her hands. "May I see it, please?"

I brought out the shawl and draped it first around her shoulders and then mine.

"It's beautiful, so beautiful. I wish I had one like it."

At that, both Old Mag and Trog burst into laughter and this time, I joined in. *Will I ever get the vision of the Iron Mistress bent over a loom out of my head* I thought, *or are the three of us destined to laugh about this forever?*

Lily's look of bewilderment prompted me to stop laughing. "Come on, Lily, help me select the yarns for another shawl. Old Mag and Trog have given me that task and I need to get started."

The four of us worked on our respective looms during the last hour of the day. Lily and I took turns filling the triangular loom with warp threads in a soft shade of yellow. Old Mag and Trog were engrossed at their looms and when Lily and I spoke to each other, we did so softly. The time passed quickly.

Although I was busy the next day, I did not forget my promise to Vance. I was thinking about trying to find him that afternoon when he entered the weave house, Lily hanging on his arm.

He greeted us all merrily and then knelt beside Old Mag. "How are you feeling? I must say you look mighty fine to me."

"Vance, I think you'll find her fit as a fiddle," chimed in Trog. "She has more energy than the rest of us put together, isn't that right, Old Mag?"

"Well if I do it's because of Vance's medications. They worked wonders for me. I just finished the last of the primrose tea you made for me. It's relieved the terrible headaches I've had since the fever left me." She gave him a hug. "Thank you, Vance. Stop in one night soon and we'll have another pie."

"I've come to ask if you can spare Callie for a little while. I want to show her the medicine room."

"Sure, the girl can go. She does more than her share of the work around here." Old Mag smiled and then added, "Be sure to be back in time to help with supper."

We said quick goodbyes and then Lily and I set out with Vance. We walked down the stagecoach road for quite a while before he led us across a field and headed toward a stand of trees. I had to look hard for his cottage. Nestled low to the ground, it was almost hidden in the dark and shady forest. A small column of smoke trailed lazily from the chimney.

He opened the door and we stepped into the small room that served as the brothers' living quarters. They had no sleeping loft and two pallets lay on the floor along one wall. It was furnished sparely; a table, several straight-back chairs, and a hutch for storing dishes. A second wall was lined with shelves similar to ours; these contained a flour crock, a few jars of canned vegetables and fruits and other items I was unable to identify. The hearth held several large iron cooking pots. This Spartan room seemed appropriate for the tall, lean men who inhabited it.

I looked up at him and wondered why I had thought him stern when I first met him. His dark eyes twinkled and a generous smile brightened his handsome face. He offered us bee balm tea and then, to my surprise, produced a plate of sugar cookies to go with it. A mid-afternoon snack was a rare treat and Lily and I enjoyed it to the utmost.

Not until I set down my empty teacup and wiped the last cookie crumb from my lips did Vance show us his medicine room. Smaller in size than the living quarters, the entire room was lined with shelves filled with jars and sacks of roots, dried plants, bark, and seeds. Plants and flowers, tied with string, were suspended from the rafters of the ceiling. In the center of the room was a wide table. It was here, he told us, that he ground and chopped the ingredients used in his medicines. An earthy odor permeated the room, mingled with that of dried plants.

His medicines filled most of the shelf space. I walked the length of the shelving looking at the large quantity of items he had. Each was labeled in a beautiful Old World penmanship, many were familiar to me, a few weren't. I had no idea parts of catnip, daffodil, hollyhock, lemon balm, lily of the valley, marjoram, marigold, strawberry, violet, and goldenrod were used to cure ailments.

He had the outer and inner bark of trees as well. I asked him about that.

"Certain parts of trees are used for different ailments. The black walnut tree is a good example. The green rind of the nuts is rubbed on ringworms. I char the bark of the twigs, add water and apply the liquid to snakebites. Another example is the sassafras tree. An excellent tea is made from the roots and used for both medicinal purposes as well as a refreshing drink. Wood chips from the sassafras are used in blanket chests to keep moths from dining on woolen fabrics. Women often used parts of those trees as well to produce nice fabric dyes. The hulls of ripened walnuts produces a brown dye used on wool and the charred tree bark will produce a black dye. The bark of the sassafras produces an excellent orange color that doesn't fade in the sun."

He shared more information as I slowly made my way around the room. "My mother had a huge herb garden and she'd walk me around it and talk about the medicines her mother made from each plant. She fussed all the time about the importance of heirloom seeds and I try to use those whenever I can."

"What are heirloom seeds?" asked Lily.

"Seeds that are handed down from mother to daughter, one generation after another. Those plants are strong and healthy. Old Mag uses heirloom seeds when she plants her herb garden." I looked questioningly at him and he added, "She gets them from me."

Vance continued, "I lived for a while with a tribe of Mohawk Indians and they showed me how to use the parts of trees for medicines. As you can see, I keep my room well stocked."

I nodded in agreement. His collection of medicines was impressive but what impressed me more was his knowledge about how to use them.

"Is it possible to use the wrong medicine?" I asked.

"It certainly is. Just like with Old Mag. The first treatments I used weren't strong enough. But I've learned from experience that if one treatment doesn't work, something else will. Camphor is one of the best medicines for a chest cold and that's what I thought she had."

"That vile stuff I had to put in a sack? How did you make that?"

"I boiled lard, camphor and a few other ingredients down to a paste. It's important to put it in a sack, though, before placing it on anyone's chest. The salve must never be placed on the bare skin."

"Why is that?"

"Oh, Callie, even I know the answer to that," chimed in Lily. "If you rub that salve on your bare chest, you'll have blisters on your skin in the morning. That stuff is really strong."

I grimaced at the thought. "That's nice to know."

"Do you know what else is good to use, Vance, and I don't see any around here?" Lily continued. "Salt meat, that's what. Once I stepped on a piece of wood that had a long nail in it. The nail went right up through my shoe and into my heel. It went in so deep I couldn't pull it out. I had to go home with the wood flapping against my foot. Mama pulled it out. The hole was deep and ugly looking. She put a small slab of salt meat against my heel, wrapped it in a mullein leaf and put my sock over it. I had to keep it on all night but the next morning, that hole was almost turned inside out. Mama said the salt meat sucked out all the poisons from the nail."

"Your mama was right, little girl."

I shuddered at the image of Lily walking home, a board attached to her heel with a nail flopping under her shoe.

"A medicine man has to be very careful. I have to accurately identify the trees and bushes. There are lots of poisons growing under our feet and over our heads."

"Poisons? As in kill people?" I asked.

"As in kill people. Water hemlock is a very poisonous plant that grows in wet, swampy areas. When cut, the root oozes a yellow oil that is very dangerous. If a case of poisoning is caught in time, an emetic may be used to prevent death. Elder bark or muskrat skin with the hair on, chopped fine, are both excellent emetics for hemlock poisoning. May apple is also quite deadly. The plant grows to about a foot or so in height, has beautiful leaves, white flowers and produces a yellow fruit. Oddly enough, the fruit is edible; has a sour but pleasant taste. The roots and seeds of the plant are highly poisonous. Again, if caught in time, an emetic may be administered. Both these plants have medicinal value also but the medicine man must use every caution and know exactly what he is doing. I choose not to use them at all. I have tried and true concoctions that I rely on. I want to heal people, not kill them."

At that comment, we all laughed. "The plants in this area are Taw's. He uses many of the same things on animals that I use on people. I do all the plant collecting because he's not as good at that as I. I also prepare the medicines and tonics from the materials I collect. He administers them to an animal as needed and, I might add, is quite skilled at what he does."

"As are you, Vance. If I get sick I'll know I'm in very good hands."

We walked into the living area and held our hands in front of the fire to warm them. I glanced out a window and noticed how dark the forest seemed.

"Lily, I think it is time for us to be on our way. Your mother probably has chores for you to do and I know Old Mag is expecting me to help her with supper. Thanks, Vance. I'm glad you came for me. I have enjoyed hearing all about your medicines and Taw's too."

Fearful that we might not find our way, Vance walked us back to the village. Lily chattered away but my brain was boggled. Even after seeing his medicine room I still didn't have much faith in a weed as a healing agent. I found myself silently repeating a little chant to the cadence of my footsteps. *I won't get sick! I won't get sick!*

# Chapter 17

The days passed quickly. The sun followed a lower path across the sky and Chance sprawled in the patches of sunlight on the weave house floor. Lily came almost daily to help with the yellow shawl. The crimson shawl was tucked away in Old Mag's blanket chest awaiting a special occasion for me to wear it. Old Mag and I laundered and shaped it with gentle hands. Washing it softened the wool fibers and added an extra sheen to the vibrant color. I was proud of the shawl and was eager to wear it.

Rune was very busy now and was not always able to meet me for a stroll after supper. When he did, we wrapped our arms about each other's waists and pulled ourselves so close together our shadows seemed as one.

On one such evening, we walked for a while along Stagecoach Road, and then backtracked somewhat to stroll past the workers' cottages. There was a fingernail moon high in the sky, just a small cream sliver dangling for us to see. It was quiet and still, just the sounds of our feet hitting the earth and the brush of my skirt against a few shriveled blades of dried grass.

As we approached the cottages, we heard dogs barking. Not just one or two dogs but a cacophony of barks; it seemed that every dog in the village had something to say.

"What's the matter with the dogs?" Rune asked. "They are certainly wound up."

"I can't imagine," I replied. "It can't be the moon."

Rune looked about cautiously. "I hope a bear hasn't decided to come into the village for one last meal before he tucks himself into hibernation."

A small trickle of fear ran down my spine and I clutched his waist more tightly. "Do you think that's why the dogs are barking, Rune? Do you really think a bear has come into the village?"

"Of course not, silly. But I'll say anything to get a few more squeezes like the one you just gave me." He laughed and then continued. "Will you squeeze me again if I tell you I'm afraid of dogs, especially barking dogs?"

I gave him a playful shove and then quickly pulled him to me and kissed him on the lips. "Don't make fun of me, Rune. Those dogs are barking for a reason. Maybe we should turn back."

"Come on, Callie, they could be barking at a raccoon or an opossum. Listen. They've quieted somewhat."

I had to agree the barking had lessened considerably but that did not prevent me from looking cautiously at each dark shadow. As we passed the cottages, I noticed that not a single window was lighted. Everyone in the village was tucked into bed.

As we neared the end of the U, two figures popped around the corner of the last house and ran toward us. My heart skipped several beats; I was tempted to turn around and race for home until I heard laughing and giggling. I recognized Lily and one of her brothers.

"Lily, you two are out awfully late. Is something wrong?"

Lily covered her mouth with one hand and looked at me. "We-we-we're out running an errand for Ma," she blurted out. Her brother nodded his head emphatically in agreement. "She sent us to get something she needed from one of the neighbor's." The two of them stood facing us, awkwardly balancing first on one foot, then on the other. "Come on, we'd better get back. Ma told us not to dawdle." And with those words the two of them scampered away. Their laughter drifted back to us.

I turned to watch them go. "Rune, do you see a light on in Lily's house?"

He peered intently at the houses. "No, Callie, I don't, but maybe the curtains are drawn so tightly no light shows. Surely those two wouldn't be out at this hour without permission." He paused. "But then again, knowing Lily, it's hard to tell. That girl is always up to something."

We completed our circle of the village and were halfway back to my cottage when we saw someone heading toward us. Taw. There was something unmistakable about the way he carried himself that made him readily identifiable even with the poorest of light.

"Good evening, Taw," I called out softly. "Are you out for a stroll, too?"

He chuckled. "No, but had I known you two were out and about, I would have joined you."

"We've finished our walk for this evening, Taw. We're ready to go in for a cup of hot tea. Would you care to join us?"

Taw punched Rune playfully on the shoulder. "What, and spoil the rest of your evening? I think not."

The three of us laughed and then Taw continued. "I'm checking out the village. Did you hear all those dogs barking? I wondered if a bear had decided to take up residence. You two didn't see anything unusual, did you?"

"We thought about a bear, too, but saw nothing. Didn't smell a bear either. I had to hang on tight to Callie because I knew if a bear showed up on the path she'd outrun it and me. She'd run right on in to Snow Hill and Trog would have to fetch her in the wagon tomorrow morning."

Rune and Taw laughed loudly at the thought of me outrunning a bear. I had to admit, the mental picture was funny. We stood a few minutes longer chatting before Taw headed back the way he had come.

Trog and Old Mag had retired for the evening. The fire had been banked but a pot of water simmered over the coals. I fixed us each a cup of chamomile tea while Rune pulled the rocker up close to the hearth.

"Do you want a little honey in your tea?" I asked.

He pulled me onto his lap. "You're all the sweetness I need," he murmured, burying his face in my neck. "You're all I need."

Later, as I climbed into the loft, all thoughts of Lily and her brother had fled my mind.

In the morning, Trog asked about the barking dogs. "I'll bet they roused everyone in the village. Did you and Rune see anything odd going on?"

Before I could reply, Old Mag chimed in. "Well, I didn't hear dogs last night. Why do you think the girl heard them? When she and Rune go out, they have eyes and ears only for each other." She gave me a broad wink.

"Now Mag, how could they not have heard the dogs?" Trog laughed. "Seriously, Callie, did you see anything last night?"

"No Trog, I didn't. All the cottages were dark. We heard them barking, though. They barked so much Taw got out of bed to investigate. We met him on the path just before we came in for tea. He thought a bear had wandered into the village but the three of us decided a smaller animal had most likely created the uproar."

The subject was dropped as the three of us went about our chores. Old Mag and I got breakfast while Trog went to the weave house to light a fire in the fireplace, as he did each morning. After breakfast, we did the dishes and straightened the cottage before heading to the weave house. By that time, it was warm and cozy.

We each went to work immediately on our projects. The table runner was nearing completion. Old Mag had decided to do several more but no two would be identical. Trog was weaving the top of a very detailed pillow covering. His work was so intricate it looked more like a tapestry than weaving.

The yellow shawl was soft as butter under my fingers. It too was almost finished. I was amazed at how easy weaving on the triangular loom now seemed. My hands flew over the work and I seldom made an error.

We had been working several hours when Trog stood up and stretched. "I'm going to take a breather," he said, "get a little fresh air. I think I'll stop by the store to ask if anyone knows why the dogs were barking last night."

"Are you still harping about all the racket those dogs made?" asked Old Mag. "The girl said all the houses were dark so who's going to know why they barked."

"I don't know but there's no harm in asking," he replied as he walked out the door.

Shortly after Trog left, Lily dropped by. She had a basket full of fabric strips to sew together for a weaving project and after a quick greeting, got right to work. She even ignored Chance who tried his best to get her to play with him.

I was just about to ask her if the cat had her tongue when Trog returned. He had a huge grin on his face and I could tell he was eager to impart whatever news he had found out. Old Mag and I looked at each other briefly; she rolled her eyes upward and gave me a little smile. We didn't say anything to him nor did Lily.

He busied himself at his loom for a few minutes; the silence in the air was heavy with expectation. Finally, he could stand it no longer.

He turned on his stool to look at us. "Does anyone wish to know what happened in the village last night?"

"I know what happened, Trog, I know," said Old Mag. "The dogs were talking to each other and one said something the others didn't like." She cackled with glee at her remark.

Trog sighed and shook his head at his mother. "Better than that, Mag. Somebody played a switching game. Every family around the U was affected."

"A switching game?"

"What is that?"

Old Mag and I asked our questions simultaneously.

"It seems a mischievous little imp went out last night and switched the animals around. Mrs. Brown went out to milk her cow and found a goat in the stall. Same thing

113

happened at the Monroe's. The Tuttles went out to their henhouse and found all the chickens had been replaced with…"

I tuned Trog out and looked at Lily. Her big, brown eyes were wide and innocent. But I knew. And she knew that I knew. My lips curved upward in a smile. She returned it warmly. Her thank you was unspoken but I received it. We were conspirators.

"…and how that change was made," continued Trog, "without a lot of squawking and quacking, I'll never know. Oh, I must tell you about the dogs. Every dog that was tied outside last night was swapped with another dog. Now wonder they were barking."

He paused for a second and I began to laugh uncontrollably. The image of Lily and her brother running around in the dark, switching animals from one place to another was just too much. I laughed until tears rolled down my cheeks and my sides ached. And still I laughed.

The others joined me, whether from contagion or because they truly thought it was funny. It was quite a while before we got ourselves under control and went back to work.

Neither Lily nor I mentioned the switching game again. It was our secret and served to strengthen the bond of friendship that tied the two of us together.

# Chapter 18

The weather turned surprisingly warm during the second week of November. Trog lit the fire in the weave house long enough to remove the chill and then we opened the windows and the door. I gazed out the windows longingly and found myself making one mistake after another in my work. I ripped out the weaving with audible sighs until Old Mag in exasperation suggested I put aside the project and take a walk.

"I think you have spring fever in November, Girl. Many more mistakes and that wool won't be fit for weaving. Go on, get away from here for awhile."

She didn't have to tell me twice; I was out the door in a heartbeat. I stood outside the cottage for a few minutes pondering where I should go. I wanted to run but there were too many people out and about. I didn't want to go down to the canal because I'd have to pass by the furnace and I always worried about flying sparks and cinders in the stack area.

I finally decided to walk toward the blacksmith shop in hopes of finding Taw. He was busy with two horses Master Dodd had recently purchased. Trog had told me they were very unmanageable and Taw was trying to gentle them. I was curious to see how a horse whisperer worked.

I chatted briefly with several women busy readying their gardens for winter. As always, their warmth and friendliness uplifted my spirits. The feelings of isolation and emptiness I had experienced when I first arrived in the village had dissipated and I no longer felt I had been displaced in time. True, Trog and Old Mag, Taw, Vance, Lily and Rune, of course, had done a lot to ease my emotional pain. But I deserved a lot of credit, too. I had grown in ways I could not fathom and deep inside the core of me I knew I belonged here. This simple life satisfied me and I was truly happy.

There was, however, one dark shadow on my happiness. Jack. Even now my stomach clutched when I thought of him. We had shared many wonderful times and he deserved better than to have me just disappear. There had to be closure for both of us. But when? And how?

*Why am I thinking such thoughts on this beautiful day? Push those deep and disturbing questions aside until you have to deal with them. You'll know when the time comes. For now, enjoy yourself.*

I was so deep in thought I was upon the blacksmith shop before I knew it. I hesitated, unsure what to do or where to go. A large man stood in the doorway, arms akimbo, staring at me. A long black apron covered his torso and his shirtsleeves were rolled up past his elbows to reveal muscular, hairy arms. His mouth was hidden in a full black beard and thick black brows shaded his green eyes.

"How may I help you, miss?" I jumped a little when I heard his booming voice.

"I'm looking for Taw. I want to see the horses he is gentling."

"And who might you be?"

Without thinking, I replied, "I'm the Weaver's Girl."

A broad smile revealed white teeth nestled in the beard. "Ah, yes, I've heard of you. Aren't you Rune's lassie?"

"That she is, Smitty. He's a sorry sight if he can't get back to the village to see her every night." Taw was suddenly beside me, laughing at my discomfort. "I'll look after her."

"Just my luck for you to show up when you did. I've heard a lot about you, Girl. Nice to have met you."

"And you, too," I replied but the smith had already turned his back and was bent over an anvil.

"Just be glad you didn't meet him because you have a toothache."

"Why? What do you mean?"

116

"He's the village dentist, didn't you know?" I shook my head in answer to his question. "If a tooth gives you a problem, he'll put a pair of tongs in your mouth and pluck it out for you. Sometimes I think he enjoys being a dentist more than he does shoeing horses."

"How awful." I shuddered to think of dental work without anesthetic or antibiotics.

Taw took me by the arm. "Callie, what a wonderful surprise. What brings you to the blacksmith shop?"

"I was looking for you, Taw. I heard you were gentling two very spirited horses and I wanted to watch you work. That is, if you don't mind."

"Of course I don't mind. I'll be happy to have you watch me work my magic."

He steered me well to the right of the blacksmith shop and headed for an area I had not yet had the opportunity to explore. In the distance I could see a low outbuilding. Two beautiful horses were prancing about in a nearby corral. As we approached they pawed the ground and snorted.

"The black beauty is Prince and he is a haughty one. The brown lad is Juniper; he's a handful, too. I've been working with them almost two weeks now and am happy to say I have made a little progress. At least they let me enter the corral. When they were first brought to me they allowed no one to enter. Your presence, Callie, will disturb them a little so I won't guarantee what you will see."

Taw found a spot for me to sit and then opened the gate to the corral. As soon as he did so, the horses shook their heads and snorted. Prince galloped around the fence, kicking his heels, mane flying. Taw opened a door in the outbuilding and Prince pranced in. Taw followed, shutting the door behind him. When he returned, he carried a bridle.

Juniper stood still, nostrils flaring, eyes rolling wildly and ears flat against his head. Taw approached him slowly, holding out the bridle. The horse pawed the

117

ground twice but allowed the bridle to be slipped over his head.

Taw talked to Juniper the entire time I watched. Sometimes I heard his voice but most of the time his murmurings were so soft they were inaudible. He led the horse around the corral so many times I lost count. At first, Juniper pranced and walked sideways forcing Taw to keep his distance but with each lap, he moved closer and closer to the animal until they were side by side.

At one point, man and beast stood nose to nose. The horse was very quiet, ears perked forward listening intently, eyes looking into Taw's. He didn't flinch when Taw gently placed a hand on his neck and stroked softly. Taw stepped very close to the animal and ran his right hand along the beast's back. The two of them made several more turns around the corral and then Taw led him to the outbuilding.

He returned with Prince. What a wild one he was. He reared on his hind legs and pawed the air with his forefeet. I held my breath in fear Taw would be struck by his flashing hooves. I don't know how Taw managed to hold on to the bridle but he did. Prince tried a variety of tricks to shake him off. He jerked his head up and down and sideways. He tried to maneuver Taw against the corral fence. He bucked. Nothing worked. He finally wore himself out and stood panting, white lather on his flanks.

Eventually the horse and man were walking side by side around the corral, Taw's arm flung lightly across the horse's back. Taw murmured the entire time. Not once did I hear a sharp word or see a sign of anything but patience on Taw's part.

When he finished with Prince, he removed the bridle and then let Juniper out of the building. The two horses ran wildly for a few minutes and then calmed, flanks quivering.

"Well, what do you think? Are you ready to try your hand with one of these critters?" Taw asked as he sat down beside me outside the corral.

"My goodness, no! They are both so huge and have such power. You looked awfully small standing in front of that prancing Prince. I was afraid you'd be struck by his hooves."

"That horse is really a handful. Most of the time I work with him is spent getting him in the mood to cooperate. Juniper is much farther along but they both still have a long way to go before I'll try to saddle them."

"I couldn't hear a word you said, Taw, yet you talked the entire time. What sort of things do you say to them? Be a good boy and I'll give you a carrot?"

"Oh, I whisper sweet nothings in their ears. I must say all the right things, too, because they listen. I'll give them carrots and other treats later. Right now I want them to accept me as boss. That's the biggest hurdle. Once I get past that, my work will be easier."

"What will you do with them next?"

"They'll have to get used to a weight on their backs. Did you notice how I draped my arm across their backs? Well, that is just the beginning. Next comes a blanket. They won't like that one bit and will do everything in their power to get it off. When they adjust to that, I'll put on a saddle. That really brings out the beast in them. I've had horses almost pull my arm out of socket when I saddled them. I remember one fellow that dropped to the ground and tried to roll the saddle off. Let me tell you, that was a funny sight. Last, but most difficult of all, is a man's weight in the saddle. Mine. Prince and Juniper are not going to like me on their backs one little bit. You thought they bucked and reared and pawed the air today but that was nothing to what they will do when I first get in the saddle. I'll hang on for dear life and when I get tossed I'll just climb right back on. Eventually, the knowledge that I'm on to stay will sink through their hard heads and then training will be over. They'll be ready to ride."

"Will you turn them over to Master Dodd then?"

"I'll ride them myself for a few days and then I'll take them to Master Dodd. He likes spirited horses so I won't take all the devilment out of them."

"Are you ever afraid?"

"No. The day I show a horse fear, I'm finished. I show the animals respect and persistence and eventually they come to respect me and do what I ask of them. Some horses take longer than others but sooner or later, I'll win them over."

"How in the world did you figure out you have a way with animals?"

"Oh, I don't know. I've always enjoyed being with critters. As a little tyke I discovered I could sort of talk to them and to my amazement, they seemed to listen. One of my first experiences involved a cat. She was a wild thing and no one could come near her let alone touch her. One day, while I was sitting on our back steps, I began murmuring to her. Before long, not only could I rub her back but she was eating out of my hand. I realized then I had a gift. When I first began working with horses, I did a lot of things wrong. Through a process of trial and error, I developed a system and it works well for me. Once in a while I get kicked or bitten but most of the time I leave the corral with nothing broken or bleeding."

I stood and brushed the dirt off my skirt. "I enjoyed watching you put Prince and Juniper through their paces. You have a lot more patience than I."

"I don't believe that for a minute, Callie. It takes a lot of patience to sit in front of a loom and weave thread in and out. Old Mag is always bragging about how good you are. She says you are making shawls to sell and trade. I think that is wonderful considering you have only been at it a couple of months. And besides that, Old Mag and Trog are real taskmasters. If they say you are good, you are."

I felt my face and neck flush under his gaze. I appreciated and welcomed his compliment but just didn't know how to handle it.

"Speaking of Old Mag and Trog, I think I'd better get back to work. Old Mag let me go out for a while because the weather is so beautiful and she'll be wondering where in the world I am."

"I think I'll walk you back to the weave house. I haven't seen the two of them in a few days. Think they might enjoy my company for a bit?"

"I know they would, Taw. You're always welcome. Come one. If we hurry, you might persuade Old Mag to give you a slice of the apple pie I saw on the shelf last night."

As we turned to walk away, I looked back for one last glimpse of Juniper and Prince. They stood quietly, observing our movements. One would never have suspected how unruly they could be.

# Chapter 19

The warm weather continued but I did not receive another reprieve. I spent my days in the weave house with Old Mag and Trog. I finished the yellow shawl and started on one using both a dark and light blue. Old Mag expected me to work on her loom a little each day and together we had completed a small stack of table runners.

We talked of many things, the three of us. Old Mag was excited about the upcoming Feast Day, scheduled to take place near the end of the month.

"Does anyone call Feast Day Thanksgiving Day?" I asked.

"No, I don't think I've heard it called that particularly by anyone in the village."

"Is it held on the same day each year?"

"No, the women just get together and decide when to have it. They usually wait until everything in their gardens has been harvested and canned. Then they celebrate with a big day of eating. All kinds of wonderful dishes are prepared and everyone eats and eats."

"Sort of like a bear gorging himself just before hibernation, is what it is," chimed in Trog. "They sure do try to out cook each other, Old Mag included."

"Like the Pilgrims celebrated their first harvest in the New World," I said.

"If you say so," replied Old Mag.

I let the subject drop and we worked for a while in silence. I had several questions I wanted to ask about Feast Day. Did each family celebrate alone or was it a community endeavor? Was part of the day spent in the church giving thanks or did each family give thanks in their own way?

The village church was located near the far end of the U and I went every Sunday morning with Trog and Old Mag. It was small with wooden floors and whitewashed walls. The pews were uncomfortable with high, straight backs and very narrow seats. It was lighted with candles and whale oil lamps and on a morning when the windows and door had to remain closed, the fumes were overpowering. Two wood stoves near the front provided heat when needed. So far this fall, neither had been lit because body heat took the chill off the room.

We had an actual preacher one Sunday a month; a circuit rider, he served a number of other churches. I enjoyed the sermons he preached. During the other Sunday services, someone in the community elaborated on the message he had given and by the time the preacher came back, we were all ready to hear a new sermon.

The music was simple, guitars, spoons and hand clapping. There was no hymnal; we sang from memory. The songs used were favorites in the village and before many Sundays had passed I knew them all.

The service was long but I enjoyed the simplicity of it. It was basic worship without all the folderol and I found myself looking forward to Sunday morning. It was also the social event of the week for the women in the village and after the service, they hung about the church, chatting and laughing. The ladies vied for the honor of having the preacher dine with them for Sunday dinner before he rode off to his next parish.

*If there is a Feast Day service, what will it be like? And who will deliver the message? Surely the preacher won't return in the middle of the week? Most important of all, will Rune be here? Wouldn't it be nice to have him around for an entire day?*

"Snap out of it, Girl. Your hands have been idle for quite some time." Old Mag interrupted my thoughts. "Have you reached a difficult spot or something?"

"No," I laughed, "I was just thinking."

"Must have been good thoughts, too, because you had a lovely smile on your face," added Trog. "I need your help, Callie. I'm ready to put new warp on my loom and I wondered if you be kind enough to help me."

"I'll be happy to," I replied. Concentrating on the intricacy of threading the warp would most certainly keep me from daydreaming. Trog and I worked diligently but the task was tedious and the morning dragged. I was glad when Old Mag suggested we take a meal break. We always took sack lunches to the weave house even though the cottage was next door. For one thing, we let the fire in the cottage go out and it was time consuming to start another. We had a cold meal at mid-day; bread with the meat left over from dinner the night before, washed down with milk or water. If the fire was burning in the weave house, we kept a kettle going for hot tea.

I passed the cloth meal sack to Old Mag and Trog and watched as they each removed a biscuit, a thick slab of salty ham, and an apple. I poured three glasses of milk before I sat on the floor in the sun from the open doorway and pulled my lunch from the sack. As soon as he heard it rustling, Chance was by my side, begging for a bite to eat.

"Okay, okay, I'll share with you but give me time to get the food out of the sack, will you?" I pulled the ham into bite size pieces and put them on the floor nearby. Chance pounced upon them quickly. I leaned against the doorjamb and bit into my biscuit.

A swarm of tiny insects hovered nearby, enjoying the warmth of the sun. Their little wings fluttered so hard and fast they were both invisible and soundless. The three of us ate wrapped in the silence of our thoughts.

I was thinking how wonderful a nap would be when a shadow fell across my face. I opened my eyes and saw Rune with Vance beside him, peering down at me.

"Rune," I cried with delight. "How wonderful to see you! What are you doing in the village in the middle of the day?"

I smiled broadly as I held out my hand for him to pull me to my feet. He did so, then put his hands on my waist, picked me up and swung me around. Chance ran

124

for the safety of his basket, taking with him the last morsel of ham.

"A little bird told me about an apple pie that's on the shelf in the weave house," said Vance, "and I decided to stop by to check it out, the pie that is. Rune decided to come with me to check out the apple of his eye."

"Well, there's no apple pie here. Taw finished it off the other day. But the girl can run along to Dusty's and get one. Here," said Old Mag, handing me a pot holder, "he probably needs another one of these by now. He burns through them regularly."

"I think I'll go with Callie; she might need help carrying the pie," said Rune. He stood aside to let me pass through the doorway and then fell into step beside me. He put his arm around me and kissed me on the cheek. "I don't know if you're prettier by moonlight or sunlight, Callie."

I felt myself blushing. "Rune, what a surprise! Do you have to go right back or will you be here for tonight, too?"

"What do you think?" he asked, giving my waist a squeeze. We walked slowly toward the bakery anxious to prolong these extra minutes we had to spend together.

The aroma of bread filled the air around the bakeshop. I let Rune select the pie and we started back toward the weave house. Rune's silver hair glistened in the sunlight. He caught me looking at him and winked lasciviously.

"You carry the pie, Callie and then I can put my arm around you."

"Why? I can wrap my arm around you just as easily," I replied, but I took the pie. As I did, I felt him draw in his breath sharply.

"What? What's the matter?" I asked, concern in my voice.

Rune stopped walking, tilted his head up and looked into the sky. I followed his gaze and was astonished to see a bright red balloon with a suspended gondola floating on the breezes above.

"What in the world is that?" asked Rune.

"A hot air balloon," I replied. "I wonder what it's doing here?"

"Hurry, let's tell the others!"

We raced to the weave house. I called through the doorway, "Quick, quick, step outside and see the hot air balloon that's flying over us."

The others joined us outside and gazed upward. As we watched, the balloon slowly began to descend from the sky. Four lines dangled from the sides of the huge basket. I could see two men waving wildly as they peered at us over the rim of the basket.

By now, many villagers had spied the balloon and a large crowd, eyes turned upward, watched in awe.

"I hope the navigator doesn't try to land that thing near the furnace," said Trog. "If he does, that'll be the end of the balloon. All it will take is one flying spark or ember to put a hole in the fabric."

The balloon seemed to hover right over the weave house as it crept toward the ground. "Hello down there!" yelled one man from the gondola. "Is it all right if we land?"

"Yes!" shouted a number of people almost in unison.

"We'll need something to tie the ropes to. Can you handle that?"

Again a resounding yes was the response. Two men raced to the blacksmith shop and returned shortly with four iron stakes and a huge mallet. The stakes were barely driven into the ground before the huge gondola hovered over our heads. Several men leaped into the air, grabbed the lines to pull the basket down and secure it to the stakes.

The men in the basket smiled broadly at us as they climbed over the side. "Thank you, thank you gentlemen, for a job well done," said one of them, nodding his head as he spoke.

We all crowded around trying to get a look. Someone pulled on my sleeve. I looked down to see Lily, standing on tiptoes, straining to see. I called to Vance. "Swing Lily up on your shoulders, Vance so she can have a look, too." He did so much to Lily's delight.

Trog stepped forward. "How can we help you gentlemen? Surely you stopped for a reason."

"That we did, kind sir, that we did. We've come from Fort McHenry and hope to return this very afternoon. Unfortunately, we are running low on charcoal. We saw your furnace and wondered if you might be able to spare a little."

A laugh rippled through the crowd. "Charcoal we got plenty of mister," someone yelled. "How much do you need?"

By this time, the furnace supervisor had arrived on the scene. He and the two men talked briefly and the supervisor sent several men to the charcoal warehouse. The rest of us pushed closer to the balloon, anxious for a look.

Rune and I maneuvered through the crowd and before long, I found myself standing right in front of the gondola. The basket looked small in the air but on the ground it was huge with more than enough room for the two men, a generous pile of charcoal and a large metal pan.

One of the men smiled at me. Encouraged, I asked, "How does this thing work?"

"Oh, it's very simple to operate. We build a charcoal fire in the brazier," he pointed to the metal pan, "and the hot air from the fire is fed into the balloon to keep it inflated." He climbed back in and pointed to a large valve fastened above the gondola. "This is a blast valve. We maintain our height by opening and closing that valve. In doing so, we control the flow of heat from the brazier to the burner. The more hot air we allow into the balloon, the higher we go. Keeping the valve closed allows us to descend."

127

"What is the balloon made of?" asked Old Mag.

"The balloon is nothing more than a huge bag made of varnished silk; it holds hot air nicely."

"Do you have to go the way the wind is blowing?" asked Rune.

"Oh, no. See these lines holding the gondola to the balloon? We pull on them to get our direction. It's really very easy once one gets the hang of it."

About that time, the crowd parted to permit a mule and wagon into the area. The needed charcoal had arrived.

"Where do you want the coal, mister?" asked the driver.

For the next few minutes the two balloonists busily directed the placing of the charcoal. "That's enough, good friends. What do we owe you?"

"Nothing," replied the furnace supervisor. "A look at your contraption was worth a little charcoal."

"Can't you stay for a bite to eat?" asked Old Mag. "I can rustle up something quick."

"Thank you dear lady, but no, we must be on our way. Darkness falls early these days."

They added charcoal to the brazier to intensify the fire. The balloon had sagged somewhat while the gondola was on the ground but more heat from the brazier caused it to swell again.

"Untie the lines and when I give you a signal, release all four at once."

There was a flurry of excitement as the lines were removed from the stakes. "Wait, wait," I cried. "Take this apple pie. You won't find another anywhere nearly as good." I held the pie up and one of the men took it from my hands as the balloon began to rise.

"Thank you lovely lady. I'm sure the pie is delicious but I'd rather have you."

There was a ripple of laughter followed by a chorus of goodbyes as the balloon slowly ascended. All around me people applauded, excited yet sad to see the adventurers glide away. I waved until the men in the gondola were no longer visible and in no time at all, the balloon was a tiny speck in the afternoon sky.

The crowd slowly dispersed and the villagers went about their business as if nothing had happened. We trooped back to the weave house, joined by Lily and Taw, who had seen the balloon from the corral and hurried in to join the crowd.

"Well, Girl, you gave away our pie. What do you think of that, Vance?"

"I think it was more than generous of her to do that. I hope they enjoy it. I know I would have."

Trog handed me another potholder. "Run over to the bakery and get another one. After that adventure, we all need something sweet."

# Chapter 20

That night Rune and I walked to the medicine house to visit Vance and Taw. We sat on blankets in front of the fire and sipped hot mint tea. Conversation flowed easily with the balloon being discussed first.

"If those men had offered me a ride in that balloon, I would have taken it," said Taw.

"Not me," said Vance. "I plan to keep my feet planted on the ground."

"Well I think it would be exciting to see the earth from high above. I'll bet everything looks different. Just think how much you could see at one time. All you'd have to do is turn around slowly in the gondola. Down here, vision is so limited. Something always blocks the view. A house or a tree. Up there, the sky's the limit. Why, I'll bet you can even feel the clouds on your face."

"Great fun, Taw, until you run out of charcoal or the balloon meets a bird with a very sharp beak."

"Come on, Vance, I would have guessed you'd be willing to fly through the air with me."

"I would have gone with you, Taw," chimed in Rune. "How about you Callie? Would you be daring enough to go?"

"Oh yes," I replied. "The view from a balloon has got to be magnificent. Better than the one from an airplane." The words slipped out of my mouth.

The three men looked at me. Taw finally spoke. "An airplane? What's an airplane? Does it fly, too?"

"Yes, it flies but it looks nothing like a hot air balloon. A plane is hard to describe but look, I'll sketch one on the table, with my fingers." I roughly drew an invisible plane with my fingers, hoping their imaginations would bridge the gap.

They studied the table intently while I described the wings, the cockpit, the cabin seating and the windows.

"Food and beverages are served, too, if the flight is long enough," I added as I finished my description.

My words were met with disbelieving silence. Rune looked at me finally and asked, "Where do they store the charcoal?"

"Planes don't use charcoal as fuel, Rune. They use a liquid fuel called gas, stored in large tanks inside the plane."

"What you describe is difficult to imagine, Callie, but if you say it's true, it is," said Vance, scratching his chin thoughtfully. "Have you ever ridden in one?"

"Yes, I have, many times." My mind reached for a parallel they could understand. "It-it's like riding in a wagon, only you're in the sky without horses." Pretty lame but that was all I could think of at the moment.

Taw guffawed heartily. "Then it's got to be a pretty bumpy ride. That balloon just floated away as smooth as you please. I'd rather be in the balloon."

I laughed, too. "Well, actually, a plane ride is pretty smooth most of the time because you're in the air. Once in a while, the plane bounces up and down because it hits air pockets and then the ride is bumpy."

"Air pockets and bumps in the sky? You aren't making all this up are you Callie?" asked Rune.

I shook my head. "No, everything I've said is true. I've never flown in a balloon but I've always wanted too. Maybe I will someday."

"I doubt I'll ever have the opportunity again. That's the first time I've seen a balloon like that but I'm going to be looking in the sky from now on," Taw laughed.

Vance refilled our cups and we sat for a few minutes in comfortable silence.

"I was in the store today," said Rune, "and McQuerrie told me the charcoaling is about ready to end. The colliers are constructing the last pits. When they burn down to charcoal, that'll be the end of it for this season."

"They've coaled longer than usual this fall due to the warm weather. I'm sure those men are ready to stop. Coaling is hard, dangerous work."

My face must have reflected my thoughts because Vance said, "You have no idea what we're talking about, do you, Callie?"

"No, not a glimmer," I replied with a laugh.

"Now you know how we felt about your airplane. Well let us give you an education in charcoaling," Rune said and the three of them filled my head with talk of fagans, billets, lapwood, mulls, and charcoal pits until my mind was totally awhirl.

"Whoa! Stop! I don't understand half of what you're saying."

"Why not? We told you everything you need to know to construct and take care of a charcoal pit."

"You've told me too much. A little information would have been just fine. Where are these charcoal pits anyway? I haven't seen anything like you just described in the village."

"Of course they're not in the village; the colliers construct those on a flat piece of ground close to the cut sections of the forest," laughed Rune. "The thing to do is to take you to a pit area and let you see the mounds first hand. Would you like that?"

"That's a great idea, Rune. I'd like to go, too, but we have to do it soon. Taw, how'd you like to go? Can you get away from Prince and Juniper for part of a day?" Vance looked at Taw, who nodded.

"Wait a minute. I'll have to check with Old Mag before I promise to go traipsing off to who knows where with you three."

"Now Callie, you know good and well Old Mag will let you go. Hasn't she always let you do what you ask?"

"That's true but there might be a first time," I said, knowing full well Old Mag wouldn't hesitate to say yes.

"Let's plan to go the day after tomorrow," suggested Rune.

By the time Rune and I left the medicine house, the four of us had made our plans. I was pretty sure Old Mag would go along with them.

The air was mild for almost the end of November. Rune and I walked side-by-side, arms around each other's waists. We stopped often to embrace and kiss.

"Callie, I love you."

Rune's words took me by surprise. I looked at him, mouth agape, struggling for something to say and over his shoulder, saw a falling star flame briefly in the heavens. The moment was magical; I was afraid if I spoke the spell would be broken.

I looked at him for long moments and then put my arms around his neck and pulled his face close to mine. "Rune, Rune, I love you, too, so very much," I whispered before his lips found mine.

I could not believe this tall, strong man loved me. Me! I wanted to sing and shout but instead, walked softly beside him, holding his hand. My heart beat erratically in my chest and my emotions were a jumble in my brain. Jack seemed as remote and disconnected as a faded childhood memory. Rune was here and now; I wanted to be with him. The time and place did not matter.

My heart was almost back to normal by the time we reached the cottage. Old Mag had retired for the night but Trog sat by the fire, smoking his pipe and reading a book. He greeted us warmly and waved a cup in our direction.

"Join me, please. I waited up for you two. I'm ready for a little conversation before I retire."

I got out two cups and filled them with the hot brew. I enjoyed the tea Trog made. It was somewhat stronger than Old Mag's and he often added herbs to provide an interesting taste. I refilled his cup before I joined the two of them at the table.

"Callie and I visited Taw and Vance this evening. We talked at length about the balloon. Did you know there were such things, Trog?" asked Rune.

"Oh yes, I've seen them frequently in Paris. I've actually been up in one but don't tell Old Mag. I was just a young fellow looking for excitement. A friend dared me to go up and I went."

"How was it?" inquired Rune.

"It was exhilarating. Everything I thought it would be and more. The balloon lifted me smoothly away from earth and before long I was above Paris, looking down at that beautiful city. For a while, I was able to identify buildings and such but as the balloon ascended, everything got smaller and smaller. I was most disappointed when I had to return to earth."

"I envy you, Trog. That must have been quite an experience."

"It surely was but it must remain our little secret. Old Mag does not like to learn of these things. You see she somehow has the idea that I have been a saint all my life. It would disappoint her greatly to learn, especially at her age, that I am not."

I gave Trog a big smile. I found it hard to imagine calm, unflappable Trog acting impulsively. "Your secret is quite safe with us, Trog. Do you have any others you wish to share?"

"I absolutely do not," he laughed, "one secret a night is surely enough."

"Callie told us about..." began Rune. I kicked him sharply under the table. I did not want a lecture tonight. Rune received my message. "Callie said she'd like to go up in a balloon, too, someday."

"Did she now?" Trog looked at me thoughtfully. "I expect she will some day. Callie pretty much does what she says she will do."

*He's knows I've mentioned something I'm not supposed to. At least Rune didn't spill the beans. Thank you, Rune. Thank you.*

134

"I was in the store today, Trog and McQuerrie told me the coaling is about to stop."

"Yes, I heard that, too. It's way past time, isn't it?"

"Yes, but with the good weather and all, the Iron Master wanted them to keep at it. This warm spell will end soon enough."

"I'd like to see the coaling, Trog. Do you think I can be spared from the weave house for an afternoon?" I asked.

"I don't see why not. Besides, those charcoal pits are impressive and I think you should see them first hand." He looked at me suspiciously. "But I guess you've already decided when you two are going. Right?"

"Right," laughed Rune. "Taw and Vance are going, too. We have a pit area in mind and thought we'd go day after tomorrow. But Callie insisted she had to check with you and Old Mag first, before she'd agree to go."

Trog gave me a warm smile. "You've checked, Girl, and go with my blessing. But first you have to finish helping me put new warp on my loom. Now please refill our tea cups; mine has gotten quite cold."

The two men kept the conversation flowing; I chimed in every now and then to make them think I was listening intently. But I wasn't. My thoughts were out on the path from the medicine house to the cottage and the words "I love you, Callie" played an incessant tune in my head.

I stayed up long after Trog had climbed to the sleeping loft and Rune had gone home. The fire slowly died to twinkling embers. I stared at them with unseeing eyes, wrapped in a cocoon of ecstasy, Chance curled contentedly in my lap.

"Girl, you'd better come to bed soon. You won't be fit to weave tomorrow if you don't." Old Mag called out from the loft. Her voice broke the spell. I was aware of the chill in the room and rubbed my arms vigorously.

"I'll be right up, Old Mag, " I replied softly as I got to my feet. I turned down the lamp and carried it and Chance up the ladder.

I fell asleep immediately and dreamed of walking with Rune under a canopy of moonbeams and falling stars.

# Chapter 21

Old Mag and Trog kept me busy the following day. I spent the morning helping Trog with the warp on his loom. My back ached by the time the last thread was passed through the eye of the heddle and securely fastened. That completed, Old Mag asked me to finish weaving a colorful table runner. It was mid-afternoon by the time I sat down at the triangular loom to work on the blue shawl.

"Hello, everybody," chirped Lily as she breezed in, bringing in a draft of cool air. The weather had changed drastically overnight and the air was quite nippy.

"Lily, child, sit down," replied Old Mag with a broad smile. "Have you brought work to do? If not, I'm sure the girl can find something to keep your hands busy."

"I have some sewing but to be honest, Old Mag, I'd like you to show me how to weave on your loom. You let Callie do it and I know I can, too. Do you mind?"

"Of course I mind, child but seeing as how it's you doing the asking, I'll let you weave a row or two before you get down to your own work."

"Thank you, thank you," cried Lily exuberantly as she threw her arms around Old Mag's neck.

"Child, child, such thanks is not necessary but is appreciated. Here, sit down next to me and I'll show you." Lily did as she was asked. "Goodness gracious, your feet do not reach the pedals so I'll have to do that part for you. Now here's what you do."

I smiled at the sight of their heads bent eagerly over the loom and then bent mine to my work. I wanted to finish the shawl this afternoon because a villager had inquired about it earlier in the week. Old Mag had displayed the yellow shawl; it was purchased the same day she put it up. The woman traded a lot for it, too; milk for a month and several jars of vegetables.

Old Mag allowed Lily to weave several rows and then shooed her my way. She sat beside me and pulled out a pretty piece of needlework. The design was of a little cottage with flowers growing all around. Her stitches were tiny and straight.

"Where did you get that design, Lily?" I asked.

"I drew it. Ma didn't have to help me one little bit. Do you like it?"

This small, eight year old child never ceased to amaze me. I tousled her hair. "I think it's beautiful. I wish my embroidery looked as neat as yours. Somehow mine is always messy, especially on the underside. Let me see the back of yours."

She turned the fabric over for my inspection. The back was as neat as the front.

"Ma taught me how to keep the back of my work tidy. She says the back of a needlework picture is almost as important as the front. When I first started sewing fancy work, she made me rip out a lot of stitches because she didn't like how the back looked."

"I'll bet you don't have to rip out many stitches now," I commented.

Lily shook her head. "Just once in a while, especially if Ma's teaching me a new stitch."

"Do you think you could teach me, Lily? I'd like to be able to embroider as neatly as you."

Trog interrupted. "You two need to get to work. Callie doesn't have time to think about embroidery right now. She needs to complete that shawl. Right, Callie?"

I nodded and bent my head to the loom. Lily giggled as she threaded her needle with bright red thread. "Trog tries to sound mean but we know different, don't we Callie?" she whispered.

I smiled and nodded. Trog was right. I needed to apply myself to the task because tomorrow I planned to be tramping through the forest with Rune and the others. The silence in the weave house was comfortably broken only by the crackling of the fire and the thump of the beaters on the two looms.

The shadows began to lengthen and I knew the work-day would soon end. My fingers flew. I had just a little more fringe to add to the shawl and I was determined I would finish it before I left the weave house for the day. Lily sensed my intensity and remained silent, moving her needle in and out with dexterity. Just as Old Mag stood at her loom and stretched, I tied off the last of the fringe. The shawl lay in my lap, ready to be washed and shaped.

"I've finished this one too, Old Mag." I held it up proudly for her to see.

She took the shawl from my hands, carried it to a window and scrutinized it carefully, nodding her head as she did so. I waited anxiously for her approval.

"Looks fine to me, Girl. We'll get it washed and shaped tonight." I basked in her approval. "Look at this, Trog. Every stitch is even. She has a real knack for weaving, doesn't she?"

Trog ran his hand over the shawl. "Yes, she does, Old Mag. We'll have no difficulty selling her work."

"She kind of reminds me of you Trog, when you first started weaving. You took to it right away and before long, you were the best. Still are as far as I'm con-cerned." Old Mag gave him a pat on the shoulder. "Course, I guess that's because you had a wonderful teacher. Me!" She cackled with delight and one by one the three of us began to laugh, too.

That's right, Mag, you have to have the best to get the best." Trog gave her a big hug. "Now let's think about a little supper if you don't mind."

I watched the two of them with admiration. Both were excellent weavers but Trog was by far the better of the two. I had often marveled at the delicate and intricate stitches he produced on his loom. Like a musician, the ideas were in his head and when he sat down to weave, he transposed them onto thread.

Old Mag and Trog left for the cottage while Lily and I tidied the weave house, rearranged the embers in the fireplace, and turned down the lamps. I said goodnight to Lily on the doorstep and then Chance and I hurried to the cottage to help with supper.

That night I dreamed of Jack. He was standing on the opposite bank of the canal, arms stretched out toward me. I went to him, laughing as the water splashed above my waist, soaking my skirts. We embraced and the familiar scent of his cologne filled my nostrils. I ran my fingers through his hair and over his face. It was wonderful to see him, to hold him. We fell gently to the ground and kissed passionately, arms wrapped tightly around each other. My heart raced and I felt my head begin to swim with desire.

*Jack, Jack. I love you,* I murmured in my dream. *Don't leave me here. Take me with you.*

"Callie, Callie, wake up, Girl. It's time to get up."

I was jostled on my pallet. Jack slowly faded into the recesses of my mind as I opened my eyes and focused on Old Mag holding a lamp. I blinked several times to clear my head.

"Get up, Girl. We have a lot to do to get you ready to go tramping through the forest. You are still planning to go, aren't you?"

"I'm awake."

Old Mag set the lamp on the floor. "I'm going downstairs and get breakfast started. Don't be long." She disappeared down the loft ladder.

I lay in bed for a few moments trying to recall the dream that was still vivid in my mind. My brain felt thick and I couldn't think clearly. I was torn between two worlds and couldn't make up my mind which one I wanted. I wasn't sure I could walk away from Jack. There needed to be closure. How could that happen if I didn't return? *Oh, Lord, what a mess! Life is complicated enough without adding extras.*

I sighed heavily, threw the covers aside and rose to my feet. The loft was cold and I dressed quickly. The smell of frying bacon greeted me as I descended the ladder. Trog came in through the door carrying an armload of firewood.

"Good morning, Callie. Did you sleep well?"

"Good morning to you, Trog. Yes, I slept well, thank you." The dream of Jack tried to push its way into my mind. I clenched my teeth and forced it back.

"I can tell you it is absolutely beautiful outside. You will have a wonderful day for hiking to the charcoal pits."

"Would you like to go too, Trog?" I asked thinking I detected a little envy.

"I'd love to go and thank you for asking. But I really must stay here and work on my new project."

"Why don't you let that project rest for a day, Trog? Go with the girl and the lads. A good tramp in the woods might do wonders for you. Remember how your best work always came after spending a day roaming the fields and hills?" Old Mag looked thoughtfully at Trog.

He hesitated a few seconds and then replied, "I believe you're right, Mag. I'm overdue for a day in the fresh air and sunshine. Thank you Callie. I'll be happy to join you."

I looked at Old Mag with questioning eyes. She read my mind and before I could open my mouth, said, "Don't even think it, Girl. There's no way I'm going to traipse through the woods. Was a time I could do it, mind you, but those days are long past. I'll stay here and keep the weave house open."

After breakfast, Old Mag and I prepared the sack meals. We put in extra bacon and biscuits because there was no telling how long we'd be out. While we did that, Trog brought in several more armloads of wood. We had barely finished those preparations when the door opened and the three men walked in accompanied by Lily.

141

"Ma says I can go, Callie, if it's all right with you. Please say yes, please!"

"Stop begging Lily," I laughed. "Of course it's all right. Trog is going too."

That announcement brought whoops of glee from Taw and Vance. Rune patted Trog enthusiastically on the back and then looked at Old Mag. "Want to come too and make a real party of the day?"

She hesitated a second too long. "Come on Old Mag, we'll slow down when you need to rest," said Taw.

"What do you mean, you'll slow down. I'll have you know I can keep up with the best of you on a bad day."

"I dare you to show us," laughed Vance.

She put her hands on her hips and looked around the room. She frowned a little but her eyes twinkled. "Okay, I'll just do that. Give the girl and me a few minutes to get several more sacks of food ready and we'll be off."

"Oh," squealed Lily, "this is going to be so much fun, isn't it Callie?"

I nodded my head in agreement as I fetched the biscuits from the shelf. In no time at all, the seven of us were out the door and on our way.

Trog was right. The day was beautiful. The sky above us was cloudless and there was no wind. Before long, I was too warm and was forced to remove my cloak. I tied it as best I could around my waist and then helped Lily do the same.

Rune led the way and headed in an unfamiliar direction. At first we chattered like magpies, calling back and forth to each other. That banter gave way to singing. By the time we reached a thick stand of forest, we had tired of both and were silent for the most part.

"Let's stop here for a few minutes rest," Rune suggested. "We'll have quite a hike through this stand of trees. In places the walking will be rough but we'll take all the time we need. Before long we'll come to a wood-hauler's road and the going will be a lot easier. We'll follow that road right to the charcoal pits."

"Anybody need a little snack before we go into the forest?" asked Old Mag.

We all shook our heads. "All right, let's go," said Rune and one by one we stepped into the forest, single file, Rune leading the way.

He was right. The going was rough. A thick carpet of leaves blanketed the ground hiding branches and twigs lying in wait for the careless step. At no time did Rune seem to follow a straight path. Instead he chose one that wound through the trees in a seemingly haphazard fashion. There was no bantering or singing. It was all we could do to stay upright.

Bright sunlight filtered through the bare branches above us dappling the forest floor with strange patterns. Rune stopped once and dug in the leaves to expose a tiny green vine bearing red berries.

"Teaberry," exclaimed Old Mag. "Pluck a leaf and inhale the aroma."

"Smells good," said Lily.

*Smells like teaberry gum,* I thought, trying to remember the last time I had seen that flavor for sale in a store.

"It's better than good," said Vance. "The leaves from this little vine are used as both an antiseptic and a liniment. In fact, the entire plant may be eaten."

We spent a few minutes admiring the glossy plant and then plodded on in silence. Eventually the forest began to thin somewhat and the ground seemed less treacherous.

Rune pointed ahead. "There's the woodhauler's road. Let's have a bite to eat here and then follow the road to the pits."

# Chapter 22

I sank to the ground gratefully. My legs were tired from picking my way cautiously through the trees. I looked at Old Mag but could see no signs of stress on her face. I opened my sack and pulled out a biscuit, two slabs of bacon and put them together to make a sandwich. I leaned back against a tree, took a good-sized bite and exhaled with a long sigh.

"Feels good to rest, doesn't it?" asked Taw. "My legs were getting mighty tired at the end."

"When you say rough, Rune, you mean it, don't you?" asked Trog. He glanced at his mother. "How're you doing, Mag?"

"No one has to carry me yet," she exclaimed before taking a bite of her sandwich. "How bout you, Lily? You doing okay, child?"

"No one has to carry me yet, either," she replied.

"Well I'm thinking about asking someone to carry me," joked Taw. We all laughed.

For a few minutes we were silent, busy eating our meal. Trog took out his pipe and soon the sweet aroma of his tobacco filled the air around us. Old Mag passed a rabbit skin bag of water around. I was thirsty and the moisture felt good trickling down my throat.

"I had forgotten how wonderful a walk in the woods is," said Old Mag. "Being out in the brisk, fresh air is better than any tonic."

"I agree," said Vance. "How much farther, Rune?"

"Not much. And the walking will be easy. The pits are just off this road. Everybody ready to push on?"

I stood, brushed the crumbs from my skirt, and tied my food bag to the drawstring. I was cool from sitting on the ground and wrapped my cloak around my shoulders. We moved out of the forest onto the deeply rutted road.

"What is this road used for," I asked.

"The woodhaulers bring in the wood the colliers need to build the charcoal pits. They use large sleds pulled by mules or horses. By the time enough wood is hauled in, the road is pretty well established and will stay that way for quite a spell." Rune fell into step beside me. Trog, Vance and Taw took the lead and Old Mag and Lily brought up the rear. "I saw this site the other day. Four pits were already built but I think we'll be in time to see the last one erected. Let's hope so, anyway."

"How many pits will there be in this location," I asked. "And how many colliers?"

"Four colliers usually take care of nine pits. But let me tell you it's hard and dangerous work. I've seen those men on top of the pits stomping out a blaze with their feet. No thank you, I'll stick to what I do."

"Listen," said Taw, "do I hear voices up ahead?"

We all stopped on the road to listen. "I hear them, too, Taw, I hear them," exclaimed Lily.

Lily's excitement was catching. Our footsteps along the road quickened in anticipation. In no time at all, we reached a turnoff through a thin stand of trees. I was not prepared for what I saw. I expected to see large holes in the ground. Instead, eight huge mounds loomed in view and the ninth was almost completely constructed. Each was built a distance from the others. Four colliers were working the site.

"Are those mounds the charcoal pits?" I asked in amazement.

"That's right," replied Rune.

Each pit was 30 to 40 feet in diameter and stood about 20 feet high. Lightly rounded at the top, the pit continually widened until it reached the bottom. A pole protruded from a hole in the top of each. The eight completed pits were covered with a thick coat of dust. The wood used to construct the ninth pit was fully exposed and the four men were busy applying the final pieces of wood. I was amazed at the intricate construction. As far as I could tell, there was no hole in the ground at all.

Rune began to fill us in. "The pole extending from the center is called a fagan and is made of green wood so it won't burn. Two lengths of wood are used to construct a pit. A billet is 4 feet long and is usually cut from tree trunks. Shorter lengths are called lapwood and are generally cut from tree branches. You can't see the chimney that surrounds the fagan. Triangular in shape, it is fashioned with lapwood. Look at the bottom of the pit. See the billets standing vertically all the way around? The first level of billets is the foot and the second level is the waist. The next two levels, the shoulder and head, are fashioned with lapwood placed horizontally around the pit. Once that is completed all the cracks and spaces are filled in with the lapwood. Any questions?"

"What goes inside the chimney," asked Trog.

"Small stuff like twigs and leaves. They'll even dump charcoal dust in if they have some to use. The fire will be lit in the chimney and they'll use things that will burn easily. Look, they're taking stuff up now."

Using a crude ladder fashioned from a notched log, the colliers climbed to the top of the last pit carrying baskets filled with small debris. Once the chimney was filled, lapwood was used to cover the hole at the top. Next, they used long handled shovels to spread the dust cover. It was several inches thick on the sides and about a foot deep on the head and shoulders. When they were satisfied that the covering was sufficient, they began to light the pits.

The dust and leaves were removed from the opening at the top of each pit, as were several pieces of lapwood. Hot coals from the collier's cooking fire were placed on top of the kindling in the chimney and the lapwood and dust were carefully replaced. Once the lighting was completed, one of the colliers approached us.

"Here comes Snoop, the collier in charge." Rune quickly extended his hand. "Hello Snoop, remember me?"

"Of course I do. You said you might bring some folks by and you sure enough did." Snoop made eye contact with each of us as Rune did the introductions. He was a burly man with a thick shock of red hair and closely set hazel eyes. A bristly red beard covered his chin. He was covered in grimy, black dust and when he smiled, his teeth gleamed whitely. He was tall but next to Rune, Taw and Vance he seemed short.

"I filled them in as best I could, Snoop. But they might have a question or two."

"Where do you live?" asked Lily. "It's a long way out here. Do you go back and forth every day like my pa does?"

"No, child. We live out here. See that little hut?" He pointed to a crude building low to the ground with a stovepipe sticking through the roof.

We nodded. "That's our house. There's room enough for four pallets and a stove. We eat what we can find. The pits will take up all our time, day and night, until they burn down and are ready to be raked. We have to watch them carefully and make sure they smolder instead of burn."

"What happens if they burn?" asked Taw.

"We have to climb on the top and stomp the blaze out. Then we have to dump more dust on the area that burned. Let me tell you, nine pits keep us pretty busy. Tonight will be the last full night's sleep we'll get until the charcoal is ready to be raked."

"Why?" asked Old Mag.

"The pit fires don't burn too hot the first few hours. We try to light the pits late in the day. By tomorrow this time, we'll be very busy watching for blazes."

"But you've shut off all the air," said Trog. "How does the fire blaze?"

"Oh, we'll poke draft vents here and there. We can easily open those and then fill them in if need be. We just want the wood to smolder under the covering. In a little less than two weeks, the wood will have turned

147

into charcoal. Remember, the wood has to burn from the head to the foot. The first draft vents are poked a little higher but as the fire nears the foot, we lower the vents, too."

"How can you tell when the wood has burned down and has become charcoal?" asked Vance.

"The pit will begin to shrink. We help it along, too, by constantly ramming the fagan deeper into the chimney to make sure the fire gets down to the foot. The smoke coming from the vents will tell us whether we have a good burn or not. A blue smoke means the pit is burning evenly. White smoke means there's too much draft or the wood is too old and the fire is burning too fast. That causes the pit to burn unevenly. We try to keep the surface of the pit level but sometimes winds and rains work to make the fire too hot. When the wood has charred, we rake it out and haul it out to fuel the furnace."

"Why do you call the mounds charcoal pits? Pit to me means something down in the ground. These don't go down in the ground, do they?" I inquired.

"Good question," replied Snoop. "Many years ago the first pits probably were in the ground but eventually somebody figured out how to make charcoal without digging a pit. The name just stuck, I guess."

The men continued to ask Snoop questions but Old Mag, Lily, and I had lost interest. We wandered away. I couldn't take my eyes off the huge pits. It was hard to believe a fire was burning inside each one and that all the wood I had seen under the covering would soon be charcoal.

"Wow," said Lily, "those men are really dirty. I think they are blacker than Pa when he comes home from the furnace."

"I think you're right, Lily," Old Mag said. "I don't imagine they take many baths during the coaling season. For one thing, there is no water near by. For another, I don't think they care."

The three of us laughed at that remark causing the men to look at us. Rune gestured for us to come closer.

"We need to head for home soon. I'd like to get through that stretch of woods before dark."

We said our goodbyes to Snoop and the others and made our way back to the woodhauler's road. In no time at all, we reached our entry point into the forest. The way back didn't seem as long or as difficult. The sun was no longer overhead and the forest seemed a little darker but we made excellent time. We stopped once to eat the apples that remained in our food sacks.

I was proud of Old Mag. She kept up even though the pace was brisk. I knew she had to be tired but she did not complain. Nor did Lily. *These folks are not wimps,* I thought. *They are made of tough stuff.*

# Chapter 23

The sun had not yet dipped below the horizon by the time we cleared the forest and we quickened our steps in the gathering twilight. Old Mag worried about supper.

"I have enough stew left to feed us all and plenty of bread. But we'll have to get the fire going and that will take some time."

"I'll help you, Old Mag," I reminded her.

"I know you will, Girl, but I just don't want to be eating supper too late. It's bad for my indigestion."

Trog interrupted. "Mag, you won't have a problem with indigestion tonight. Not after all the walking and fresh air you've had."

"I'll say one thing, Old Mag," said Vance, "you sure did keep up with the best of us."

"Well spoken, Vance," laughed Taw. "I wish we'd put you in the lead. If we had, we'd have finished supper by now."

"Old Mag's the best," chimed in Lily.

"You all better stop chit-chatting and move your feet. It's going to be dark before we know it," cautioned Old Mag. "Move, move."

We stopped talking and did as she requested. Rune and I dropped back to bring up the rear. He reached for my hand and held it tightly. "Are you warm enough, Callie? Your hand feels cold."

"I'm fine," I replied looking at him. As I did so, I stumbled, and had it not been for his hand, I would have fallen.

"You two need to watch where you're going," cautioned Trog. "If you get hurt now we're all too tired to carry you home."

"I'm too tired to laugh at that remark," said Vance but he did and the rest of us joined him.

We plodded along in silence, one foot in front of the other, all anxious for a hot meal and a long rest.

Trog stopped so suddenly Vance bumped into him. "I'm sorry, Trog, I . . ."

"Stop, everyone," said Trog in a strangely calm voice. "Take a deep breath and tell me what you smell."

We did as he asked and for a few seconds could hear each other inhaling and exhaling.

"I smell smoke," said Vance. "I don't think it's wood smoke because the scent is too strong."

"It's not the smoke from the furnace either," replied Taw.

"Fire!" yelled Old Mag. "A cottage must be on fire!"

Before the words were out of her mouth the four men began to run, covering the ground quickly with their long strides. I began to run, too, leaving Old Mag and Lily to get back to the village as best they could. The closer I got to the village, the stronger the smell of smoke. Just before I reached the last small stand of trees, I could see two red glows in the sky. One was the furnace, the second had to be a cottage. My heart pounded in my chest from both exertion and fear. *How in the world will we deal with a major fire?* I thought. *No fire engines, no hoses to pump a steady stream of water. The cottages are so close together that if one goes, they all will go. Thank God there isn't a heavy wind blowing.*

I reached the outskirts of the village shortly after the men. The cottage on the far end of the U was completely ablaze. The villagers were doing their best to keep the fire contained in that one cottage. Water was being thrown on the blazing cottage as well as on the sides and roof of the one next to it. Men and women had formed a bucket brigade from the canal to the U. Children of all ages formed a second brigade and passed the empty buckets back to the canal. I squeezed into line and passed one bucket of water after another.

I don't know how long I passed the buckets. My arms were numb; my back and shoulders ached from the strain. The woman to my left gave a small moan and fainted. The woman next to her stepped sideways toward me and the procession of buckets did not falter. The next time I looked at the fallen woman she was gone. I didn't know if she walked away or was carried, so intent was I on the job at hand.

The women in the line were silent. Just an occasional grunt or groan from those nearest me reached my ears. Other noises filled my head. Horses screaming in fear, dogs barking, children crying for their parents, men yelling hoarsely for more water.

I wondered where the others were. The men were most likely handling water and Old Mag was probably comforting the tenants of the burning cottage. I worried most about Lily. I was certain she was in the thick of things; that's the kind of child she was. Her house was near the center of the U and at this time was in no danger of burning but the story might be different an hour from now. *An hour from now! Can I last that long?* I wondered.

"Move over, Callie and let me in." I was surprised to see Old Mag standing next to me.

"Where's Lily?"

"She's right behind us in the other line. That child tried to go right to the fire. It was all I could do to persuade her to stay with me. Even so, she wanted to get in this line, next to you. 'Absolutely not,' I told her. 'The buckets are much too heavy for you to handle.' She put up an argument but for once, I won."

I breathed a sigh of relief before asking, "How bad is it?"

"The one cottage is just about gone. The men have been concentrating on the one next to it and I think it will be spared. Everything has been hauled out of it, though, just in case."

We both fell silent, too tired to continue the conversation. It was all I could do to pass the buckets, swing my arms to the right and take a bucket in both hands, swing my arms to the woman on my left and pass the bucket to her, swing my arms to the right and repeat the process over and over again.

Water from the buckets sloshed down the front of my bodice and skirt. I was wet and cold and tired and hungry but saving a cottage was more important than any of those things.

A loud cheer went up from the vicinity of the U. Old Mag and I looked at each other. "Do you think the fire is out?" I asked.

"Out or close to out."

The buckets continued to be passed up the hill until someone yelled that no more water was needed. A few women and children dropped their buckets and jumped up and down, screaming with joy. Old Mag and I sank to the ground. Weariness was etched on her face. I stretched out on my back with a long sigh, tensing and releasing my muscles. The pain burned unbearably.

Trog appeared as if from nowhere. "Fortunately, the men were able to contain the fire to the Miller's cottage. Unfortunately, it has burned to the ground. They saved nothing."

Old Mag raised herself to a sitting position. "I'd better get busy and find them a place to stay."

Trog put a hand on her arm. "It's all been taken care of Mag. They're to live with Dusty Jacobs and his wife until they figure out what they want to do. If they decide to stay, a new cottage will be built for them. You, however, look tired to the bone. Let's go home and see if we can get a little bite to eat. I think that will make us feel better."

He turned to Lily. "Child, your mother has been frantic with worry. I assured her you were in good hands but I know she won't stop fretting until she sees you in person. Get along home with you."

"Go straight home, too," I admonished. "No stopping by to see what's left of the blaze."

Lily gave me an 'I hear you' look before she made her way up the hill toward her home. The sun had dropped behind the trees in the far west and dusk was beginning to settle. Lights appeared in several of the cottage windows. I looked back toward the U and saw glowing embers where the Miller's home had been. I didn't know any of them well but Mrs. Miller had always waved and smiled whenever I passed by. Tears filled my eyes and I squeezed my eyelids tight to hold them back.

Trog put his arm across Old Mag's shoulders as we trudged toward our cottage. "Do we have anything cold to eat?" he inquired. "I don't want you cooking if you're too tired."

"Well, I can cook up something, Trog, if Old Mag needs to take a rest."

"You'll do no such thing, Girl. We're going to have that stew I told you about. It will heat up just fine. That is if Trog will stop worrying about me and get the fire going. Can't cook without a fire, can I?"

"Mag, you're a tough old bird, I'll give you that," laughed Trog. "I don't mind saying I am tired."

"Not too tired to light a fire, I hope. I remember one of the girl's fires. Filled the whole house with smoke, she did. If it hadn't been for Lily I'd a died of smoke inhalation. I don't think she's gotten much better since then and I don't want her to start practicing tonight"

It was wonderful to be home after such a long and strange day. Trog got the fire going quickly. I washed my face and hands before I set the table. I felt grimy all over and if my clothing was an indication, I was as dirty as I felt.

"Lay out plates for Rune and the others," Old Mag reminded me. "They'll be along shortly. I know they must be starved."

The stew soon bubbled in the pot. I got out tea and honey and then sliced a loaf of bread. We sat in front of the fire, Old Mag in her rocker, Trog and I at the table. Old Mag rocked gently, eyes closed, hands folded quietly in her lap. Trog lit his pipe and the smoke curled around his head like a halo. We were silent, each locked in private thoughts.

The scuffling of feet outside the door broke my reverie. Rune entered first, followed by Taw and then Vance. Their faces were black with soot as was their clothing.

Taw immediately apologized. "I'm sorry we took so long. I hoped you'd eat without us but I'm glad you waited."

"Smells good," said Vance taking off his coat. "Shall we leave our coats outside fellows? They smell smoky."

"Sounds like a good idea to me," replied Rune. He took the three coats and put them just outside the door.

No one seemed to be in the mood for joking and we ate quietly for the most part. Exhaustion showed on everyone's face. I could barely lift my fork. Old Mag and I cleaned up the table and the dishes after we had finished. She brought out the cups while I set the tea box in front of Trog. She set a little bottle of rum beside the box.

Trog puffed his pipe thoughtfully while he selected the tea. I filled each cup with boiling water and the aroma of the leaves mingled with the smoke from the pipe. He held up the bottle of spirits and each of us nodded. He poured a small splash into each cup before passing one to each of us.

"Well lads, what was the situation when you came in?" he asked.

Rune spoke first. "The major blaze is completely out but the embers will have to be watched all night. Most of the men have volunteered to spend an hour or so keeping watch. The entire area around the cottage is ringed with buckets of water as a precaution. We're going to get a little sleep before we take our turn."

"Nothing was saved," added Taw. "The Miller's are lucky they all got out. Someone got burned but I'm not sure who."

"I hope it wasn't one of the little ones." Trog puffed his pipe thoughtfully as he spoke.

"And Dusty took them in?" inquired Old Mag.

Taw nodded.

"That man has a heart of gold," added Old Mag. "He barely has enough room for his family. The Miller's have how many children? Five? Yes, I think it's five and another one on the way." She rocked back and forth. "The girl and I will take some things to them tomorrow. I'm too tuckered out to think about it tonight."

Taw and Vance rose from the table. "Thanks for supper, Old Mag" said Vance, "it hit the spot." He gave her a hug.

So did Taw. "I think I'll be on my way, too. I need a little rest before I have to watch the embers." The two of them walked toward the door.

Rune rose, too. "I'm going to be right behind you, fellows. I just want to say goodnight to Callie."

I stepped outside with him. The night air was cold and our breath hung in front of us. Off toward the west I saw a crescent moon hanging in the sky. I kissed him goodnight before he started down the path. I watched his shadowy figure until I could no longer see it.

# Chapter 24

I slept late the next morning. Chance roused me instead of Old Mag. I looked toward their pallets and determined they were both downstairs. I felt guilty for being a lay-a-bed. My back and shoulders screamed as I descended the loft ladder. Old Mag and Trog were seated at the table in front of the fire. Bright sunshine streamed in through the kitchen windows.

"I'm sorry I over. . ." I began to apologize but Old Mag cut me off in mid-sentence.

"We all overslept, child. Trog and I have been up just long enough to get the fire going. I hope you're not in a hurry for breakfast because I'm moving mighty slow."

"So am I. I wasn't sure I could handle coming down the ladder. Everything on me hurts when I move."

Old Mag rose from the table and made her way slowly to the pantry shelves. I joined her and the two of us brought out the crock of oatmeal, a pitcher of milk and a loaf of bread. While she made the oatmeal, I set the table.

During breakfast, our conversation turned to last night's fire. "We need to look on our shelves, Girl, and see what we can fix up to take to the Miller's. The women of the village will all send food to them but we try not to all do it on the same day. We also need to hunt for clothes in that chest of mine."

"While you two do that I'm going to go down to the U to see what the situation is now. Maybe I can lend a hand there. If not, I'll be back shortly with a report." Trog put on his hat and coat; he gave us a smile before he went out the door.

He was gone almost an hour. By the time he returned Old Mag and I had a hearty soup simmering over the fire. She had found several small cloaks and three pairs of leather shoes to donate to the Miller's.

"With five young ones, these things are bound to fit somebody," she said. "I'm glad now I didn't cut the cloaks up for use in the weave house. Now Trog, tell us the news."

"Master Dodd has assigned a number of men to begin tearing down what remains of the burned structure and once the furnace shuts down for the winter, rebuilding will begin. If there had to be a fire it certainly happened at the most opportune time."

"What news do you have of the Millers?" I asked. "Are they planning to stay here or will they move on to somewhere else?"

"They plan to stay. Tom Miller is busy tearing down his former home right now. In fact, he has been put in charge of the operation. You should see him. He has a determined look on his face, one that means 'this won't get me down.' He's keeping the other fellows hustling, believe me."

"Does anyone know how the fire started?" I queried.

"One of the children added a log to the fire. In doing so, she pushed a burning log out onto the floor and a rug caught fire. The place went up like a tinderbox. Fortunately, no one was in the sleeping loft. Mrs. Miller has a few burns on her arms and hands but other than that no one was hurt. Vance took her several salves last night."

"Well, that's comforting to know. The girl and I will take the soup and the clothing to the Millers a little later. Right now I think we all best get ourselves to the weave house and get busy." Old Mag wrapped herself in her cloak as she spoke.

Trog and I agreed with her and before many minutes had passed the three of us were hard at work on our projects. Trog had lit the fire before he went down to the U and the little cottage was warm and cozy. Chance found a large patch of sunshine on the floor near my feet and curled himself into a tight ball. For several hours, the only sounds in the room were the thump, thump of the beaters on the two looms.

I broke the silence. "I enjoyed going to the pit area. With the exception of the fire, the day was wonderful. And I'm glad the two of you went. That made the day even more special."

"Thank you, Callie," replied Trog, clearing his throat a little. "Yes, the pits are a sight to behold. First time I've seen them. I don't know how four men manage to take care of nine of those monstrosities at a time but they do. The furnace never seems to run short of charcoal."

Trog and Old Mag made a few more comments about charcoal pits as well as about the fire. I listened at first but became engrossed in the shawl I was weaving and tuned them out. Occasionally I glanced at them. They looked none the worse for wear while I was still tired beyond belief.

I had slept well the night before in spite of my exhaustion. I barely remembered undressing and crawling under the blankets. My sleep was deep and dreamless but my overtaxed muscles needed more rest than I had gotten. And now it was catching up with me. I was glad when Old Mag announced it was time for the noon meal.

We stopped a little earlier than usual in the afternoon so Old Mag and I could take the soup and clothing to the Millers. The Jacobs' cottage sat directly behind the bakeshop; the smell of freshly baked bread permeated the area around the front door.

Mrs. Jacobs greeted us and asked us to step in. The room was crowded with well-wishers, mostly women and children of various ages. I spied Mrs. Miller near the fireplace and went over to express my sympathy. Her burned arms were smeared with a salve that glistened in the firelight. Her fingers had swollen to the size of sausages and she held her hands in the air to relieve the pressure. Pain was etched on her face but she smiled brightly and thanked me through swollen lips for coming. Her hair was singed, her eyebrows and lashes gone and she had a small burn on one cheek.

159

*Oh for a bucket of ice,* I thought, wincing at the suffering I saw in her eyes. *At home she'd be in a burn unit getting special treatment and pain medication.* I looked at her hands and wondered if she'd fully recover her use of them. Her arms would definitely be badly scarred.

The table was laden with offerings of food. Old Mag added the bread to the bounty and put the kettle of soup on the hearth. I placed the clothing on a small mound of garments piled in a corner. We didn't stay long; the cottage was unbearably hot and we had work to do in the weave house. Mrs. Jacobs hugged Old Mag warmly before we left.

"Old Mag, I don't know how you do it. Your generosity in times of need is always overwhelming. Thank you for everything you brought."

"You and the Miller's are most welcome to anything I have. But don't just thank me. The girl here had a hand in this, too."

"Thank you dear, thank you," Mrs. Jacobs murmured giving me a smile. That's all she had time to say because two more women were on the doorstep waiting to come in.

"While we're out, let's walk over to the U to survey the damage," suggested Old Mag and we turned to walk in that direction. "That poor women is in for quite a time of it. My heart aches for her. I've seen others with lesser burns have hands that were useless after the healing."

"I thought the same thing, Old Mag. She appeared to be in great pain. Doesn't Vance have a concoction for that?" I asked.

"I'm sure he does, Girl, and he has probably already taken her something. But she may have decided not to take what he offered. Some folks are funny that way. When the pain gets to be too bad for her, she'll gladly take what he brings."

We caught a whiff of charred wood as we neared the U. A dozen or so men were hard at work on what was left of the Miller's house, pulling charred timbers from the ruins and tossing them into the back of a wagon. We joined a small cluster of women watching the activity.

"Have you been to see Mrs. Miller, Old Mag?" asked a lady in a pink mobcap.

"Yes, the girl and I have just been. She's quite poorly but had a kind word to say to each of us."

"She's a brave woman, that she is," said another. "She got those burns trying to save a quilt that had belonged to her mother. Ran right back into the flaming house, she did with all the men screaming for her to stay back. She just ignored their warnings and dashed in. She was on fire when she came out carrying the burning quilt. Only thing she had left of her mother's. Sad, sad."

A murmur of agreement ran through the little crowd. The women conversed with each other in hushed tones. I noticed a lot of nodding and shaking of heads.

Old Mag and I watched the cleaning up process briefly before heading back toward the weave house. Trog was busy at his loom when we entered.

"I had just about given up on you two," he said with a smile. "How's Mrs. Miller?"

"Her condition isn't too good," said Old Mag and the two of us described our visit to Dusty's as well as to the site of the fire. He stopped weaving and gave us his full attention.

"I'm sure Vance gave her something for pain. She's foolish not to take it." We agreed with him.

"The girl and I are going home to get supper started, Trog. How much longer do you think you'll stay?"

"I'll be along shortly. I have several more rows I want to weave while the pattern is fixed in my mind and then I'll be along."

Old Mag and I had supper just about ready by the time Trog put in an appearance. As we sat around the table I noticed how tired and drawn they both looked. The strain of the day before had taken a toll on all of us. I looked at our cheery fire blazing in the fireplace and gave a small shudder. *What happened to the Miller's could happen to anyone's cottage, even ours. One care-less mistake and that friendly fire would become a fear-some enemy. No wonder Old Mag doesn't want me pok-ing around the fire. I haven't had enough experience. If a log rolled out I don't know what I'd do.*

That evening, Rune and I walked down the hill, past the furnace and took the towpath that ran beside the ca-nal. The night air was cold and I wrapped my cloak tightly. No barges went up and down the canal at night. The sound of the rushing water was soothing. In no time at all we reached the wooden lock that raised the water level in the canal to that of the tidal waters in the creek.

"I'd like to come here in the daytime, Rune. I'd like to see the lock in operation."

"Easy as pie," he replied. "A barge goes in the lock, water drains in and the barge rises and then sails into the creek." He gave me a kiss. "Too busy down here in the daytime for the likes of you. You'd be a big distraction." He kissed me again. "The best time to see it is at night. With me. Understand?"

"M-m-m-m," I murmured in reply.

# Chapter 25

The last week in November was very cold. The wind blew through the cracks and crevices in both the cottage and the weave house. Trog and I brought in armload after armload of firewood but it seemed to burn as rapidly as we brought it in. My hands were stiff and I had difficulty weaving.

Early in the morning on December first, I opened the cottage door to discover a world of white. It had snowed lightly during the night, just enough to cover everything with a coat of dazzling white so bright it hurt my eyes. By noon, the snow was gone, blown away on the wind. The little that was left was blackened with the soot and embers from the furnace or churned into the earth by the livestock. The sky was ominous for several days, threatening to dump more snow upon us, but none came.

The time passed quickly. My days were spent in the weave house and the evenings, after supper, with Rune. Occasionally we stayed in the cottage with Old Mag and Trog but usually we bundled up and walked around the site, whispering sweet nothings to each other, stopping often for hugs and long, passionate kisses. The cold and damp did not seem to hamper our good feelings about spending time together.

Taw and Vance were frequent visitors at both the cottage and the weave house. Taw proudly related that Master and Mistress Dodd were riding the horses he had recently broken and so far there had been no mishap for either of them. He was working with two more wild ones for someone on a neighboring farm. Vance was busy fixing medicines for the sickly in the community. I did not need to be told that winter was probably the busiest time of the year for him.

One evening Rune and I visited the two men at the medicine house. The place was cozy and warm in spite of the howling wind outside. We sat around the fire and talked, our hands wrapped around cups of fragrant hot tea.

"The woodhaulers will be busy keeping the community supplied with wood. I noticed there are now two community piles, one at the U and one near your cottage, Callie," remarked Taw. "The wood is used quickly, though, in cold weather like this."

"The woodpile near us is really handy," I added. "I like being able to pop out for wood and pop right back into the cottage before I have time to get too cold."

The men laughed. "We have an even shorter walk, Callie," said Vance. "We just step outside the door and get our wood."

"I thought you had to get yours from the pile near the U."

"We did but we have a friend who made arrangements with a woodhauler to keep us supplied. Dumps it right outside our door. It's nice to know important people."

"You do? And who might that be?"

Vance lightly punched Rune on the upper arm. Rune laughed. "That's the least I could do considering all you two do for me."

"What did you do to make a deal like that with the woodhauler?" I asked Rune.

"That's my little secret," he replied with a broad grin. "These two have tried to pry it out of me but I'm not telling. Not even you."

"Wood is not all that's going to disappear during this cold spell. That furnace will be burning charcoal at a rate you won't believe in order to keep up the temperature in the stack. And the charcoalers are finished; when the supply is gone, it's gone. I saw Snoop at the Boarding House the other day. Hardly recognized him, he was so clean."

My heart gave a lurch. "Does that mean when the charcoal is used up the furnace will shut down?" I queried.

"Right," replied Vance. "Won't be long now, maybe a day or two. A week at the most."

*Decision time* I thought. *I'm going to have to make a decision. Do I go or do I stay?* My mind whirled with thoughts of leaving, of saying goodbye to Rune, of seeing Jack.

My inner turmoil must have shown on my face because Taw leaned toward me. "Are you all right, Callie? You've turned pale as a ghost."

I smiled wanly. "Of course I'm all right. I was just wondering what this town will be like without the noise and soot and embers from the furnace. I'll probably have a headache for three days from the quiet."

"It'll be quiet all right," added Vance. "So quiet you'll be able to hear yourself think. Funny how the noise just becomes a part of you and you don't even hear it until it stops. Leastways that's how it affects me."

"Me, too," chimed in Taw. "I'll have to get used to the noise all over again when the stack is fired up in the spring."

"I think it's about time I took Callie home," said Rune. He rose to his feet and drank the last of the tea from his cup. "Are you about ready to go?"

"Yes, I am," I replied. I looked at Vance and Taw. "Thank you so much for a wonderful evening. I always enjoy my visits with you. Stop by the cottage or the weave house soon."

There was handshaking and thumps on the back as we bid our adieus and then Rune and I stepped out into the night. Stars twinkled brightly through the trees as we moved toward home, shoulder to shoulder, arms around each other's waists.

"Something upset you back there, Callie. Do you mind sharing with me?"

I was silent for a few minutes before I replied. "I was thinking about a decision I'm going to have to make when the furnace stops."

"You mean whether to go or stay?"

"Yes, that's exactly what I mean." I turned to face him and wrapped my arms around him tightly. "I don't know what I'm going to do, Rune. Part of me wants to leave but a big part of me wants to stay." Tears stung my eyelids and I squeezed them shut.

"Am I part of your reason for wanting to stay?" He cupped my chin gently in his hand and tilted my face toward him.

"Yes, yes, you know you are. Every part of my being wants to stay with you."

"Then it seems to me the decision is easy. Stay."

"It isn't that simple, Rune. There are things at home I need to take care of, bring to closure. Then I'll be free to stay."

"Closure? What does that mean?"

"Closure means to bring something to an end or con-clusion."

"You have something back home that is that impor-tant?"

"Yes, Rune, I do. I can't talk about it but I do."

We walked in silence to the U. A few cottages showed lights in the windows but most of them were dark.

"Does this something you have to do concern a man, Callie?" His question hung on the air between us.

"Does that matter?"

"No, of course not. But I'm not so stupid as to think a beautiful woman like you would not have a man in her life."

"Rune, you'd be totally surprised at how many beau-tiful women in the 21$^{st}$ century do not have a man in their lives and they make out just fine."

"Without a man?"

"Absolutely."

"You still haven't answered my question, Callie and that tells me there is a man. It makes no difference to me. I love you, Callie and I can't imagine being here without you."

"Oh, Rune, I love you too. So very, very much. And that's why I'm so torn. I'm not sure I can be happy without you in my life."

We had reached the cottage door and Rune wrapped me in his arms. I pressed my body into his as we kissed. And then he was gone. My heart was sad as I watched him head down the pathway toward the U.

Old Mag and Trog were up and waiting for me. The expressions on their faces told me they wanted to talk. I poured myself a cup of tea and sat down at the table with them. Chance hopped into my lap and curled into a ball, purring loudly. Trog puffed a little on his pipe before he began speaking.

"Now that the weather has turned cold, Callie, the furnace will be shutting down."

"I know, Trog. I've just come from the medicine house and we've been talking about that."

"Did the lads mention how soon?"

"Yes. They seemed to think a matter of days. No more than a week at the most."

"They are most likely correct with that assessment. This knowledge brings us to you and your problem."

"My problem?"

"Yes Girl, your problem." Old Mag joined the conversation. "Do you not want to go home?"

"Of course I want to go home. But does it have to be as soon as the furnace shuts down? Is my window of opportunity for return that narrow?" My voice rose in pitch as I spoke and sounded shrill to my ears.

"Callie, Callie," said Trog soothingly, "calm down. Old Mag and I are not trying to rush you. We've enjoyed your company greatly and will both be very unhappy to have you leave. But it is time to think about as well as discuss what you plan to do. In that way we can be ready to help you return to your home safely."

Tears welled into my eyes and spilled onto my cheeks. There was nothing I could do to stop them. Old Mag moved next to me and put her arms around my shoulders. "Go ahead, Girl. Let your frustrations come out. You'll be none the worse for it. Trog and I are here for you."

I leaned into her warm arms and sobbed quietly for several minutes. She patted me on the back and crooned soothingly. When the tears stopped, she pressed a hand-kerchief into my hands. I snuffled and snorted and wiped my eyes, trying to cover my embarrassment.

"Drink your tea, Girl. It'll make you feel better." Old Mag pushed my cup toward me.

I did as she asked. The warm liquid seemed to have a calming effect on me and I was able to look at her and smile.

"Thank you, Old Mag, and you too, Trog," I mumbled. I took several more swallows of tea before I spoke again. "I'm not sure what I want to do. I love it here. And I love the two of you. You've been wonderful to me. But I need to go home to finish up a few matters, things that can't be left the way they are."

"Does Rune enter into this picture, Callie?" asked Trog. "You two are doing what I call keeping company and have been for quite a while."

"Rune and I were discussing how we feel about each other on the way home. Of course he's in the picture, front and center. I'm in love with him. That's why the decision is so difficult to make."

Trog puffed on his pipe and blew a stream of hazy, blue smoke toward the ceiling. It circled lazily around his head.

"Do I have to go now or can I wait a little longer?" Trog nodded his head as I spoke. "If I leave, will I be able to return? All I want to do is straighten out a few things and then I want to come back here to live with you. That is, if you want me back."

"We'll always welcome you, Girl. You know that," added Old Mag. She looked at me thoughtfully. "Your decision does not have to made tonight, Girl. Think on it. Sleep on it. Sometime during the next few weeks you will know what to do. And when that time comes, Trog and I will help you in every way we can."

"That's right, Callie. You'll have several months in which to make your decision. When the furnace shuts down it won't refire until early March. That's long enough for you to make up your mind, don't you think?"

I nodded. "I'm sure I'll have an answer by then."

"Well Girl, let me say this," interrupted Old Mag. "Think through this problem carefully. You want to make the right decision. Do what is best for you. Don't let your heart rule your head." Her green eyes seemed to be looking into my soul. I returned her gaze for several long moments.

She spoke again. "Now, I think it's time we all went to bed."

Sleep was elusive for a long time after I crawled under my blanket. I didn't want to think about my decision but knew I had to. I couldn't have it both ways. I went home or I stayed. It was just that simple. When the time came I was certain I would make the right decision. *Until then,* I promised myself, *I will not dwell upon it.* Immediately after that thought, I drifted off to sleep.

# Chapter 26

Four days later I woke to an eerie silence. I lay in my pallet and tried to figure out what was wrong. And then I knew. The clack, clack, clack of the bellows no longer filled the air. The furnace had shut down.

*Vance certainly knew what he was talking about,* I thought, *and so did the others.*

Old Mag greeted me with a cheerful smile as I descended the loft ladder. "Doesn't that quiet sound nice, Girl? It'll take some getting used to, I'll grant you that. But not having that blasted noise going day in and day out is a blessing. Almost makes me feel like dancing this morning."

"Old Mag, you can dance anytime you want to with or without the noise of the bellows. In fact, I'd like to see how far you can kick up your heels," I challenged with a laugh. "Well, I'm waiting."

She looked at me and grinned and then proceeded to do a soft shuffle around the room, holding the hearth broom in her arms. Trog entered with an armload of wood.

"Are we dancing before breakfast, Old Mag? Will you give us each a lesson?" His eyes twinkled merrily.

"No, I will not. We're going to eat and then we're going to weave. And that is that."

I cleared my throat. "Before we eat I have something to say to both of you." They looked at me expectantly. "I'm not going to think about making a decision yet. But I think when the time comes, I'll know what to do and I'll make the right one. Does that make sense?"

"Yes, Girl, it does. It's a woman's way. Now, let's eat."

A little later, the three of us were busy in the weave house when Lily entered. "Guess what, guess what? Feast Day is set for this Saturday! Isn't that wonderful?

Oh, Callie, you're going to love Feast Day. Let me tell you all about it."

"Whoa, child, whoa. Sit down and take a breath," interrupted Old Mag. Lily did as she was asked. "Now, who decided Feast Day is to be Saturday?"

"Master Dodd. Ma heard it at the store early this morning."

"We talked about Feast Day earlier, Callie. Do you remember?" I nodded. "Well, we celebrate several things at the same time. The most important reason for celebrating is the gathering of the harvest from the gardens. Everything possible has been canned and preserved. The pantry shelves in each cottage are stocked as they well should be because that food is necessary to survive the coming winter. The other reason for celebrating is the shutdown of the furnace."

"Oh, Callie, you'll love Feast Day. We have so much fun," interrupted Lily.

"That we do, Lily," said Trog. "Why don't you tell Callie what happens."

"First we go to church. The preacher stays the entire day and sometimes he spends the night too. We sing all our favorite hymns. After church, the children play outdoor games until time for dinner. After dinner, we all play indoor games until time to go to bed. It's almost the most exciting day of the year, Callie!"

Lily's enthusiasm was catching and I found myself smiling broadly. "I'm anxious to hear about the games you play. Do the grown-ups get to play games, too?"

"They do, Callie. A lot of father's play outside with their children. But the mother's and big sisters are mostly inside helping get dinner ready."

"The dinner is very special, Girl. You have never seen the likes of the food that is put out on the tables. Sometimes we eat leftovers for almost a week!" added Old Mag.

"Until we are thoroughly sick of them," laughed Trog.

"Anyway," continued Lily, "Ma is going to invite all of you and Rune and Taw and Vance, too. Will you come, Old Mag? Please say yes!"

"Child, child, stop prattling on so. I'll talk to your mother. We'll get all the details worked out. Now, enough. Get yourself settled down and work on your sewing," said Old Mag.

Lily moved next to me and got out her sewing. I looked at her and gave her a big, slow wink. She giggled under her breath but did as Old Mag asked. Soon the only sound to be heard in the weave house was the thump of the beaters on the big looms.

That afternoon Old Mag and I visited Lily's mother to discuss our contributions to the Feast Day meal. Rose met us at the door with a big smile and warm hugs for each of us.

"I see Lily has already shared the news. It's impossible to keep a secret with that child around."

Rose was quite pretty with long dark hair and brown eyes. She had laugh lines at the corners of her eyes and her mouth turned up in a smile. "Please sit and have some tea with me." As she spoke, Rose removed garments from the chairs around the table.

I gazed about the cottage while Rose prepared the tea. Everywhere I looked I saw a child peering at me. They were all busy with something. Several of the girls were sewing. Two boys worked on an old skirt, ripping it into long strips to be sewn together later and used for weaving. By the time I had my tea in front of me, the children, with the exception of Lily, had lost interest in us.

Lily sat beside me, small hands wrapped around a cup of hot tea, and listened intently to everything that was said. The conversation eventually got around to the big dinner.

"Rune and his friends are hoping to shoot a deer this week. Venison will be a nice addition to the menu, don't you think, Old Mag?" She nodded in agreement. "They hope to get several so meat can be put in the smoke house, too. We'll also have rabbit stew. That's one of Lily's favorites."

"M-m-m-m." Lily rubbed her stomach in anticipation of her favorite dish.

"And I'll prepare several vegetable dishes, too. Potatoes, peas and carrots," Rose continued.

"The girl and I will bring turkey stew, loaves of bread and four or five vegetable dishes. We'll also bring several pies, too. Oh yes, and Trog will provide the spirits to slosh into our after dinner tea and coffee. Sounds like we'll have quite a feast."

"It certainly does," said Rose. "I'm so happy you will be able to join us. I must tell you that Lily is the one who suggested it. She is quite fond of you, Callie, and talks about you all the time."

I squeezed Lily closer to me. "She has a soft spot in my heart, too. I don't know what I'd do without her to keep me company."

"We all love Lily," added Old Mag. "And the three of us are more than delighted to be asked to join your family for Feast Day." She rose from the table. "And now Girl, it is time to go back to work. We have several things to finish before supper."

We said our goodbyes and started back toward the weave house. Old Mag spoke first. "My goodness, that woman has her hands full with all those children. How many are there?"

"Ten."

"No wonder she is so thin and scrawny. I doubt Lily is much help to her. She spends too much time with us. She didn't do that before you came along, Girl. Now, I'm not complaining. But I wonder sometimes if her mother doesn't need her to help out more at home."

I agreed but wondered how much an eight year old was expected to do.

"Is the Feast Day dinner all planned to your satisfaction, Mag?" Trog asked when we entered the weave house.

"You'll have to trade a small rug or a mat for a turkey, Trog. Do you think you'll be able to get us one? I told Rose we'd bring a turkey stew."

"Turkey stew. I love turkey stew, Mag. Thanks for putting it on the menu." He gave his mother a big smile. "I think I can manage to find us a turkey. In fact, if you ladies don't mind, I'll see to it right now. A little stroll about the town will do me good, too. I've been cooped up in here all day and need some fresh air. I probably won't be back until time for supper. Can you manage without me?"

"Get along with you, Trog. Of course we can manage without you. Why, we probably wouldn't notice you were gone if you hadn't told us you were going."

Trog chuckled as he put on his coat and went out the door. I watched him as he started down the path toward the U. He took long strides and in no time at all was hidden from my view.

Lily's enthusiasm for Feast Day remained with me for the rest of the afternoon. I tried to imagine eating dinner with seven adults and ten children. Plus me. Eighteen people! I wondered how Rose would manage to squeeze us all in. *The more the merrier,* I thought. *There won't be a dull moment. Or room to turn around.*

Old Mag began making preparations for Feast Day that night after supper. We sat around the kitchen table and discussed the vegetable dishes we'd prepare.

"Let's have baked yams and succotash," she suggested. "Everyone likes those dishes, especially the way I prepare them."

"And don't forget creamed corn, Mag. No one here makes it like you do," added Trog.

"Good, good," said Old Mag. "Can you think of anything else?"

174

"I'd like stewed tomatoes, Old Mag," I said. "I love your stewed tomatoes."

"Thank you, Girl. We'll have stewed tomatoes, too. Plus the turkey stew, the bread and the pies. First thing tomorrow morning Girl, you visit Dusty and put in an order for five pies and six loaves. You pick out the kinds you want."

"Get an apple pie or two, Callie. Those are big favorites and one won't be enough," suggested Trog. "And get both wheat and white bread."

"What shall I take to trade?" I asked.

"You know what we have in the weave house. This is a special occasion. Trade for whatever he wants." His confidence in me warmed my heart and I smiled at him gratefully.

"Did you find us a nice turkey, Trog?" queried Old Mag.

"Indeed I did. Tom Warren is going hunting in a couple of days. Said he'd bag one for me. I told him I'd give him an extra mat if his wife would dress it for us." He looked at me and winked. "Unless you want to show Callie how to get the feathers off a bird."

"I do not," declared Old Mag emphatically. "You know how much I hate cleaning birds. Only do it when no one else is around to do it for me. Besides, I'll bet the girl will be no better at cleaning birds than she is at lighting cooking fires." She looked at me with a twinkle in her green eyes.

"You're probably right, Old Mag," I replied before I began to giggle at the thought of stripping feathers from a turkey. *I'd much rather buy one from a supermarket,* I thought.

We were still discussing our contributions to the dinner when Rune arrived. He joined us at the table with his tea. "Lily was certainly full of herself this afternoon. She insisted I take her to see both Taw and Vance so she could personally deliver their Feast Day invitations. That girl gets so excited she takes my breath away."

175

"She does have a way about her," agreed Trog. "She keeps us on our toes in the weave house, that's for sure."

We shared our plans with Rune. "I'm already hungry. What a feast we are going to have. Vance and Taw are going deer hunting with me. Taw is good with a bow and arrow. So good, in fact, he rarely misses. Vance is pretty good, too. The three of us ought to be able to bag several deer. One for Feast Day and two for the smoke-house."

Trog lit his pipe and puffed contentedly, sending spirals of smoke into the air. "Maybe Callie would like to go hunting with you."

Rune looked my way but before he could ask, I replied, "No thank you, I think I'll pass on that outing. I'd just be in your way." *And I'd probably cry when I saw you shoot an arrow into one,* I thought. *How can anyone kill an animal with such beautiful eyes?*

"I passed by the Miller's place tonight. Now that the furnace is shut down, that place will be rebuilt in a hurry. They might even be in by Feast Day," related Rune.

"That will be a blessing," said Old Mag. "Mrs. Miller sure needs one, too. Her hands have not yet completely healed and though she doesn't complain, I think she is still in considerable pain. I'm wondering if she's well enough to take care of her own home. Mrs. Jacob's told me she could barely dress herself her fingers are so bad."

We were all silent, thinking of Mrs. Miller. Her hands and arms had healed badly and were covered with ugly scar tissue. Mobility in both hands was limited and she was still unable to do simple chores.

The conversation turned to other events occurring in the community. I sat, drinking tea, contentedly listening to the murmur of their voices. Thoughts of going home did not enter my mind. I was content, wrapped in the warmth and comfort of their friendship and love. *This is my family,* I thought *and I love them all dearly.*

# Chapter 27

Saturday dawned crisp and clear with a bright sun that promised a beautiful day. Old Mag called me from my pallet earlier than usual. She wanted breakfast out of the way so we could begin work on Feast Day dinner preparations. She hurried us through the morning meal; even Trog complained that he had no time for a cup of tea and a smoke. She brushed his complaints aside.

"Go on with you and bring in plenty of firewood. The girl and I have to get the turkey stew going before we go to church. What's more important, your pipe and tea or that turkey stew you've been hankering for?"

He didn't bother to reply; just shook his head and went out for more firewood.

Old Mag kept me busy for the next several hours. I peeled and chopped and sliced the vegetables that went into the stew. She was pleased with the plumpness of the turkey. She rubbed it with lard and plopped it into a large kettle of boiling water. To that she added onion and a bag of spices. Soon the aroma of stewing turkey filled the cottage.

"What kinds of spices are in the bag, Old Mag?"

"I can't tell you that, Girl. That's what makes my turkey stew better than everyone else's. My mother always did that and so did her mother. We've never shared the contents of the little bag with anyone."

"Well, whatever it is, it sure smells delicious."

"It does, doesn't it, Callie? Ma's turkey stew is truly the best." Trog dumped another load of firewood on the floor near the fireplace. "And now, Ma, if you don't mind, I'm going to have hot tea and smoke my pipe. I won't take up much space or get in your way. I promise."

She pulled the pot of turkey a little away from the fire. "We'll just let this fellow stew while we get the vegetables and spices out for the side dishes. We need to do that before we go to church."

We worked quickly and before long everything was ready. "Let's have a cup of tea before we head for church," said Old Mag. "You fix it while I look for something in my blanket chest."

She rummaged through the garments in the chest and breathed a sigh of relief when she found what she wanted. "Look at these, Girl. Aren't they beautiful?"

She put two pairs of pockets on the table. They were exquisitely embroidered in a swirl of delicate stitches and colors that covered the entire front side of each. Every woman in the community wore pockets. They were fashioned from two pieces of coarse, unbleached muslin sewn together. A long slit was cut in the front side of each pocket. A string was run through a loop at the top of each pocket and then tied around the waist. The pockets were then positioned one over each hip, with the slit in each pocket aligned with the slit on each side of the skirt. I had a handkerchief in the pocket on my right and when I needed it, I slipped my hand through the slit in my skirt and then into the slit in the pocket. In my left pocket, I tucked a small sachet filled with a fragrant potpourri. Old Mag did the same.

"I've never seen anything so pretty, Old Mag. Why haven't you been wearing them?"

"I do, Girl, but just for special occasions. And today is special. The extra set is for you."

"Thank you." I ran my hand lovingly over the stitches. "It seems a shame to hide something so beautiful under a skirt."

"Oh, we'll wear these pockets on the outside, over our skirts. You'll see a lot of them today. Every woman who does fancy needlework has a pair of these. They only wear them once or twice a year to keep them nice."

"I didn't know you did fancy needlework, Old Mag. You are full of surprises."

"I used to do a lot more before I got involved with weaving. I guess I just have a knack for working with yarns and threads. And now Girl, let's get ready. Trog will be in here before we know it."

I took off my apron and hiked up my skirt to remove the pockets I wore everyday. I carefully smoothed the front of my skirt before tying the embroidered pockets around my waist after tucking in the handkerchief and sachet. Old Mag did the same.

"Well, don't my ladies look especially nice," said Trog from the door. "You two will be the envy of the town."

We wrapped our cloaks around our shoulders and set off for the church. As we neared the U other people began emerging from their cottages. There was much laughter and calling of greetings along the way.

The doors to the little church were wide open to welcome the worshipers. We entered to find the pews rapidly filling. I spied Lily standing on the right about halfway up toward the altar. She waved and indicated she had seats saved for us. We made our way down the aisle and squeezed into our places. Both woodstoves at the front of the church were lit and I knew our location in the sanctuary would be comfortable. Too close to the stoves was miserably hot; too far in the back was unbearably cold. Lily's family had selected a good spot.

The wooden pews were uncomfortable. The seats were narrow, the backs straight and there was not much legroom between each row. It was difficult to sit still for any length of time without squiggling. I hoped the service would be brief but knew better.

Bright sunshine poured in through the windows on each side of the sanctuary and the whale oil lamps were not lit. I was glad because the smoke from the lamps often gave me a wretched headache. The building was soon filled to capacity and the latecomers stayed outside in a cluster. There was a soft murmur of conversation that died quickly as the circuit preacher strode to the pulpit and the service began. He talked of giving thanks for the many blessings of the year; the bountiful harvest from the gardens, the successful year of operation for the furnace and the safe shutting down for the winter season. He talked about the blessings bestowed upon each of us as individuals and as he did so I found my mind wandering.

I looked about me with interest. Old Mag was right. The women had removed their cloaks and I saw lovely pockets adorning the skirts of many of them. Even Lily's were covered with pretty stitches. She squeezed my arm and I gave her a big smile.

All around me people seemed rapt in what the preacher was saying. *Am I the only one not listening?* I wondered. Then I spied Rune sitting with Taw and Vance. He gave me a wink and I returned the gesture. I felt Old Mag stiffen against me and knew she'd seen the exchange and did not approve. I had to lower my head to keep her from seeing the smile that lit up my face.

Eventually the sermon ended and the singing, my favorite part of the service, began. There was no musical accompaniment, everything was sung a cappella. I was amazed at the beauty of the voices around me. Somehow they blended together in a pleasing harmony. I added my soprano to the hymns I knew.

And then the service was over. The atmosphere of reverence was replaced with one of joviality. People greeted each other with hugs and slaps on the back and handshakes. We made our way slowly to the door and exited into the bright sunshine. The area in front of the church was filled with people; many seemed reluctant to head for home but wanted instead to prolong this pleasant morning.

Old Mag and I worked our way through the crowd, stopping often to chat. No one seemed to be in a hurry to get home. Trog finally caught up with us just before we reached the U.

"Everyone is in a jolly mood," he said. "It was hard to get away."

"The whole atmosphere in the community seems to have changed," I added. "Is it because it is Feast Day?"

"Partly," he replied, "but the furnace shutting down for the winter adds to the feeling of good will. The men were anxious for a break from the backbreaking, dangerous work of smelting pig iron. They are looking forward to repairing things at home, hunting and playing with their children."

The delicious aroma of turkey stew filled our cottage. Trog sniffed appreciatively. Old Mag and I removed our fancy pockets, donned our aprons, and began to work on the vegetable dishes.

The time passed quickly. I was engrossed in my work when Lily's cheerful voice startled me. She was standing at my elbow looking up at me. "You didn't hear a word I said, did you Callie?"

I looked at her and smiled. "No, I didn't. Old Mag is keeping me so busy my ears are closed."

"Oh, Callie, how can your ears close?" Lily queried. "Anyway, I want to know if you can come outside for awhile. I need a partner for the game of graces."

"The game of graces?" I shot Old Mag a questioning glance. "I'm not sure I know how to play that. Besides, I've too much to do here."

"Well, Girl, we seem to be pretty well caught up. I can finish what you are doing and the rest is up to the cooking pots. Why don't you go out with Lily for a while? Rune's probably out there too, pining away. I wouldn't be surprised to find out he sent Lily in here to get you. Go on, go on, you two."

"Thank you, Old Mag, thank you," cried Lily, throwing her arms around Old Mag's waist.

I took off my apron and put on my cloak. Old Mag was chuckling as we went out the door. I was surprised to see the area near the U full of people engaged in all sorts of fun activities. Their shouts and laughter drifted toward us as I walked along, Lily skipping happily by my side.

Just before we reached the U, Rune fell into step beside us. He put his arm around my waist and gave me a little squeeze. "I was hoping Old Mag would let you come out and about. I decided she'd give in to Lily's begging and I was right."

"Wrong," I replied. "Old Mag saw right through your little scheme. She's probably looking out the window right now laughing. Don't you dare turn around to look."

The area was a beehive of activity. A large group of children played hide and seek. We watched for several minutes and then moved on. Four boys rolled iron hoops in an area near the church. I marveled at how adept they were at controlling the hoop with a piece of wood. Watching them it seemed easy but when I tried it, I had difficulty keeping the hoop upright. I finally resorted to using my hand for control instead of the stick and made out much better. I gave up when I tripped and sprawled flat on my face. I don't know which was more embarrassing; falling or enduring the laughter of Rune and Lily.

"There are my friends, Callie, playing the game of graces." Lily pointed to a group of girls just in front of the church.

The game of graces involved hoops, too. Narrow wooden hoops, not unlike large embroidery hoops, bedecked with brightly colored fabric streamers tied in three or four places on the hoop. As I watched, two girls sent the hoops flying high in the air toward each other, streamers trailing. With quick, deft movements, each girl caught the hoop on a pair of pointed sticks, paused a second and then sent it flying again.

"Come on, Callie, I'll teach you how to play," said Lily enthusiastically. She pulled me toward the group. "May Callie and I play with these?" she inquired, picking up the hoops and sticks not in use.

We stepped to one side and I received excellent instructions in playing the game. "Hold one stick in each hand and stretch your arms out in front of you," Lily directed as she demonstrated. "Put the sticks through the hoop. That's right. Now cross one stick over the other and raise them. Good, Callie. Swing the sticks apart and lift up like this."

She pulled the sticks apart in a scissoring motion. As she did so, her hoop sailed toward me. I had to duck to avoid being hit. "Go ahead, Callie, you try it."

I did as she asked but my hoop did not go as far as hers. Rune stepped in to help. "Get a little more lift in your arms. Don't try to push with your body. Let your arms and the sticks do the work."

I practiced several times with Rune helping. In no time at all, my hoop was sailing right toward her.

"Now the next step is to catch my hoop with your sticks. Send your hoop to me and I'll show you how."

I did as she asked and sent her a well-placed hoop, high in the air. She gave a little jump and caught the hoop neatly on the sticks.

"Now you try it." My first several attempts were not good but suddenly I got the hang of it. Before long I was tossing and catching the hoops just as well as the other girls playing the game. Lily and I teamed up with six other girls to form a large circle and toss the hoops back and forth from one person to another.

"I have to stop," I told Lily. "My arms are so tired I don't think I can toss any more."

"That's okay, Callie. You were good. Wasn't she Rune?"

"That she was, Lily. Let's move on down to the horseshoe pit. Taw and Vance have a match today and I'd like to see them play."

## Chapter 28

As we walked toward the blacksmith shop, the clang of metal on metal reached our ears, followed by the shouts of onlookers. A ring of spectators had gathered to watch the game and the three of us found a spot that allowed us to see. The horseshoe pit was about forty feet long with a foot high stake protruding from the ground at each end. Two men were standing at each stake. Each held two horseshoes and tossed them, one at a time, toward the opposite stake, hoping the shoe would ring the stake.

The men played well. Many of their tosses were ringers. Excitement and tension filled the air as the players assumed a tossing position, took aim and let the shoe fly. Applause greeted each ringer. After each toss, points were announced by a man standing on the sidelines.

"Do you understand the game, Callie," Rune inquired.

"Yes, but I'm not sure about the scoring."

"A ringer is three points. If there is no ringer, the shoe closest to the stake gets one point. The first team to reach fifty points wins."

As he spoke, a loud cheer went up from the crowd. The match was over. There was much handshaking and back thumping as the four men left the pit. Vance, Taw, and two other men stepped into the pit.

"Good," said Rune. "I was afraid we'd missed their match."

The men in the pit began to take warm-up tosses with the horseshoes and while they did so, the crowd shuffled about. Lily tugged on my skirt. "Look, Callie, isn't that Snoop over there?"

I looked where she was pointing. "Yes, that's Snoop. He looks different doesn't he, Lily?"

"I think it's because he's so clean," she replied. "I wonder how long he had to scrub to get all that dirt off?"

The two of us giggled. I had to admit she was right. He was filthy when we had last seen him. As I looked his way, he caught my eye and waved. I smiled back and then turned my attention to the pit and the match that was about to begin.

A hush fell over the crowd as the players determined which team would go first. The men opposite Taw and Vance won the draw and the match began. The men were evenly matched and ringer after ringer was tossed by both teams.

"How in the world will one team be declared the winner? No one seems to be missing the stake," I commented to Rune.

"They'll play two consecutive games and if the teams are tied at that time there will be a challenge. The team that wins the challenge will be declared the winner."

"A challenge?" I questioned.

"Yes, each team will toss until a player fails to ring the spike. And then, the game will be over."

"Oh, you mean a sudden death playoff?"

"What? A sudden what?"

"Never mind. It means the same thing. I'll explain it to you later."

Silence reined. Although the crowd was large not a sound other than metal clanging against metal could be heard. I held my breath each time Vance and Taw tossed. Their tosses were straight and true. But so were the other team's. At the end of two matches, the score was tied.

"Challenge, challenge," the crowd began to chant. The players nodded in agreement and the challenge began. Taw tossed first, followed by an opponent. Four shoes, four ringers. Vance tossed as did his opponent. Four shoes, four ringers. The match continued in this fashion for a number of minutes and then it happened. Taw tossed. His first shoe was a ringer but the second bounced against the stake and teetered for a few seconds. My breath caught in my throat. The shoe slowly

185

wobbled down and wrapped itself around the stake. A ringer!

I blew out a long sigh of relief. Taw's opponent tossed a shoe. A ringer. He tossed a second time and the shoe flew a little wide of the stake. It fell on the ground, no part touching the stake.

A loud cheer went up from the crowd. The bystanders crowded around the players yelling enthusiastically. Lily jumped up and down with excitement. "I knew they'd win! I knew it! I just knew it!"

Rune put his arm around my waist and pulled me close to him. "Wasn't that a great match?" he asked.

"Indeed it was. Do Taw and Vance ever play each other?"

"Oh my, no," he replied. "They want to stay friends as well as brothers. They only play as a team."

*Smart men,* I thought. *Competing against each other would surely cause hard feelings.*

Another match was set to begin but I had had enough of horseshoes for one day. "I need to head back to the cottage, Rune. Old Mag might need my help."

"Wait just a few minutes, Callie. The fellows will join us in a minute. They'll be happy to find out you watched the match."

We began to walk slowly toward the U. Vance and Taw soon caught up with us, wide grins on their faces.

"Hey, you two," I said, "that was quite a game of horseshoes you played. The other fellows didn't stand a chance."

"They sure did. When I saw that shoe teetering and wobbling I thought we'd lost the match for sure," replied Taw. "I think you and Lily brought us luck."

"I know we did," cried Lily. "But I knew you two were going to win. I just knew it."

Vance lifted Lily onto his shoulders. "We appreciate your confidence in us, Lily. From now on we'll make sure you attend every match."

I left Lily and the men at the U and hurried to the cottage. Old Mag and Trog were sitting at the table, he smoking his pipe, she gazing into the fire. Both greeted me with smiles.

"Have a cup of tea, Girl, and tell us about the games," said Old Mag. "We have a few minutes before we go to Rose's."

They listened intently as I related the events of the afternoon. "I wish I'd known Vance and Taw had a match. I'd have gone to see it. I understand they are excellent players." Trog puffed on his pipe as he spoke.

Chance jumped into my lap and purred contentedly. "They are, Trog, they are. I wish you could have seen Taw's last toss. It took my breath away." I stroked Chance's back gently. "I enjoyed the afternoon. The children seemed to be having a wonderful time."

"I'm glad they were," said Old Mag. She sipped her tea. "They don't have much time to play. It seems to me they are always working."

We chatted a few more minutes before Old Mag announced it was time to begin taking food to Rose's. I looked at what was assembled on the table and wondered how many trips the three of us would have to make.

I needn't have worried. By the time we were ready to go, Rune, Vance, and Taw were at the front door. In no time at all, Old Mag had filled their hands with baskets and sacks and the six of us were off. Rune and I made one extra trip to get the turkey stew and the pies.

I took a deep breath as I stepped into the cottage. It was a beehive of activity. Rose and Old Mag scurried about doing last minute tasks; Trog and Tom, Rose's husband, sat in a corner near the fire, smoking pipes and chatting. Vance and Taw were engaged in tussling with several of Lily's brothers. Children seemed to be everywhere at once, talking and laughing.

Tom had extended the table with sawhorses topped with wide planks of wood to make it long enough to accommodate eighteen. The table was covered with several brightly colored cloths and was so laden with food it seemed to sag. The room was lit with oil lamps and dozens of candles burned brightly, casting a cheery, warm glow. The scene looked like something from a picture book.

In no time at all, we were squeezed around the table inhaling the aroma from the bounty set before us. The adults sat at one end of the long table, the children at the other with the exception of the smallest child. Rose positioned him in a special chair next to her.

"Let's all join hands for the blessing," said Tom. "I'll begin and then I'd like for each adult to also say a few words."

"May I say something too, Pa?" asked Lily.

"Yes, you may. Now, let's bow our heads and give thanks for family and friends."

One by one we each offered our thanks for the food on the table, for good health and for good weather. When it was my turn I lifted my voice in prayer. "Oh Lord, thank you for the bountiful feast you have spread before us. Bless those that gather around this table, Lord. I humbly ask that you keep us all safe under your sheltering wings. Amen." As the words left my lips, I felt them deep in my heart.

The final amen was echoed by others around the table. "We'll fill the children's plates first," said Rose, "and then we'll pass our plates to the right. Put a spoonful of whatever's in front of you on the plate being passed."

Old Mag and I helped Rose fill the children's plates and then we took our places. In no time at all, the only sound in the room was that of eating utensils scraping crockery. I looked at the heaping plate in front of me and wondered how in the world I could eat all of it. I needn't have worried. I was famished and like everyone else, ate with gusto. Everything was delicious and I was sorry I had no room for seconds.

One by one the children were excused from the table. They amused themselves for the most part while they waited for us to finish. Three of them were too tired to stay up and Rose sent them to the sleeping loft. The smallest child fell asleep at the table. Tom gently picked him up and carried him to his pallet.

Lily and I helped Old Mag and Rose clean up the table. A generous portion of the leftover food was put into crocks to be taken home by Vance and Old Mag. Lily and I did the dishes; I washed, she dried. By the time we were finished I felt I had washed every dish and pot in the cottage.

Rune and Taw took down the sawhorses and the planks and put them outside the cottage door. The children were occupied with several indoor games. Lily and a brother played checkers on a large, wooden checkerboard. Four of her brothers played marbles in a corner of the room.

They used a long, thin strip of cloth to form the circle. Each boy placed five marbles in the center of the circle and took turns trying to shoot the marbles out. To do that, they held a marble called a shooter between their thumb and index finger and used their thumb to project the shooter at the marbles within the circle. Marbles knocked out of the circle belonged to the boy doing the shooting. Each boy kept his marbles in a little cloth sack tied with a drawstring.

Rune wanted to play and was heartily welcomed into the game. Each boy gave him a marble from his sack and one little fellow offered Rune a beautiful bluish-green shooter. He squatted on the floor like the boys and made a big show of selecting which marble he wanted to send out of the ring. They were delighted to have him play and when he finally sent a marble outside the ring, they cheered loudly. *I'm proud of him,* I thought. *He can whip those little fellows blindfolded but he knows how important it is for them to win.*

Rose gave the children pie and sent them off to bed. Lily put up a little fuss but her mother was firm and a teary-eyed Lily joined her brothers in the sleeping loft.

"Now, let's sit down and relax with our pie and tea," Rose said. "What kind of pie would you like?"

We made our selections and sat in comfortable silence around the table. Rose poured tea into our cups. Trog brought out a bottle of rum and passed it around the table. We each poured a little slosh into our cups.

The day was drawing to a close. And what a wonderful day it had been. I couldn't remember a happier family occasion. Rune's hand found mine under the table. He gave it a little squeeze. His white hair framed his face like a shining halo. He returned my smile and the dimples in his cheeks deepened. My heart skipped several beats. Thoughts of Jack did not enter my mind.

# Chapter 29

The days following Feast Day were busy and passed quickly. Old Mag and I worked nonstop on table runners, hot mats and small rugs. I worked on shawls at every opportunity and took great pride in the fact that no two were alike. Cooler weather increased the demand and my shawls were purchased before I finished them.

We were several weeks into December when Old Mag announced that, weather permitting, we'd be spending the following day in Snow Hill. "We'll leave early, before dawn most likely, and won't return until that night."

"What is the occasion," I asked.

"The Christmas season is almost upon us, Girl, and I have a gift or two to buy. We'll take the things we've made to Mr. Lapp's store and sell them. That fine gentleman does not refuse an item we weave."

"Do you mean sell, Old Mag? Or will we trade."

"We'll most likely do a little of both," Trog chimed in. "If we need something he doesn't have, he'll give us coins."

"Well, we're going to make a day of it," said Old Mag. "We'll have a big meal at Miss Pansy's. After that we'll shop at Lapp's. There'll be time to browse in the other little shops, too. Before we return, we'll have pie at Miss Pansy's. Sound like fun, Girl?"

"Oh my, yes, Old Mag. I do have one question, though. Will I have to ride into town hidden under a blanket?"

Trog whooped in delight. "No, Callie, you don't. This time you can sit up and enjoy the ride like the rest of us."

"The rest of us?"

"Yes, Girl, we're going to make a party of it. I've invited Lily and Rune and I think Vance and Taw want to go, too. Now, enough of this chatter. We have to decide on the things we're taking to trade."

Old Mag and I spent the larger part of the afternoon selecting the items we wanted to take into town. Trog added four exquisite wall hangings and a table runner to the stack of woven goods. I ran my hands appreciatively over the woven threads.

"Your work is especially beautiful, Trog. It's so delicate and fine. I'll never be able to weave like you do."

"Your work is beautiful, too, Callie. I don't think I've ever seen shawls quite like yours. The women around here certainly seem to like them. Don't be too hard on yourself. I didn't always weave like I do now. Your weaving technique will change with time and practice."

Old Mag set several table runners aside. "Add these to your shawls, Girl. You did most of the work on them. They're yours to trade or sell."

I looked at her in surprise. "Thank you, Old Mag. That's very generous of you. But I was planning to put my shawls with your things."

"You'll do no such thing. We have plenty to trade, don't we Trog? Besides, you might want to buy a gift."

He nodded in agreement. "May I give you a word to the wise, Callie? Trade your things for what they're worth. Get a figure in your mind and keep it there. Don't let Mr. Lapp or anyone else take advantage of you."

"Thank you, Trog. And you too, Old Mag."

I wanted to thank him for his compliment about my weaving but Lily burst into the room. "Ma just told me I'm going with you tomorrow. We'll have such fun, Callie, won't we?" She jumped up and down with excitement.

I hugged her. "That we will, Lily."

The remainder of the workday passed quickly. It was almost dark by the time Old Mag rose from her loom. I sent Lily on her way and then tidied my workspace. Chance waited patiently at the door. I scooped him up on my way out and carried him in my arms to the cottage.

After the supper dishes were cleared away, Trog and I returned to the weave house to pick up the things we planned to take to Snow Hill. We returned to the cottage to find Rune, sitting at the table, Chance on his lap, a cup of tea in his hands.

"I was going to help you but Old Mag persuaded me to stay," he grinned broadly.

"And I'll bet it didn't take much persuasion. You look mighty comfortable to me," I said, returning his grin. "Trog and I managed to bring it in one trip. I'm surprised, too, because we have quite a bit to take."

"Have some tea," suggested Old Mag, "and then we'll make plans for tomorrow."

By the time Rune and I were ready for our nightly stroll, everything had been decided. "I'm staying with Vance and Taw tonight. We'll escort Lily in the morning." He smiled at Old Mag and Trog. "I'm looking forward to going. Thank you for including me."

The prospect of a day in town had me too excited to sleep. I tossed and turned far into the night before I drifted off. It was very dark when Old Mag wakened me. I hurriedly dressed and descended the ladder into the kitchen, shivering with both cold and excitement.

I helped Old Mag set out a cold breakfast. Trog went for the wagon afterward while Old Mag and I packed extra food in a sack. Biscuits, ham, apples and several chunks of cheese. I caught her adding a handful of penny candy to the sack and looked at her inquiringly.

"I declare I can't get away with anything, Girl. You're always one step ahead of me. I've been saving this for a special occasion. McQuerrie gave it to me a few weeks ago. It'll be a surprise treat for everyone."

"I won't tell a soul, Old Mag. I'll be just as surprised as everyone else." The two of us exchanged sly grins just as Trog entered.

"What are you two up to?" he asked.

"None of your business," replied Old Mag. "Can't a couple of womenfolk have a secret?"

"Secret? What secret?" exclaimed Lily as she burst into the room.

"Don't you be worrying about a secret. Let's all get our things into the wagon and get going. Out with you, Lily. Find a spot in the wagon and stay put while the girl and I get ready."

I put my cloak around my shoulders and picked up the heavy sack of food. "Aren't you going to wear the red shawl?" asked Old Mag. "You'll be the envy of all the women in Miss Pansy's with that wrapped around your shoulders. Get it, Girl, and put it on under your cloak."

I did as I was told and then stepped outside into the dark, cold air. Trog had wrapped the woven goods in cloth and neatly stowed them in the bed of the wagon. Lily, Taw, and Vance sat with their backs against the wooden sides, blankets tucked around them. Rune and I joined them. Trog and Old Mag sat on the seat up front. He gave the horse a gentle tap with the reins and we were off.

The trip was delightful. We sang songs and told funny stories in the pre-dawn darkness. The road was uneven and we bounced and jostled in the bed of the wagon. Rune put his arm around my shoulders and I leaned into him savoring the moment.

The sky overhead was a canopy of black velvet, not a star twinkling. We were one lone wagon traveling east. I felt like a pioneer seeking a new land, a new beginning, a new life. I closed my eyes and nestled closer to Rune.

"Look, Callie. The sun is waking up." Lily shook me from my reverie.

Sure enough, colors were streaking across the horizon, pink and gray and gold. The leafless trees standing sentinel by the side of the road were stark skeletons against the morning sky. Slowly, slowly the sun rose. At first just a small arc of color and then in the blink of an eye, the entire golden orb crested the horizon. It was a beautiful sight.

Old Mag passed the food sack. My fingers searched for a piece of candy but found none. *You rascal you,* I thought. *You've taken them out and saved them for later.* Rune and I shared a small chunk of cheese and a biscuit. I was hungry and the snack tasted especially good.

Other wagons appeared on the road. We called out and waved to the passengers in each one we saw. All were strangers but they greeted us like old friends, with enthusiasm and genuine delight.

The town of Snow Hill appeared in the distance. We began to make plans for the day.

"Let's split up into small groups and go where we want to go before the noon meal," said Old Mag. "There's plenty to see. Afterward we'll do our trading and shopping. Is that agreeable with everyone?"

"I'm going with Callie," said Lily.

"Of course you are," I replied giving her a hug.

As we approached the town, wagon traffic thickened. So did the pedestrians. There were people everywhere, bundled in coats and cloaks against the chill. Numerous houses and cottages lined the route into town, smoke from their chimneys filling the air with a woody scent.

"The town lies on the banks of the Pocomoke River for a good reason. Access to water was important when towns were constructed. The river generates a lot of commerce for the town and allows goods to come in and go out easily. In fact, the pig iron we smelt at Furnace Town is shipped down the Pocomoke to the Chesapeake Bay. Lots of business men come here on sailing ships," said Trog. "Many residents in the area have large tracts of land used for growing tobacco. It is shipped out to other areas. Some local landowners have become quite wealthy raising the plant."

"Is tobacco the only product shipped out?" asked Taw.

195

"No, cypress is very much in demand. It's hauled out of the swampy areas and sold. Feathers and fertilizers are also exported."

"Feathers?" I asked. "Are there that many feathers around here?"

"Indeed so. All kinds of waterfowl are found in this area and their feathers are much in demand."

"The ships don't come in here empty," said Vance. "What goods do they bring in?"

"Rum, sugar, spices and other products too numerous to mention. This is quite a bustling little seaport."

We crossed the bridge into the town. I was surprised at the width of the river. I looked to the right and saw three and four-masted schooners tied up along the waterfront. To the left I saw elegant houses with backyards extending to the river. The smell of salt water reached my nostrils and I inhaled deeply.

"Have you decided what you're going to do?" asked Old Mag.

"I think so," replied Rune. "We're going to take a look at the waterfront first and then we'll mosey into the shops."

Trog stopped the wagon in front of Miss Pansy's and we climbed down. "We'll meet here at noon," he said, checking his pocket watch. "It's now ten so you'll have two hours."

He and Old Mag secured the horse and wagon and disappeared into Miss Pansy's. The five of us turned in the direction of the river. We had several blocks to walk before the docks came into view.

I cast admiring looks at the schooners. They were sleek and majestic as they lay in the water. The nearest one was taking on cargo. Men bustled up and down her gangplank carrying boxes and bales on their shoulders. They were a cheerful lot, too, with their laughter and catcalling. Many smaller boats plied the water in and around the tall schooners. Everyone seemed to know what he was doing.

"Tall ships have always fascinated me," said Rune. "I'd like to sail on one someday."

"Me too," added Taw.

We stood on the dock and watched for a few minutes and then turned back toward the center of town. Taw had promised Smitty he'd deliver a message to the local blacksmith and Vance decided to go with him. The two of them asked a passerby for directions and left us on the corner facing Lapp's Yarn and Textile Shop.

Rune, Lily, and I walked along slowly looking in the shop windows. We stopped at the milliner's shop to admire the fancy, feathered hats in the window. Lily begged to go in but I refused. Trying on hats with no intention of buying was not my idea of fun.

We ventured into a small shop that sold scrimshaw. The tiny trinkets carved from ivory were beautiful. I handled several and admired the delicate handiwork. I particularly liked a folding knife. The blade was silver and the handle was carved with an intricate ship sailing the sea. I rubbed my thumb over the handle; it felt good to my touch.

Lily loved the doll shop. She *oohed* and *aahed* over so many I lost track. When I asked her to show me her favorite, she couldn't but replied, "I like them all, Callie."

"Surely you must see one you like better than the others."

"No, these are all pretty dolls. They're for show, Callie. I wouldn't be able to play with one of these. She'd just get dirty and wouldn't be pretty anymore. I want a doll I can play with." Rune and I agreed with her.

The tea shop was fun. The proprietor was named Ling and he told us he sold authentic oriental teas. We sniffed at the leaves trying to determine which one we liked best. Ling gave us a sample of a tea he had brewing in the fireplace. It had a spicy aroma and the liquid was dark when he poured the brew into tiny cups. I took a sip and nodded at the pleasant tang.

The time passed quickly. We barely made it back to Miss Pansy's by noon. The others were waiting for us on the doorstep. I was more than ready to sit down and be waited on.

# Chapter 30

Miss Pansy welcomed us with a big smile. She took our outer garments and then led us to a table. Old Mag, Trog, and Vance sat on one side of the table. Rune, Lily, and I sat opposite them.

"Callie, you have on your beautiful shawl," exclaimed Lily. "May I wear it? I do believe I feel a draft on my shoulders."

"Lily, you are a sly one," I laughed as I removed the shawl and draped it around her small body. "Just be careful that you do not spill anything on it."

"I won't, I'll treat it just like it's mine. I promise."

Vance tweaked one of Lily's ears. "The shawl looks almost as pretty on you as it does on Callie."

The two serving girls set platters of food in front of us; ham, rabbit stew, yams, greens, beets, carrots in a cream sauce, freshly baked bread with butter and an assortment of jellies. Everything looked and smelled delicious. We filled our plates and ate heartily.

Miss Pansy's was very popular. At times, all the tables were full and people were waiting to be seated. Miss Pansy asked if two people could sit at the ends of our table but rather than do that, Trog moved to one end and let the couple sit together at the other. They were shy and spoke only when spoken to and I soon gave up trying to engage them in conversation.

Old Mag and I finished eating before the others. I looked around the room while I waited. It was plain with just a needlework sampler or two on the whitewashed walls and two large portraits over the huge, stone fireplace. The fire blazed brightly and I was glad we were not seated near it. The mantel held both oil lamps and candles. Sconces on each wall also held oil lamps. The wide planked floor was scuffed and worn.

The room was filled with the clatter of crockery and the laughter of the diners. Everyone seemed to be having a merry time. I smiled as I looked around the room. My thoughts were on the gifts I planned to buy. I hoped I could trade for what I wanted.

"A kiss for your thoughts," whispered Rune.

"I'm thinking what a happy place this is," I whispered in reply. "I'm glad we came here today."

It was almost two o'clock by the time we finished eating and were back on the street. We agreed to meet at Miss Pansy's at half-past four. I had two shawls and three runners to trade. I hoped it was enough. I wrapped the goods in a large piece of fabric and prepared to go shopping.

"May I go with you, Callie?" inquired Lily.

"Not this time, Lily. I need to shop alone." For once she didn't pout and put up a fuss. I looked at the faces around me and smiled. "I'll see you all later."

My first stop was the shop that sold the scrimshaw. I wanted to buy the knife for Rune. There were several customers in the shop and I had to wait. I didn't mind; I enjoyed looked at the beautiful carved pieces.

When it was my turn, I asked the shopkeeper to show me the knife. I handled it carefully, opening and closing the blade and rubbing the intricate carving with my thumb. *Rune will love this,* I thought. *A tall ship in his pocket.*

"I'd like to buy this," I said, "but I don't have money. Will you trade it for something I have?"

I opened my package of goods and spread them out on the counter. He fingered each one and then nodded. He selected a butter yellow shawl and said, "This will do."

I gave him a big smile. *That was easy,* I thought. *I hope I do as well everywhere else.*

He wrapped the knife in brown waxed paper and tied it with red string. "Did you weave the shawl young lady?" he asked as he handed me the package.

I nodded in reply.

"I'm not familiar with your work. I haven't seen shawls edged the way yours are. Do you work in this area?"

"Yes, I live and work in the furnace community."

He smiled. "Then you must know Trog and Old Mag. What weavers they are!" He paused briefly. "Don't tell me you work with them."

I nodded once again as I opened the door.

"Well, you have the very best of tutors. My daughter will love this shawl. Stop in again."

I hurried to the tea shop. A little bell over the door tinkled merrily as I entered. Ling appeared from a back room hidden by a heavy curtain of beads. He bowed graciously and let me wander around the room looking at the tea selection. I sniffed little sacks of leaves until I could no longer distinguish one aroma from another. I finally selected four teas I thought Vance would like. I placed a green and white table runner on the counter and asked if he'd trade. He fingered it appreciatively and nodded. He wrapped the tea in a paper packet and bowed once more.

A general store was two doors down from the tea shop. I stepped into a large area crammed with all types of merchandise. A number of people were also shopping and I scanned them quickly looking for familiar faces. Seeing none, I breathed a sigh of relief. I stood for a second and inhaled the pleasant aroma of the store. I couldn't identify one scent from another; all blended together to form a smell only a general store has.

I was amazed at the variety of items in stock. One area held bolts and bolts of fabrics; coarse muslins to fine silks and satins. Feathery boas dangled from a nearby shelf. Lace and bead trimmings were in a bin nearby. The household section contained large bins of flour, sugar, and salt. Barrels of molasses stood next to shelves of crockery and iron pots. Huge baskets heaped with oranges and apples sat on the floor near the bins.

Woven baskets hung from iron hooks nailed to a tall pole.

I spied a basket of hand made soaps. The bars were delicate shades of pink, blue, and green. I lifted one to my nose and the scent of lavender filled my nostrils. Another smelled like roses and a third had the lovely aroma of lemon. I removed a basket from a hook and put in the three bars of soap. *The perfect gift for Old Mag,* I thought as I moved to another area, *and this basket will be my shopping cart.*

I found just the right pipe tobacco for Trog. The aroma was quite different from the one he usually smoked, not as pungent but more woodsy. I fell in love with a brown leather tobacco pouch, too. It was soft and pliable to my touch and I knew Trog would enjoy using it. I added the tobacco and pouch to the basket.

I was surprised to find a section with paraphernalia for horses. I thought immediately of Taw and looked through the area in earnest. Beautiful saddles with silver trappings were displayed on sawhorses and colorful blankets hung from hooks under the shelves. I saw liniments, salves, and tins of the blacking used to polish a horse's hooves. I poked about idly and then I saw the curry brushes. One in particular caught my eye. The handle was made of a dark wood, highly polished and carved with the figure of a running horse, tail and mane flying in the wind. It was beautiful. I picked it up and held it in my hands. The wood felt like satin under my touch. *Taw will enjoy using this,* I thought as I placed it gently in the basket.

*Now for Lily.* I wandered aimlessly about the store but saw nothing I thought she would like. There were a few dolls in one corner but none had much appeal. I decided to take another look in the doll shop so made my way to the counter to pay for my purchases. On the way, I passed the oranges and selected seven nice ones. The storekeeper helped me remove the things from the basket.

"Quite a nice selection you have here," he said. "Do you want the basket too?"

"No thank you. I just used it to carry my selections. I hope you don't mind." I hesitated and then added, "I have several woven goods in my parcel. Will you be willing to trade?"

"Let me see what you have."

I untied the parcel and spread out the remaining shawl and two runners. He picked each one up and looked at it carefully. I held my breath in fear he was going to say no but he nodded his head and selected the blue shawl and a red and gold runner. I had one runner left.

"These will do nicely." He wrapped each purchase individually in brown paper and put them all in a cloth sack tied with a drawstring.

"Thank you. I've enjoyed shopping in your store," I told him as I left the counter. He didn't have time to reply because another customer had taken my place in front of him.

Another look around the doll shop confirmed my suspicions that I would find nothing for Lily on the premises. The dolls were just too pretty and not at all suitable for an eight year old. With a heavy heart I left empty handed.

I passed Lapp's Yarn and Textile Shop on my way back to Miss Pansy's. *Did I see dolls in here the last time I visited?* I wondered. I decided to go in. The smell of yarns and fabrics was familiar to me and made me feel at home. I looked for Old Mag or Trog but saw neither of them. Mr. Lapp was busy waiting on a customer so I wandered a bit on my own. There were fabrics, yarn, laces, threads, but no dolls. I stood with heavy heart, clutching my parcels and sack wondering what to do. *I'll have to make her one,* I thought.

"May I help you, miss?" I was so deep in thought I hadn't heard Mr. Lapp approach me. I gave him a startled look.

"Oh, dear, I didn't mean to frighten you. Please excuse me. Why, I remember you. You're related to Old Mag, are you not? Are you looking for her? She was in earlier." He gave me a big smile.

"Yes, I'm with Old Mag but I'm not looking for her. Right now, that is. What I'm looking for is a doll, a rag doll. Do you happen to have them for sale in the store?"

"Let me see, I think we had some over here." He walked toward the window. "No, they're gone. Where else might they be?" He stood thinking, one hand under his chin.

Finally, he looked up. I followed his gaze and there, on the top shelf, sat a lone rag doll.

"That might be the last one. Let me get it down for you." He put a wooden ladder against the shelf and climbed up to retrieve the doll.

As soon as he put it in my hands I knew it was the right one. The doll was about eighteen inches high and wore a blue dress trimmed with lace at the neck and sleeves. She had blond yarn braids, brown button eyes, and pink cheeks. White stockings and tiny black leather shoes covered her feet. A white, lace trimmed petticoat peeked from under the hem of the dress. Pink ribbons on the braids completed her outfit.

I held the doll. She was soft and pliable and fit the curve of my arm. She was just right for Lily.

"She's just what I was looking for," I exclaimed.

"Let's see," said Mr. Lapp, "there was a little sack of clothing that went with that doll. I wonder where it is? Hm-m-m. Let me think."

Once again, he stood deep in thought, chin resting in one hand. "I know." He ascended the ladder once more and poked around on the shelf where the doll had been sitting. He extracted a little sack and waved it merrily. "Here 'tis," he said triumphantly.

The little sack contained extra clothing for the doll. There was a red velvet dress trimmed with sparkling black beads, a black cloak edged with tiny feathers, a crisp, white apron, a dainty mob cap and two red hair ribbons. I was amazed at the beautiful handiwork. The stitches in the garments were so tiny they were difficult to see. I could barely contain my excitement.

"I'll take it all," I cried happily as I followed Mr. Lapp to the counter. I pulled the last table runner from the wrapper. "Will this be enough?"

He looked at the runner and then at me. I felt my heart beating in my chest and my breath caught in my throat. I was good at reading people. *It's not going to be enough.*

He shook his head. "I'm sorry but I'll need more than a runner. Do you have anything else?"

"No, no, I don't," I began. "Wait. I do have something else." I put down my parcels and took off my cloak. "Will you take this shawl?"

With trembling fingers I removed the red shawl and handed it to him. He stroked it gently and then held it in the air while he examined it carefully.

"This is beautiful," he said. "I haven't seen another like it and I've handled a lot of shawls." He was silent for a few moments and then added, "The doll must be for a very special person for you to part with this."

"Yes, she is," I replied.

He wrapped the doll and her accessories in brown paper and passed the package to me. I took one last look at the red shawl.

"Thank you, Mr. Lapp.'

"No, my dear, thank you. I hope to see you the next time you folks come to town."

Shopping completed, I turned my steps toward Miss Pansy's. I spied our wagon, too, and placed my parcels carefully in the wagon bed, covering them with a blanket. I didn't have long to wait for the others.

# Chapter 31

We gathered in front of Miss Pansy's, all present but Old Mag. Trog told us she had one more errand to run but we were not to wait for her. So in we went. Miss Pansy collected our cloaks and coats and I hoped no one would notice the missing shawl. We were barely seated before Lily asked about it.

"Callie, where is your shawl? I was going to wear it again."

"It must have come off with my cloak, Lily. But let's not bother with it now. It's mixed in with all our outer garments and will be difficult to locate. Let's think about the pie we are going to have."

"I'm all for that," said Vance.

We all had tea while we waited for Old Mag to join us. She arrived somewhat breathless, her cheeks rosy from being out in the brisk air.

"Did everyone have a jolly time?" she asked when she was seated.

"Yes," cried Lily. "Rune and I had lots of fun. We took a little sail on the river. Didn't we Rune?"

"We certainly did. We were standing on the docks looking wistful, I guess, and a kind-hearted captain asked us if we'd like to sail with him to get something from another ship. We took him up on his offer."

"May I tell the rest, Rune? May I?" Without waiting for him to reply, Lily continued with the story. "He picked up a monkey from the other ship, a cute little monkey with a long tail. It had on a red coat with brass buttons and a tiny hat with a strap under the chin. It was the captain's pet and sat on his shoulder all the way back to shore."

Lily's eyes sparkled with excitement and her enthusiasm for the monkey was catching. We spent the next few minutes questioning her about the animal.

Miss Pansy stopped by our table to recite the pie menu for the day: apple, peach, mince, and pumpkin. She went round the table taking our orders. Apple, peach and pumpkin were the favorites but I asked for a slice of mince.

"A slice, Callie? Just a slice?" asked Trog. "Well I for one can eat more than a slice. How about the rest of you?"

A chorus of 'me too's' greeted his question. In no time at all, Miss Pansy's girls brought us our dessert, an apple pie, a peach pie, a pumpkin pie, and a slice of mince pie. I had the mince and a tiny sliver of each of the other pies as well. That plus the tea I consumed filled me to the point of being uncomfortable but I enjoyed every bite and swallow.

It was dark when we finally climbed into the wagon to head for home. The night air was cold and we snuggled deep into our blankets to keep warm. Rune and I wrapped our arms around each other, too, and kissed in the darkness.

Once we crossed the bridge, we sang a few songs to help pass the time. Trog lit his pipe and every now and then I caught a whiff of smoke. Old Mag passed the food sack. I searched for a candy and found one. I savored it on my tongue for a long time before it completely dissolved.

One by one we fell silent. The moon rose and illuminated the wagon bed. The others slept, heads bobbing to the rhythm of the wagon as it rolled along the rutted road. I leaned into Rune and nestled my head on his shoulder. My breath hung in the air before me like a spirit leading the way.

My thoughts turned inward. *I've changed somehow. The things that have happened to me in the past several months have made me a different person, a better person. I like who and what I am, right now at this moment in time. My friends here have nothing, but they are rich in so many ways. They have taught me so much about kindness and generosity. Yes, and about life and how to live it. I mustn't forget that.*

I blew each of them a kiss in the darkness and then snuggled closer to Rune. I closed my eyes and listened to the clop, clop of the horse's hooves. The rhythm was soothing and I drifted off to sleep.

It was late when we arrived at the cottage. Rune carried a sleeping Lily home. Taw and Vance helped us unload the wagon and then took it to the stable on their way home. The cottage was icy and the three of us didn't tarry downstairs but climbed the ladder to the sleeping loft and burrowed gratefully into our pallets.

The next several days were busy. We had visitors in the weave house every day and Old Mag and Trog did a lot of trading for things we needed; jars of canned goods, butter, ham, and salt pork filled our pantry shelves. We were promised venison, turkeys, and rabbits by the wives of several hunters.

Old Mag was pleased. "It's important to have a skill that others need, Girl. That way you work hard at something you like to do but still get the necessities. I'd much rather weave than work in a garden most of the year."

I agreed. I had seen the women and children laboring in the gardens when I first arrived. They worked from sunup to sundown, planting, hoeing, weeding and harvesting. Watering the garden was a backbreaking endeavor. Bucket after bucket of water was brought from the large pond that fed the canal. The children did that task. They wore yokes across their shoulders with a wooden bucket suspended from each side. Trog told me a gallon of water weighed eight pounds and each bucket held five gallons. Those youngsters carried up to eighty pounds of water with the aid of the yoke. I was not anxious to trade places with them or their mothers.

That evening after supper Old Mag announced it was time to do a little decorating for Christmas. "We'll go out in the forest tomorrow and gather mistletoe and other greens. I like pine because it makes the cottage smell fresh but spruce is good, too. Some folks have a Christmas tree but Trog and I don't. I'm scared of the candles tucked in among the branches. Each year somebody loses a cottage because they left a candle burning on a tree. When Rune stops by tonight, ask him if he'd like to go with us."

"Can we put up a Christmas tree without candles?" I asked.

Old Mag looked at me thoughtfully. "I guess we can. But what will you put on it?"

"Oh, I can think of lots of things, Old Mag. Yarn, pine cones, acorns, even buttons."

"I think that sounds like fun, Callie," said Trog, puffing on his pipe. "I'll be glad to help you put up a tree."

"That settles it then," said Old Mag. "We'll look for a nice tree, too. And we'll all trim it."

The next morning, shortly after breakfast, Trog, Old Mag, Rune, and I entered the forest beyond the furnace to search for greenery. Rune took us through a stand of scrub pines. The trees were short and their branches were easy to cut. He led us through a stand of hardwoods, too, and there we found an abundance of mistletoe. He had to scramble up into the trees to get it, though, and we laughed at his antics as he climbed.

"You didn't learn much from that sea captain's monkey, did you?" asked Trog.

"Well, I didn't see him climb higher than the captain's shoulder. Considering that I think I'm doing very well thank you."

"Let's try to find some tea berry," I suggested. "A few sprigs of it will be pretty in a jar."

"We'll look," replied Rune, "but I'm not sure where to find it. We can get holly, though. I saw a tree the other day and it was loaded with berries."

"We need a tree to decorate," I added.

"We'll find one closer to home," said Trog. "No need to cut one way out here. It will be difficult to drag it home. You and Rune can look for one this afternoon."

209

We filled our baskets easily and were back at the cottage in time for the noon meal. Old Mag put on the teakettle while I put out bread and cheese. The four of us gathered around the table.

"Christmas has certainly come quickly. Hard to believe it's just a couple of days away," said Old Mag.

*A couple of days away! I've lost all track of time,* I thought as I nibbled on a chunk of cheese. And in that instant I heard Jack calling to me from across time. My eyes filled with tears. *Not now, Jack. Not now. I can't deal with you yet. I need more time...time...time.*

"Are you all right, Girl?" asked Old Mag. "You have a glazed look in your eyes."

I quickly swallowed a bite of cheese and faked a little cough. "I'm okay. A little cheese went down the wrong way."

Rune thumped me on the back while Trog fetched a cup of water. "Thank you, thank you. It's gone down." I wiped the tears from my eyes with the back of my hand and smiled at them gratefully.

"Finish your tea, Girl," said Old Mag, "and then be off. Bring back a nice tree. While you're gone, Trog and I will decide where to put it."

Rune and I did as we were instructed. "I think I know just the place to find a nice cedar tree," he said. "I was out this way not long ago and saw several that might do."

We walked a short distance down the road before he pointed to a small stand of trees. "Let's look in here."

A tangle of briars blocked my passage and for a few minutes walking was difficult. The thorns grabbed at the hem of my skirt and I had to use my fingers to pry them away from the cloth. I was ready to give up and suggest another spot when Rune called out.

"Look ahead of you, Callie. See those cedars a little to the left. What do you think about one of those?"

I raised my eyes from the briars and looked into the woods. Three beautiful cedars were growing side by side. Any one of them would be perfect in the cottage.

"Oh Rune, they're beautiful," I cried as I tried to jump out of the briar patch. "But I think I need a little help. I can't seem to take a step in these briars."

He turned back to help me. "My goodness, Callie, how did you get so mired in these things?"

He bent to help me extract the thorns and then tramped the briars to the ground. I gave a little jump and was finally free of the area. My skirt, however, had not fared well at all. I noticed several rips above the hemline.

We approached the cedars and inspected them carefully. They were beautiful, standing gracefully in the dappled sunlight. It seemed a shame to cut one. I almost changed my mind. Rune was no help at all but stood looking at me as I tried to make a decision.

He finally said, "You know, Callie, at some point in the near future, these little trees will be cut down and thrown away. They won't be used to make charcoal or as firewood. Why not take one home and enjoy it?"

That convinced me. I selected the one in the middle and watched him chop it down. We sang Christmas carols as we hauled it back to the cottage.

# Chapter 32

Old Mag was delighted with the cedar tree. "It will do just fine, Girl. You and Rune selected the perfect one for our cottage. For now though, Rune, we'd best stick it in a barrel of water until we're ready to trim it. Oh yes, and while you're out there pick up a few pine cones and acorns and anything else you think we can use for tree decorations."

Rune and Trog took the tree outside. I looked around the cottage in amazement. Old Mag had done wonders with the greenery while I was gone. Boughs of pine and spruce covered the windowsills and the mantel. Candles were tucked in among the boughs, as were sprigs of berry-laden holly.

"How did you manage to do all this in such a short time?" I asked, shaking my head in astonishment. "It's beautiful."

"You forget I've done this before, Girl. But I want you to add the finishing touches. What else do you think we need to do?"

"We could add bows of red ribbon or yarn to the greenery. And under the candles, too," I suggested.

"Let's try it," said Old Mag. "Run over to the weave house and bring back whatever you think we can use."

We spent the next hour adding red bows to the boughs of spruce and pine on the windowsills. I tied yarn bows around the lamps and the wall sconces. Old Mag looked through her blanket chest, brought out a beautiful Christmas runner, and held it up for me to see.

"Trog wove this a few years back. It was too beautiful to sell but even so I had a terrible time convincing him to let me keep it."

"What exquisite work, Old Mag. He never ceases to amaze me."

The runner was woven in soft colors with the nativity scene depicted on both ends. I ran my hands lovingly over the fine threads. The faces of Mary and the Baby seemed to leap from the fabric. The Star of Bethlehem, in the very center of the runner, was done in a gold thread so brilliant it seemed to twinkle.

"We need a centerpiece, Old Mag. What shall we use?"

"I'll put fruit in a large wooden bowl. I have apples that will do." She went to the pantry for the bowl and the fruit. "We can add a little holly, too, for extra color."

"I can add to the fruit bowl," I said as I climbed the ladder to the sleeping loft. In a few minutes I returned with the seven oranges I had purchased in Snow Hill. I spread them out on the table. "I was saving these as a surprise for Christmas morning."

"How nice," exclaimed Old Mag. "We don't have oranges often. We'll keep them in the bowl for now but we'll certainly eat them Christmas Day." She made room in the bowl for the oranges. "Seven of them. One each for Trog, Rune, Lily, Taw, Vance, you and me. Am I right, Girl?"

I laughingly nodded.

"Well," Old Mag added, "I'll miss smelling them tonight when I go to bed."

At that remark, we both burst into laughter.

The cottage was very festive by the time Rune and Trog returned with the items for the tree. The four of us spent the remainder of the afternoon tying red yarn around pinecones and acorns. Trog filled a small keg with earth and the trunk of the small cedar was 'planted' in that. We moved it all around the room looking for the best spot and finally settled on a corner between a window and the door.

We had a wonderful time trimming the tree. Each ornament was hung with care in exactly the right spot. Needless to say, the right spot for one of us was not necessarily the right spot for the rest of us and there was a lot of laughter as each ornament was moved about. Old Mag produced a long strip of yellow lace to be used as a garland. An extra large bow of red satin ribbon became a tree topper.

Dusk had fallen by the time we sat down to admire our handiwork. "We've done a fine job, haven't we? I can't remember when the cottage looked this nice at Christmas," said Old Mag. "What do you think, Trog?"

"I agree, Mag. It seems to be especially beautiful this year thanks to Callie. And Rune, too." Trog leaned his head back and blew a smoke ring. It looped lazily above him and I was tempted to catch it around a finger.

"Stay for supper, Rune," said Old Mag. "You've earned it, all the work you've done for us today. I've got plenty of rabbit stew and enough apple pie."

"Thank you, Old Mag. I'll be happy to stay." Rune gave my hand a squeeze under the table. "I think I'll bring in more firewood, too. It's going to be cold tonight."

"Feels like snow to me," commented Trog. "Do you need help with the wood?"

"No, just sit and enjoy your pipe. It won't take me long."

Old Mag and I had supper on the table in no time at all. Everything was delicious. I used a piece of bread to wipe my plate clean, ready for the apple pie. Old Mag served it covered with warm milk sprinkled generously with cinnamon.

"Nothing like apple pie and warm milk on a cold night, Mag," said Trog.

"The cinnamon made it even tastier," I added as I poured hot tea into our cups.

We sat in comfortable silence, sipping our tea, each wrapped in thoughts of Christmases past. The snapping of the fire was mesmerizing. Pinpoints of light from the flames danced across the walls and the lanterns and candles cast a soft glow upon the boughs of greenery.

Trog and Rune helped with the cleanup after supper. Old Mag protested noisily but we won out and in the end, she sat in her rocking chair, supervising the three of us.

"I'll sweep the floor, Girl. You and Rune go out for your walk. If we're not up when you get back, shake down the fire before you go to bed."

Rune and I donned our outer garments and stepped outside into the cold, night air. The sky above was black with neither moon nor stars visible. Our feet crunched across the frozen earth as we trekked toward the furnace.

Arm in arm, we crossed the footbridge that spanned the canal, turned right and walked along the towpath toward the lock. Silence surrounded us. The furnace loomed ahead, a quiet sentinel keeping watch in the night. I missed the sound of water flowing through the millrace and tumbling over the waterwheel now dark and still. A sudden rustling in the branches of a tree in the swamp caused me to start in fright. I shivered and moved closer to Rune.

"That was only a bird, Callie. Probably an owl hunting for his dinner." He wrapped both arms around me, pulled me to him and kissed me long and hard on the lips. I leaned into him savoring the moment. The darkness settled around us as we continued along the towpath.

"Are you warm enough, Callie?" Rune asked.

"I am as long as you hold me tight."

"Just you try to get away," he replied laughing, pulling me even closer. "If this cold weather holds the pond will freeze. Can you ice skate?"

"I've never tried," I answered. Without thinking I added, "But I can roller skate. Ice skating must be similar."

"Roller skate?" he asked. "What are roller skates?"

"Skates on wheels. You put them on and roll along. Instead of skating on ice you skate on a wood floor or the street or the sidewalk."

"Hold on. I can't imagine what you are talking about."

He listened intently while I explained skates on little wheels. By the time I finished we reached the locks. We stood looking at the water.

"Does the canal freeze, too?" I asked.

"No, it doesn't. This part of the canal is fed by an underground spring. In the daylight, you can see the little swirls where the water seeps in. I guess the motion keeps the water from freezing. When the pond freezes, lots of people use this water for drinking and cooking."

"Listen," I said kneeling on the bank, "I think I can hear the water burbling a little."

Rune knelt beside me. "I hear it too, Callie, just barely. What good ears you have."

"The better to hear you with my dear," I replied laughing as I kissed him on the cheek. "Let's start back. I'm getting cold."

Rune helped me to my feet. "Not only is it cold but the air feels very damp. I think it might snow before morning."

"Oh, wouldn't that be wonderful, Rune. Snow for Christmas Eve." I clapped my hands. "I'd like that."

We hadn't taken many steps when we heard someone else walking the towpath. Two figures loomed into view just in front of us. "We thought we might find you out here. Trog said you had gone for a walk," said Taw. "Hello, Callie."

"Hi, Taw, Vance. We've been down to the locks. Sure is peaceful and quiet down there."

We chatted for a few minutes before I said, "We're heading back to the cottage. Why don't you two join us? Hot tea by the fire sounds great right now."

"I could use a little warming up," said Vance. "The cold seems to go right through my clothing." He stomped his feet on the ground as he spoke.

Once again we walked in the direction of the cottage. The first snowflakes began to fall just as we reached the furnace. They floated lazily from the sky and dropped soundlessly to the ground.

"You were right, Rune. You were right," I cried, jumping up and down with delight. "It's snowing."

Rune grinned sheepishly at Taw and Vance. "I told Callie I thought it might snow tonight. Looks like I was right."

"It's felt like snow all day," said Taw. "The horse I was working sensed it too. He was a little skittish about being outside in the corral. I ended up working him in the barn."

The conversation turned to animals and their uncanny sense of weather changes and danger. By the time we reached the cottage, the snowflakes had thickened and a light dusting covered the ground.

The cottage was warm and toasty after the damp cold of outside. Old Mag and Trog had retired for the night. Rune added several logs to the fire and the four of us held our hands eagerly toward the blaze. I spread a blanket on the floor in front of the fireplace.

"Let's sit here," I said. "We'll be a lot warmer."

The three men dropped to the blanket and tucked their legs under them Indian fashion. I put water on to boil and in to time at all, we each held a steaming cup of tea. I sat on the blanket beside Rune.

"The decorations in here are beautiful, Callie. When did you do all this?" asked Vance.

"We did it today. Rune helped, too. He knew where a perfect Christmas tree was and went with me to get it."

"Callie. Callie." Trog called to me from the sleeping loft.

I climbed halfway up the ladder and answered softly. "Yes?"

"Get out my bottle of spirits and slosh a wee bit in each cup. That'll get your blood flowing."

"Thanks, Trog," I said. "Oh, and Trog, it's snowing."

The next hour passed quickly. The men predicted how deep the snow would be by morning. That led to sharing funny snow stories. We each tried to outdo the other and as the time passed, the events related became more and more unbelievable. *If I didn't know better, I'd think I was at a liar's convention,* I thought.

At some point I fell silent and let the conversation flow around me. My gaze fell on each man in turn. The flickering firelight gave a surreal appearance to each face, adding planes and angles not seen in the daylight. These were handsome men, yes, but their faces showed strength of character and kindness. I knew I could trust each one of them with my life if need be. I was glad they were my friends.

Taw and Vance finally stood to go. Rune helped me to my feet and I walked them to the door. When it opened, I saw a world covered in a thick blanket of white with more falling. We said our goodbyes and watched them set off toward the U. In just a few steps, they disappeared into the curtain of white.

Rune and I stood silently in the open door. It was eerily quiet and this time, I heard the snow when it hit the ground.

# Chapter 33

Christmas Eve dawned clear and bright. A little more than two feet of snow covered the ground creating a world so dazzling, I had to shade my eyes when I looked out the windows. After breakfast, Trog and I shoveled a path to the community woodpile and another to the weave house. The snow was wet and heavy and we were forced to rest frequently.

Our work was made light by the gaiety around us. Men and women were out clearing pathways from their cottages to the woodpile. The sounds of their voices filled the air and drifted our way. Children were everywhere; throwing snowballs, building snowmen of all shapes and sizes, tumbling in the snow. They were enjoying the first big snowfall of the year and their shouts and laughter were music to my ears.

"This snow won't last long," predicted Trog.

He was right. The temperature climbed steadily during the day and by mid-afternoon, snow melted rapidly from the rooftops. Patches of brown earth showed through on the shoveled pathways.

We had projects to complete for several people and spent a large portion of the day in the weave house. Our customers had big smiles on their faces and a cheery *Merry Christmas* on their lips. Each one brought us a gift and by the end of the day, the little table in the corner was laden with a variety of canned goods as well as a few pieces of fancy embroidery. My heart swelled with pride at the generosity shown us. The women who traded for our goods worked hard and had very little to spare.

Lily dropped in, too, excited and bubbly about Christmas. She pulled out a handkerchief bordered with delicate embroidery.

"I need to finish this, Callie. And I can't work on it at home because Ma will see it."

Old Mag and I complimented her on her handiwork. When Trog asked to see it, she showed it to him hesitantly.

"You have a wonderful eye for color, Lily," he said as he held the piece of fabric. "That is rare in one so young."

"I know. That's what Ma's says, too," she answered.

"If you get it finished this afternoon, Lily," said Old Mag, "come home with us and I'll iron it for you."

"Oh, thank you, Old Mag. I'd like that very much. Rune says you're all decorated for Christmas. We haven't started yet. Ma says we'll put up the pine and spruce in between supper and church. We get to stay up late tonight because of church. Are you going to the service, Callie?"

"I certainly am, Lily. Will you save seats for us?"

Lily nodded. She took her usual seat beside me and began to embroider in earnest. Chance, always ready to play, was fascinated by the movement of the embroidery thread and left his place in the sun to investigate.

"Shoo. Shoo, Chance. I haven't got time to play with you now." Lily gently pushed him away to no avail.

"Lily, you know you can't win a battle with that cat," I said, laughing.

"Yes I can," she replied. She cut off a length of thread and tossed it to him. He skittered around on the weave house floor chasing his thread, her work forgotten. "See. He's stopped bothering me."

I let her have the last word and turned back to my work. Old Mag and Trog finished their last projects and decided to go home, Trog to get the fire started and Old Mag to start supper. I stayed with Lily while she put the finishing touches on the handkerchief. It was dark by the time we closed up the weave house and walked to the cottage.

Old Mag had two flat irons heating on the hearth. "Take off your cloak, Lily. There's a cup of warm milk for you on the end of the table. I'll have the kerchief ironed in no time at all."

"I want to iron it, Old Mag," said Lily. "Do you mind if I do it?"

"Of course not, child. Let's use this end of the table. Have you ironed before?"

Lily nodded.

"Then you know what to do so go ahead. Wrap the hot mat around the handle, though, so your fingers don't get burned."

The iron was heavy and hard to slide across the fabric. Lily concentrated on the task, the tip of her pink tongue protruding from between her lips. It was obvious she had done quite a bit of ironing. Each time she picked up an iron from the hearth, she licked her index finger and put it quickly on the bottom. If the water on her finger sizzled, she used the iron. If it didn't, she replaced it on the hearth and allowed it to heat a little longer.

"Look in the blanket chest, Girl, and see if you can find a scrap of brown paper large enough to wrap around the kerchief," said Old Mag. "A present needs to be wrapped. There might be a piece of yarn in there, too."

I found paper and yarn in the chest and helped Lily wrap her mother's gift. The smile on her face was more than enough thanks. She looked around the room at the decorations.

"It's pretty in here. I love the tree, too. I hope we have one. Ma is afraid of them and if we have one, we'll only be able to light the candles on the branches when Pa is home."

Trog walked Lily home. While he was gone, Old Mag and I put supper on the table; hot corn soup and fresh biscuits, washed down with plenty of hot tea.

"I think you'll enjoy the Christmas Eve service, Callie," said Trog. "It is quite different from the Sunday service. The scriptures are read and favorite carols are sung by request only."

"The church will be decorated, too, with greens and extra candles," added Old Mag.

"Who decorated it, Old Mag?"

"The women take turns. I can't remember whose turn it is this year but it will be pretty. And it will smell nice, too. The boughs of spruce and pine will soften the rank odor of the whale oil lamps. That's always a blessing."

After the table was cleared and the dishes were done, Old Mag opened her blanket chest and took out a light blue skirt. "This is for you, Girl. I noticed you ripped your skirt while you were out getting the Christmas tree."

"But I can keep wearing it. The tears are hidden by my apron."

"Well, that skirt was worn thin anyway. As soon as it is washed, those small rips will become large ones. Put on this one." She handed me the skirt. "We'll tear your old one into strips and use them in the weave house."

"Thank you, Old Mag," I said gratefully. I slipped out of the old skirt and into the new one.

"The fancy embroidered pockets will look nice on that blue color," said Old Mag. "Don't forget to put them on before we go. And your red shawl, too."

Old Mag swept the floor while Trog and I made several trips to the woodpile. The air was cold and crisp and I huddled into my cloak. Frozen icicles hung like stalactites along the edge of the roof. Trog brought out the broom and swept them from the area over the door. They tinkled like crystal bells when they fell to the ground and shattered.

We sat by the fire until it was time to go to church. Old Mag dozed in her rocking chair, Trog puffed contentedly on his pipe and I sipped a cup of tea. Rune's knock on the cottage door startled me.

I quickly threw my cloak around my shoulders as I went to let him in. I didn't want to answer any questions about my missing red shawl. *I'll deal with that tomorrow,* I thought.

I was surprised to see Rune carrying a lighted lantern. He smiled as he stepped into the room. "You won't need to take a lantern, Trog. I have one. The moon is almost full and adds a lot of light, too."

"Walking on frozen snow can be treacherous, Rune. I'll feel better if we have a lantern along with the moon," replied Trog. "Do you mind if I carry the lantern? I don't want Mag to slip and fall."

"Of course not," replied Rune, handing him the lantern. "You lead the way. Callie and I will follow."

We stepped into a night world as bright as a sunny day. The moon was high in the sky and illuminated the snow. I looked around to let my eyes adjust and off to my left saw the silhouette of the furnace, stark and black against the background of white.

The area around the U reminded me of a fantasyland. Shadowy figures carried a myriad of moving lanterns as the villagers made their way toward the little church on the far side of the U. Their voices carried clearly on the crisp night air, "Merry Christmas, Merry Christmas."

I was suddenly filled with a feeling of happiness so great I wasn't sure I could keep my feet on the ground. The scene before me was so beautiful I was amazed to find myself a part of it. Tears of joy filled my eyes. I squeezed Rune's hand tightly. He wrapped his right arm around me and hugged me close for a moment.

"Are you all right?" he whispered.

"Yes. I'm just overwhelmed with the beauty of the snow and the lanterns and the moon."

"I know what you mean," he replied softly before he kissed me on the forehead.

Trog and Old Mag walked just a little ahead of us, the lantern lighting the path before them. He held her firmly by the arm. In just a few minutes, our lantern bobbed along with the others as we joined the small throng of people walking toward the church.

There were no seats left in the small church. Lily spied us standing in the back and made her way to us.

"Take my seat, Old Mag. I'd rather stand here with Callie."

"Thank you, child," Old Mag replied. She turned to Trog and said, "Wait for me after the service."

As she made her way to Lily's seat, Vance and Taw stepped into the church and joined us. Lily stood in front of me. I put my hands on her shoulders and looked around. The sanctuary was beautiful. Fragrant boughs of spruce and pine covered the windowsills and the altar rail. Holly laden with berries filled several vases on the pulpit. Candles of all sizes were tucked in among the greens and their flickering light cast dancing shadows across the walls and ceiling.

The service was impressive. Master Dodd read the scriptures in a deep baritone voice. While he spoke, not a sound was heard in the church; the worshipers seemed to hang onto his every word. The church resounded with the timbre of his voice as he recited the story of the birth of the Christ child. Christmas carols were sung *a cappella* between the readings and we lifted our voices with joy and praise.

I looked at the rapt faces of the people around me. Their heads nodded and they smiled. They kept time to the music with tapping feet and fingers. Their cares and worries seemed to have been lifted from them as they listened and sang.

I was sorry when the service ended. It left a wonderful feeling in my heart, a feeling of warmth and security, of goodness and love, of peace and tranquility, and yes, of hope. Hope that in the end all things will turn out right.

It was after midnight when we stepped outside the church to go home. Clusters of people walked toward their cottages, chatting and laughing. Vance and Taw bid us goodnight but Rune walked back with us. We stopped at Lily's long enough to see her safely inside and then continued on.

Trog stirred the embers in the fireplace and added a few more logs. "Let's have tea with a slosh before we turn in."

We sat in front of the fire with our tea laced with rum and talked about the service. It had affected the others in the same way it had me.

"The Christmas service is the best one of the year for me," said Rune. "I don't want to say it's magical but that's the best word I can use to explain it."

"I understand what you're saying, Rune," said Old Mag from her rocking chair. "Magical is a good word for this time of year. Folks generally behave differently toward one another. It's a hard feeling to put into words. But everyone in the church tonight had that feeling."

"Well put, Mag," said Trog. He blew two smoke rings and smiled. "I for one am going to call it a day. Merry Christmas, Callie, Merry Christmas, Rune, and Merry Christmas, Ma. May all your dreams be pleasant."

"I'm going up, too," said Old Mag. "Put another log or two on the fire, Rune. The room feels chilly." She started up the ladder. "Merry Christmas."

Rune added logs to the fire while I spread a blanket in front of the hearth. We lay on the blanket, wrapped in each other's arms, watching the fire slowly die to embers. We covered each other with kisses and when we spoke, it was in whispers so as not to disturb Trog and Old Mag.

I lay there alone long after he had gone and gazed into the shimmering bed of red coals. I felt as one with ancient peoples who had stared into a fire as I was now doing. In my mind's eye they appeared before me like a reel of silent film, huddled around a bonfire in a dark cave.

The embers had burned out when Chance awakened me. The room was cold and the lone lamp was sputtering, about to run out of oil.

225

"Oh, Chance, why didn't you wake me sooner?" I whispered. My knees cracked when I stood and my back ached.

I quickly folded the blanket and returned it to the chest. Then I crept up the ladder to the loft and brought down the sacks of Christmas gifts. I handled each one lovingly as I placed them under the tree. I smiled as I envisioned each recipient tearing off the wrapping to reveal my gift from the heart.

Old Mag and Trog snored gently as Chance and I finally crawled into our pallet. He purred himself to sleep immediately but I was like a small child on Christmas Eve and lay awake for a long time, too excited to sleep.

# Chapter 34

I heard the crackling of the fire and smelled tea brewing when I descended the ladder on Christmas morning. Trog was setting the table while Old Mag stirred oatmeal in a pot.

"Merry Christmas, Girl," Old Mag said. Her face crinkled into a big smile, green eyes twinkling.

"Merry Christmas to you, Old Mag. And to you, Trog." I smiled at both of them.

Trog nodded in reply. "You've added a lot to our Christmas this year, Callie. In fact you've made it rather exciting at times. Why Mag and I wouldn't have a tree if it weren't for you. And I can tell you it has been a long time since we've had presents under our tree on Christmas morning."

His compliments brought a blush to my face. I opened my mouth to speak but nothing came out. I felt like an awkward schoolgirl bringing a gift to a teacher, hoping her friends wouldn't notice.

Old Mag came to my rescue. "Well, the oatmeal is hot so let's eat."

I gratefully took my place at the table. We held hands while Trog asked a brief blessing. I was hungry and ate two bowls of oatmeal. When we were finished, I looked at the two of them and said, "Let's each have an orange."

"I've been waiting two days for an orange," said Trog. "How did you know oranges are my favorite fruit?" He plucked an orange from the bowl of fruit and began to peel it.

"You'd be surprised what I know, Trog," I replied laughing. "But I didn't know oranges were your favorite fruit. It was just a lucky guess."

Old Mag and I each took an orange. She peeled hers carefully. "I don't think we had oranges last year, Girl. Hmm. That does smell delicious."

The aroma of freshly peeled oranges filled the room. I broke mine apart into segments and ate them slowly, one at a time. I had forgotten how tasty an orange could be.

"Save the rinds," said Old Mag. "I'll make us a little candy with them."

"Candy? Out of orange peels? How in the world will you do that?" I asked.

"Oh, it's easy," said Old Mag. "We'll simmer the peels in sugar water until they become translucent. Then we'll dredge them in sugar until they are covered and set them out to dry for a few hours. What we don't eat right away, we'll store in a crock. They'll keep for almost a month but not to worry. Ours won't hang around that long, will they Trog?"

He chuckled. "No they won't. Next to fresh oranges my favorite fruit is candied orange peels."

Old Mag poured us each a second cup of tea. I stirred a little sugar into mine and then asked, "Will we have a big dinner today, Old Mag?"

"Just a regular supper, Girl. I have enough turkey for a stew. You'll like that, won't you Trog?"

"Sounds good to me, Mag. I could eat turkey stew every day of the week."

"Well I know better than that. Three days in a row and you're complaining," she answered with a smile. "Now, Girl, what vegetables would you like?"

I thought for a minute or two before I replied. "I love your mashed yams, Old Mag. And green beans, too. Is that too much?"

"No, Girl, it isn't. We have plenty of bread. Dusty stopped by yesterday. He brought you a present, too."

"Dusty brought me a present?"

"Indeed he did. Said you were his favorite customer." Old Mag got up from the table and went to the pantry shelves. When she returned, she set a mince pie in front of me.

"A mince pie!" I couldn't keep the delight out of my voice. "How did he know I like mince pie?"

"Same way you knew I liked oranges," laughed Trog.

"He brought us an apple pie, too, thank goodness," said Old Mag.

"Don't you care for mince pie, Old Mag?"

"I'll eat it if I have to but apple's my favorite."

I picked up the pie and returned it to the pantry shelf. Before I returned to the table, I went to the Christmas tree and picked up the gifts I had for Old Mag and Trog.

"Merry Christmas," I said handing each of them a package.

"What a surprise!" exclaimed Trog. "All wrapped up pretty and tied with a bright string." He held the package in his hands and squeezed it gently. "I'm trying to figure out what might be under the wrappings but I don't think I can."

"Well open it and see," said Old Mag.

Trog slowly unwrapped his gift. "Tobacco in a beautiful leather pouch." He gave me a thoughtful look as he opened the pouch and sniffed. The woodsy aroma drifted out. "This is wonderful, Callie. I love the smell of this tobacco. It just so happens my pipe is empty and ready for a refill. I'll do that as soon as Mag opens her gift."

Old Mag handled her package with trembling fingers. She gave a cry of delight when the three bars of soap tumbled into her lap. "These are lovely, Girl. And they smell nice, too." She sniffed each one appreciatively. "Lavender, lemon, and rose. I love fancy soaps but I don't have them often."

She rose from her seat, came to my side of the table, and wrapped her arms around me. "Thank you very much," she said, kissing me on both cheeks.

"We have something for you, Callie." Trog handed me a flat package wrapped in brown paper and tied with red string.

"Thank you," I said as I took the package from him. I deftly untied the string and let it drop to the floor. I pulled the paper aside and there lay my red shawl, the one I traded for Lily's doll, the one I thought I'd never see or wear again. My mouth dropped open in astonishment.

I jumped to my feet and draped the shawl around my shoulders. "Thank you, thank you, thank you!" I exclaimed over and over again as I waltzed around the room.

Old Mag and Trog watched me, happiness all over their faces. When I finally calmed down, I gave each of them a big hug and kiss.

"How did you know I traded the shawl?" I asked.

"Trog was in Lappe's the same time you were," replied Old Mag. "He told me what you had done so I scurried over there before dessert to get it back."

"You amaze me with your generosity, Callie. I knew how much that shawl meant to you and I was proud of you for parting with it so you could buy Lily that doll. What you did was wonderful," added Trog. "You certainly proved that people are more important than possessions. However, I knew Mag wouldn't let that shawl get away from you if she had any say in the matter."

I threw my arms around Old Mag and gave her another hug. "You're wonderful, Old Mag."

"Get along with you, Girl. You worked hard on that shawl and it should be yours to wear. Enough said. Let's get the breakfast dishes cleared up and then we'll start on dinner."

Old Mag and I spent the next several hours straightening the cottage and getting dinner underway. Soon the tantalizing aroma of turkey stew simmering in a pot mingled with that of spruce and pine. Trog made numerous trips to the woodpile before going to the U to visit friends. When he returned, we each snacked on a biscuit and hot tea.

"Did you and Rune make plans for this evening, Callie?" asked Trog. As he spoke, he packed the bowl of his pipe with the new tobacco.

"Taw and Vance have invited us for a late evening dessert. Why don't you two go with us? Vance has been anxious to show you his medicines."

"We'd better not. They might not have enough dessert and that would be embarrassing."

"Not if I took my mince pie. Please go."

Old Mag stared thoughtfully into the fire. "Let's go with them, Trog. I would like to see the medicine house. I'll bet Vance has things I've never heard of on his shelves."

"I'd be delighted to go, Old Mag," replied Trog. He puffed contentedly on his pipe, sending swirls of smoke toward the ceiling. I caught a whiff of the woodsy aroma and smiled.

He winked at me. "This tobacco tastes as good as it smells."

"Everything is under control here for the time being, Girl," said Old Mag. "Why don't we stroll over to the U. Lot's of folks seem to be out and about."

"I'd love to go," I replied. "Will you come with us, Trog?"

"I certainly will. I can't have my two lovely ladies wandering about unescorted on Christmas Day."

The three of us were busy with our cloaks and coats when there was a knock on the door. I opened it to find a beaming Lily on the doorstep.

"Merry Christmas, Callie," she cried as she fairly danced into the room carrying a tiny paper wrapped parcel in her hands. "Merry Christmas, Old Mag and Trog." She gave each of us a big hug.

"Merry Christmas to you," we replied almost in unison.

"I have a present for you Callie. May I give it to you now?" She handed me the little package.

231

"I'd love to open it now, Lily," I said, removing my cloak. "Take off your cloak and sit down."

She did as she was asked. Old Mag and Trog removed their outer garments, too.

"Would you care for a cup of hot tea, Lily?" asked Old Mag. "And a biscuit?"

"No thank you. Ma told me not to fill up on food before dinner. Open it now, Callie. I made it just for you."

I untied the red string that bound the small brown package and removed the paper. Inside the wrapping was a handkerchief embroidered with a riot of beautiful flowers. Her stitches were tiny and delicate.

I wrapped my arms around her wriggling body. "This is beautiful, Lily. I'm going to put it in my pocket and shall carry it with me always."

"Let me see," said Old Mag.

I handed her the handkerchief and while she and Trog looked at it admiringly, I retrieved Lily's gift from under the tree.

"This is for you Lily. From the three of us."

She ripped the string and paper from the doll. The look on her face was priceless. Her eyes widened and her mouth opened in a round O. For a second or two, she was speechless and then her squeals of delight filled the room.

"She's beautiful. How did you know I wanted a doll? Where did you find her? Does she have a name yet?" The questions poured from her little mouth so quickly, the three of us had no opportunity to reply.

Lily finally sat down to examine the doll. She stroked the yarn braids, admired the lace-trimmed dress, and fingered the tiny leather shoes. She lifted the dress to peek at the petticoat. She cradled the doll in her arms and kissed it many times.

"There's more, Lily," I said as I handed her the little sack of extra clothing.

The room was again shattered with an excited squeal as Lily pulled the velvet dress, cloak, and other accessories from the sack.

"A Christmas outfit, a Christmas outfit," she cried with glee. "I can change her clothes. Have you ever had a doll like this, Callie?"

We admired the doll and its clothing. Old Mag fingered the feathery trim on the tiny cloak and reminisced a little. "I had a cloak like this once. Many years ago. I loved wearing it. Feathers make a girl feel special." She stared off into space and said nothing more.

"Well, Lily, we were getting ready to go out when you popped in. I have one more gift for you and then I'm going to send you home." I gave her another hug.

"Another gift?"

I plucked an orange from the fruit bowl. "This orange is for you."

"An orange? What does it do?"

Trog laughed. "It doesn't do anything. You eat it, Lily. First you peel the rind and then you eat the fruit. You'll like it."

"I've never tasted an orange. I guess it's called an orange because of its color." She turned the orange in her hands. "I'm going to share it with my brothers and sisters and Ma and Pa. Is that all right?"

Lily's willingness to share put a warm feeling around my heart. "That's the true spirit of Christmas, Lily. Sharing what we have with others. Now put on your cloak and we'll walk you home."

# Chapter 35

Christmas Day passed quickly. Trog, Old Mag and I strolled leisurely to the U, greeting those we met with "Merry Christmas." The temperature was pleasant and the snow was rapidly melting. When we passed Lily's house, Rose came out to thank us for the doll.

"You don't know how happy you have made that child, Callie. She hasn't put the doll down since she got home. And thank you for the orange, too. We'll have that tonight as part of our dessert."

"Lily brightens my life every day, Rose. She makes me happy, too," I replied giving her a hug. "Merry Christmas."

The day was darkening by the time we returned to the cottage. We busied ourselves getting the evening meal ready. Afterward, we lingered at the table, eating pie and drinking hot tea.

"That Dusty knows how to put together a delicious pie," commented Trog. "That wasn't a plain apple pie. I think I found a walnut or two in my slice."

"I believe you're right, Trog," replied Old Mag moving from the table to her rocking chair. "We must be sure to tell him we think nuts are a good addition to apple pie."

"More tea, Callie?" asked Trog. He picked up the bottle of spirits. "I'm going to add a splash of Christmas to mine. Would you care for a little slosh, too?"

I nodded.

"How about you, Ma? Would you care for tea with a slosh?"

"No thank you, Trog. I'm going to sit here and rest a spell." She closed her eyes.

Trog poured two cups of tea, added a little dash of spirits to each, and handed one to me. He lit his pipe and puffed contentedly. We sat in a comfortable silence soon punctuated by Old Mag's soft snores.

I thought of Christmas Days long past. Looking back they seemed full of frenzy, the hurried unwrapping of gifts, the racing from one house to another with no time to sit back and enjoy the pleasure of the moment. Christmas dinners were always traumatic. Lavish and extravagant; they took hours to prepare and everything had to be ready at exactly the same time.

*I always felt disappointed and let down about something,* I thought. *I didn't get that certain gift I wanted or the new salad I made wasn't as tasty as I thought it should be or I was too tired to enjoy the guests or I really wanted to stay home but I had to visit friends and family.*

There was no letdown today. Old Mag, Trog, and I had done exactly as we wanted. We'd strolled about chatting with our neighbors and then returned here for a simple meal and good conversation.

My retrospection was interrupted by a knock on the door. I hurried to open it. Rune stood on the threshold, arms open wide. I stepped into them and returned his hug and kiss.

"Merry Christmas, Callie. I've been looking forward to this moment all day," he said.

"Me, too," I replied. "Come in." He stepped into the room and I closed the door behind him.

Old Mag and Trog greeted him, she with a hug, he with a handshake and a thump on the back. Rune walked to the fireplace and held his hands toward the blaze to warm them.

"It's getting a little chilly out there, Callie, so bundle up."

"Rune, I've invited Old Mag and Trog to accompany us. Will that be all right with Taw and Vance?"

"That will be wonderful." He looked at Trog. "Those two fellows have been itching to get you and Old Mag over to the medicine house. You're in for a treat, Old Mag and I guess you know Vance will probably talk your ears off."

While they were talking, I put the gifts for Taw and Vance in a sack along with two oranges. I retrieved the mince pie from the pantry and set it on the table.

"What's that for?" asked Rune.

"That's for in case the fellows don't have enough dessert," replied Old Mag putting on her cloak.

Rune laughed. "Don't fret, Old Mag, they have plenty, but they won't pass up the pie, either."

I put on my cloak, picked up the sack and the pie, and stepped outside. The others followed. Rune and Trog each carried a lantern to light the way. We walked briskly to the U, turned toward the blacksmith shop, and then headed for the medicine house tucked into the nearby woods.

Lighted candles in each window cast a golden sheen on the snow. Taw stood in the doorway, smiling broadly.

"Old Mag. Trog. What a pleasant surprise!" He greeted them warmly and then turned to me. "Merry Christmas, Callie."

Vance stepped into the medicine house just behind us, carrying an armful of wood. "Merry Christmas, all," he said as he knelt in front of the fire. "Let me just add a few logs to this blaze and I'll join you."

The room was warm and bright. The table was set for four but Taw quickly added two more plates and cups and before long, the six of us were seated around the table, enjoying thick slices of cherry and mince pie.

After dessert, Rune and I helped Taw clean up the dishes while Vance gave Old Mag and Trog a tour of the medicine room. Old Mag had a broad smile on her face when they returned to the eating area.

"Your brother certainly has quite a collection of herbal remedies, Taw."

"That he does, Old Mag, but better yet, he knows how and when to use them. At least, that's what he tells me."

We all laughed at Taw's remark. Old Mag warmed her hands in front of the fire for a few moments and then turned to Trog. "I think we should be heading home." To Vance and Taw she said, "I've had a wonderful time. I can't think of a nicer way to spend Christmas evening than with good friends."

Vance offered to walk back with them but Trog refused. He and Old Mag said their goodbyes at the door and stepped out into the night. I watched them go from a front window, their lantern bobbing in time to Trog's footsteps.

We settled in front of the crackling fire, cups of hot tea in our hands. The conversation flowed easily; the weather, illnesses in the village, the horses being trained, the search for herbal remedies in the forest, the trip to Snow Hill.

During a lull in the conversation, Vance handed me a package. "This is for you, Callie, from Taw and me. Merry Christmas."

"Why, thank you." The package had a little heaviness to it but when I squeezed it, it was soft and gave easily to my touch.

"Open it," said Rune, "before you kill it."

I untied the string and removed the paper wrapping to reveal a black fur muff. "Oh," I said as my breath caught in my throat, "this is beautiful. Thank you very much." I put a hand in each end of the furry piece and extended my arms outward for all to see.

"It looks beautiful on you, Callie," said Taw. "You're going to need it, too, when the weather turns cold."

"I have something for you, too," I said opening the little sack of gifts I had brought. I pulled out the oranges and handed them to Taw and Vance. "These will make a great snack," I said.

They sniffed the oranges with blissful looks on their faces. "I'm going to have mine for breakfast. Thank you very much, Callie," said Vance.

Then I handed them each a brown paper wrapped gift. They looked at me in surprise. "A second gift, Callie?!" Taw exclaimed as he ripped the paper from the curry brush. "This is very beautiful," he said as he ran his hands lovingly over the satiny wood. "I'll think of you every time I use it. Thank you."

Our eyes turned to Vance. He in turn opened his package and the aroma of tea wafted gently into the air around us. He smiled broadly as he sniffed each packet of tea. "I love tea, Callie, and you have just given me teas I would not have purchased on my own. Thank you very much."

I gave each of them a hug followed by a soft kiss on the cheek. "This has been a wonderful Christmas," I said, "and you two have helped to make it special."

Rune and I said our goodbyes to them shortly thereafter. The walk to my cottage seemed short with not nearly enough time for stolen kisses along the way. We encountered no one nor did we see lights in the cottages we passed.

Chance met us at the cottage door. I scooped him into my arms and kissed his little head. He was intrigued by the muff and sniffed it cautiously. I plucked an acorn from the tree and tossed it to him. He grabbed it in his paws and began to bat it around the floor.

Rune stirred the fire and added another log. I spread a blanket in front of the hearth and we sat Indian style for a few minutes watching the crackling blaze. He stroked my hair gently and then pulled me close. "Is it still Christmas, Callie?" he whispered.

"I think so."

He placed a small red satin sack in my hand. "This is for you, my darling."

With trembling hands I pulled open the drawstring. Out slid a gold heart-shaped brooch. Decorated with a cluster of small pearls surrounded by ornate etching, it was beautiful. Tears of happiness forced me to close my eyes. I was speechless.

"The heart opens, Callie. Here, let me show you." He took the brooch from my hand and pressed a little spring on one side of the heart. The lid swung open. Nestled inside was a lock of Rune's silver white hair.

I threw my arms around him and hugged him tightly. I never wanted to let him go. I covered his face with kisses until he laughingly pushed me away.

"I take it you like the gift," he laughed.

"I do, Rune, I do. I love it."

"Let's see what it looks like on," he said as he pinned the brooch to my bodice. "There now, I think it looks nice." He gently brushed the tears from my cheeks.

"I have something for you too, my love," I said pressing the last orange into his hands.

"Thank you. I love oranges." He looked at me and laughed.

"And something else," I handed him the gift-wrapped knife.

He kissed me and then tore off the paper. "Callie," he cried out in astonishment. He ran his fingers gently over the etching of the tall ship. He opened the blade and ran his thumb lightly along the edge. He snapped the blade closed and pulled me close to him. "I'll carry this with me always," he murmured in my ear.

We spent the last hour of Christmas day, cocooned in each other's arms, watching the slowly dying fire.

## Chapter 36

Shortly after the first of the year, winter set in with a vengeance. We had two weeks of cold weather with snow and unmerciful winds. It was miserable. Drafty air poured into the cottage around the windows and the door. Fine snow blew in around the window casements. The weave house was no better. My hands were often too cold to weave and I constantly rubbed them together to restore circulation. Trog insisted I sit closer to the fire but I, fearful a flying spark might ignite the yarn, refused to move.

It was too cold for a nightly walk and Rune and I were forced to spend our evenings in the cottage. Old Mag and Trog retired early to give us privacy and for that I was grateful but I missed our nightly strolls.

At night I burrowed deep under my blanket but even so my teeth chattered and I shook with cold. Chance disliked the cold as much as I and crept under my blanket; his little body provided extra warmth and I cuddled him as close to me as possible.

One afternoon Trog returned from McQuerrie's with interesting news. "The pond is frozen solid. I walked over there to check it out and quite a few men are busy clearing snow from the ice. There'll be skating tonight."

"That'll be a treat," replied Old Mag. "Do you skate, Girl?"

"I've never tried."

"I have no doubt that you'll catch on to it very quickly, Callie," said Trog. "Do we have skates that will fit her, Mag?"

"If I don't someone else will. Skates will be no problem. Standing up on them may be." She chuckled.

Rune and Lily stopped by just before we closed the weave house for the day. "Are you going skating tonight, Callie?" Lily bubbled enthusiastically. "We are - Ma and Pa and the whole family, even the baby."

Rune answered for me. "Of course she's going skating, Lily. I'll stop by for her right after supper."

Lily threw her arms around me. "Oh, Callie, we're going to have so much fun. Everybody will be skating." She put her arms behind her back and stepped around the room on imaginary skates.

"No Lily, everybody won't be skating because I don't know how."

"She'll skate, Lily, because I'm going to teach her. She'll be gliding about with the best of us before the evening is over."

"Suppose I don't want to skate? Do I have any say in the matter?"

A chorus of 'no's' greeted my questions. Old Mag left the weave house a little early to get supper started. Trog stayed to bank the fire while Rune and Lily accompanied me to the woodpile. The three of us carried several armfuls of wood back to the cottage in the gathering dusk.

"We'll see you later," Rune told me before he and Lily set out toward the U.

Supper was quick and the cleanup was even faster. Old Mag had miraculously found a pair of black leather skates that fit comfortably if I wore two pairs of stockings. Trog scrutinized the runners on my skates. He brought out a hasp and lightly worked on the edges of the blades to sharpen them a little. He did the same with Old Mag's skates and his as well.

The glow from the pond was visible in the night sky when we stepped outside the cottage. I could see why as we approached. Lanterns hung from poles illuminated a wide circle. A huge bonfire welcomed the skaters, many of whom were gliding across the ice. Laughter and catcalls floated across the air. Someone played a waltz on a mouth harp; the faint strains of music were barely audible. The note of festivity was unmistakable. Skating was a pleasure to which many people looked forward.

We sat on a snow bank and put on our skates. I was nervous but I needn't have been. Rune was a wonderful teacher. We skated side by side, he with his arm around my waist. He showed me how to push one foot forward and then glide; push the other foot forward and glide. I took a few spills at first but before long I got the hang of it and I was able to keep up with him as we skated round and round the circle.

When I was completely comfortable on my skates he showed me how to turn. This was somewhat more complicated as I had to cross one foot over the other while gliding. We practiced right turns; cross left foot over the right and left turns; cross right foot over the left until I could turn on command.

Stopping was the easiest lesson of all to learn. I simply pushed my heels outward and my toes inward. I thought I had it down pat until I came up behind someone and plowed into him because I couldn't remember whether my heels turned out or in. Fortunately, no one was hurt in the ensuing tangle. We all got to our feet laughing, me too in spite of my embarrassment at having been the culprit.

Lily joined us briefly as did Vance and Taw. All were much better on ice than I and I shooed them away. "Let me get my ice legs," I jokingly said. The three of them swirled away, runners flashing in the lantern light.

I noticed Trog and Old Mag once, skating on the other side of the circle. I managed a tiny wave in their direction.

That first night I didn't pay attention to the other skaters. I was too busy concentrating on keeping my feet firmly planted on the ice. Not once did Rune leave my side; I was insecure without his arm around me giving me a sense of extra standing power. My eyes stayed on my feet, willing them to do what they were supposed to do, when they were supposed to do it.

The lanterns had burned low by the time we called it a night. We warmed our hands at the bonfire before taking the path to the cottage. My feet felt leaden, too heavy to pick up and put down in my leather shoes.

Back at the cottage, we sat around the table with hot tea and biscuits, too tired to talk. Trog and Old Mag rinsed their cups and went up the ladder to bed. Rune and I lingered a few moments longer and then he kissed me goodnight and left. My legs were so fatigued I wondered if I would be able to climb the ladder to the loft.

Snug in my pallet, I let my mind replay the evening. It had been exhilarating, flying around on the ice, hair blowing, skin tingling. I was amazed at how quickly I had picked up the techniques of skating and knew that in the nights to come I would only improve.

I was stiff and sore in the morning but as the day progressed my muscles loosened and by nightfall, I was ready to return to the pond. I was a trifle rusty but Rune patiently took me through the basic techniques I had learned the previous night and in a short while I was skating comfortably.

Rune insisted that I skate alone. I didn't want to. I felt safe and secure with his arm around my waist. But he was adamant and off on my own I went, keeping him well within safe reaching distance.

I wasn't on my own for long. Lily and Old Mag joined me briefly; then Taw and Vance linked arms with me for several circles around the pond. Trog claimed a turn, too. He skated with great elegance and I was proud to be seen on his arm.

I even took a turn around the pond with Snoop. His red hair was barely contained beneath a black knit cap. I wanted to hold his arm but he insisted he put it around my waist and at times, he pulled me a little too close. He skated very well and when we completed the lap, he did a little spin and then bowed from the waist with a flourish. I giggled openly at his antics as he skated off in search of another partner.

But I spent most of my time with Rune. We skated round and round, cheeks rosy in the cold, our breath hanging in a frosty cloud in front of us. We stopped often to warm ourselves at the bonfire. The firelight flickered on Rune's handsome face and put a faint red sheen on his white hair.

One night, Master and Mistress Dodd joined the festivities at the pond. She wore a beautiful purple velvet cloak trimmed with feathers and carried a black fur mitt. His black coat had gold buttons and he wore a top hat. They were quite a handsome couple and all eyes were on them as they gracefully skated in the lamplight.

The pond was frozen solid for two weeks and during that time I became a fairly accomplished skater. I found myself much in demand by my friends as a skating partner and that pleased me very much.

"We won't have another freeze like this one," predicted Old Mag.

Her prediction was right. The end of January brought a thaw. The sun shone brightly every day and the temperature hovered well above freezing. Jagged cracks appeared in the ice and by week's end, huge chunks were all that remained of the skating rink. I was saddened every time Rune and I walked over to look at it. We'd had such a wonderful time.

Life was back to normal; weave house all day, nightly stroll with Rune and then the two of us alone in front of the cottage fireplace.

Another heavy snowfall occurred early in February; a wet snow, just right for making snowmen and having snowball fights. The morning after the snow fell, the yards were full of children and adults having fun. Snowballs zoomed everywhere and Old Mag deemed it too dangerous to go out of doors. She went anyway and gave potential culprits a look that dared them to toss a snowball in her direction.

I stopped by Lily's on my way to the basket maker and showed her how to make a snow angel.

"Lie on your back in the snow like this," I told her, demonstrating as I talked, "arms at your side and feet together. Now open and close your legs and move your arms above your head."

She did as I asked. "Now stand up and look at the impression you made in the snow."

"I made an angel, Callie. I did. Look, there is my robe and there are my wings." She hurried to demonstrate her newfound skill for her brothers.

I introduced Old Mag and Trog to snow cream. They were disbelieving when I told them I could make a dessert from the snow. I found an area that had not been walked through and scooped the snow from the top. Then I filled a bowl with clean snow. Once inside the cottage, I beat an egg until it was frothy. To the egg I added a little cream and sugar. We had no vanilla so I substituted a few drops of spearmint oil for flavoring. I poured the mixture into the bowl with the snow and stirred it well before dipping it onto our plates. Old Mag was impressed.

"I learn something new every day, Girl. That little dessert will be easy to remember. Now I'm going to show you how to make snow candy."

"You're in for a treat, Callie," said Trog.

She took a pitcher of molasses from the pantry shelf, donned her cloak, and went out the cottage door. Trog and I followed, he with a big smile on his face. Old Mag cleared a spot in the snow and then poured molasses over the cleared area. The instant the molasses hit the cold snow, it hardened and cracked into chunks. I popped one into my mouth; it was delicious.

"This is good, Old Mag," I said with my mouth full. "Can we make a lot more and bring it in for later?"

"We can take some in, Girl, but the heat in the cottage will soften it quite a bit and it won't be as tasty. It's best if you eat it right away just like the snow cream. I noticed that melted almost as fast as we ate it."

That night I told Rune about the snow cream and the molasses candy. "It was great to have something sweet to eat, Rune, something besides pie."

"How come I'm never around when you do things like that, Callie? Couldn't you make the snow cream or the candy one evening after supper?"

"Whatever your heart desires," I said in a teasing voice. "We shall have one or both of those treats tomorrow evening upon your arrival for our nightly walk. Do you have a preference?"

He was silent for a second or two and then replied, "Molasses candy. Let's make molasses candy."

And that is what we did the next evening. Old Mag made a good-sized batch. I put the leftovers in a bowl. Rune and I took it with us on our stroll and offered a chunk to each passerby we met.

## Chapter 37

Heavy rain replaced the snow. It came down in torrents for three days. Brown, muddy earth appeared; it seemed foreign after weeks of snow. Going outside was miserable. My shoes sank deep into the muck; walking was an effort. We tracked mud into the cottage and the weave house and Old Mag fussed endlessly about the mess.

The fire did little to dispel the dampness that permeated the cottage. Old Mag's rheumatism flared up and she complained constantly. She boiled a few dried roots with lard, stirred in a little honey, and rubbed her aching joints with the concoction.

Rune and I ventured out into the downpour every evening despite Old Mag's dire warnings about getting too wet. Upon my return to the cottage, I hung my cloak to dry in front of the fire, put shoetrees in my shoes, and set them on the hearth. The smell of drying wool was not pleasant.

One such night we walked toward the furnace and sought shelter under a huge cypress tree on the outskirts of the swamp. We huddled together, nuzzling each other's neck and whispering endearments. I felt his strong body against mine and ran my fingers through his silky hair.

"I love you so much, Callie."

"And I love you, Rune."

His heart beat a strong cadence against my chest. I could feel it through my heavy cloak. We stepped from under the canopy of the tree. The rain poured down upon us but I was so happy I didn't mind at all.

We all breathed a sigh of relief when the rain finally ceased. The temperature warmed somewhat; the sun shone once again and the earth slowly dried. Old Mag sent me out every day on one errand or another. Lily usually accompanied me and I enjoyed her company.

Her enthusiasm was catching and I always found myself smiling when I returned from one of our jaunts.

Early one afternoon, shortly after the noon meal, Trog sent me to McQuerrie's to fetch a pouch of tobacco. Lily had not yet arrived at the weave house and I decided to go without her.

"If you see Lily let her select a penny candy from the jar," suggested Trog. "And get one for yourself, too. Have McQuerrie put it on my account."

"Why, thank you Trog. That's very generous of you." I gave him a little pat on the shoulders as I got ready to go.

I stopped on the front steps to breathe in the fresh air. *It's only February,* I thought, *and it feels like spring.*

There weren't many customers in the store and McQuerrie was delighted to have some company. He was full of the latest gossip in the community. Mrs. Miller was at last able to do a little housework. Two boys had gotten into a fistfight and both sported black eyes. Master and Mistress Dodd were going to have a big party. I listened with one ear while I selected the tobacco and the penny candy. He was writing the amount on Trog's ledger sheet when a youngster burst into the store shouting, "The stagecoach is coming! The stagecoach is coming!"

"Well I'll be. I forgot all about that," exclaimed McQuerrie. "Several businessmen are coming to see Master Dodd. I expect they'll be staying at the boarding house."

The stagecoach passed through the area regularly and I enjoyed watching it arrive and depart. It was jolting along the road as I left McQuerrie's and I hurried to get to the stopping area. Four big horses pulled the coach, bodies lathered in sweat, blinders shading their eyes. Reins and lines jingled as they raced full tilt, the driver cracking a long whip above their heads. By the time the coach stopped, quite a crowd had gathered.

The coach was sleek, golden brown in color with red striping above the door and windows. Mac, the driver, hopped down from the seat above the coach and opened the door. Three well-dressed men stepped out, brushing dust from their clothing. Jim, who always rode with Mac, tossed down three valises. With valises in hand, the three men walked through the crowd toward the boarding house.

Jim turned his attention to the horses. A large pail of water had been placed in front of each animal and while they were drinking, he checked the harnessing. A small measure of oats was also given to each horse and as they ate they stamped their feet and swished their tails as though eager to be off to the next stop.

I was watching several brave young boys venture very close to the horses when I heard Lily call my name. "Callie! Callie!"

I looked around at the crowd but didn't see her. "Up here, Callie. Look to your left."

I did as Lily asked and saw her standing in the back of a wagon parked parallel to the stagecoach. A horse was hitched to that wagon but I saw no driver. She waved enthusiastically.

"Lily, get down," I called as I started toward her.

"No. I can see over the heads of everyone up here." She turned her attention to the horses. "I can see their eyes behind the blinders, Callie. And their tongues around the bits."

"Lily, get down, please," I yelled as I pushed my way through the gathering. "That wagon is dangerous. There's no driver."

"I'm all right, Callie. The horses hitched to this wagon are calm. Look," she pointed toward the coach, "Mac and Jim are getting ready to go."

I didn't look at the coach but kept my eyes on Lily. I was close enough to the wagon to touch it when I heard the crack of Mac's whip. It seemed to come from no-where. It startled the horses hitched to the wagon in front of me. They reared in their traces and the wagon lurched forward a few feet. Lily lost her footing and for an endless moment was suspended in mid-air as she was tossed upward. My eyes followed the somersault her little body did in the air. I tried to grab her but she was just beyond my reach. She hit the ground hard and lay motionless.

I knelt beside her crumpled form. I called her name and rubbed her arms but I knew it was hopeless. Her head lolled oddly to one side. Lily could no longer hear me. Her neck was broken.

One by one the crowd fell silent. In the distance, I heard the faint rumble of the stagecoach as it rolled toward its next stop. And then that sound, too, faded away and silence enveloped us.

I sat next to Lily, stroking her beautiful hair until her father came to get her. He cradled her in his arms and carried her home. I walked beside him, holding tightly to one of her lifeless hands.

Lily's mother wailed in despair and grief. I wanted to weep but couldn't. Not a tear pricked my eyelids. My cheeks were dry. I sat stiff backed, mute as a swan, watching people come and go, hoping this was a bad dream from which I would soon awaken.

I sensed, rather than saw, Old Mag enter the cottage. And then she was beside me. She put her arms around me and drew me close. I inhaled the familiar scent of her as she rocked me back and forth, crooning, "I'm so sorry, Girl. I'm so sorry."

The tears came in a flood. They streamed down my face and dripped onto Old Mag's bodice. Deep sobs racked my body. I cried until I could cry no more. Old Mag helped me to my feet.

"Let's go home now, Girl. We'll come back later. Do you want to say anything to Rose before we go?"

I shook my head.

I looked at Rose one more time and knew I couldn't leave without speaking. I stumbled toward her, braced by Old Mag's arm. Rose grasped my hands in hers and looked at me with swollen eyes.

"Oh, my dear Callie. Lily loved you so much." Her embrace was comforting and gave me strength. "She talked about you all the time and wanted to be just like you in every way."

To my surprise, I found I could speak. "Lily was very special, Rose. She brightened every room she entered. I loved her, too and I'm going to miss her, oh, how I'm going to miss her." I squeezed my eyelids tight to keep the tears back.

As soon as I reached the cottage I climbed into the sleeping loft and threw myself on my pallet. I cried until I could cry no more. Visions of Lily ran rampant through my mind. Lily doing her needlework in the weave house, Lily walking beside me holding my hand, Lily on ice skates, Lily seeing her doll for the first time at Christmas. I opened my eyes but the visions persisted.

*Why? Why? Lily had so much to offer. She was a little treasure here on earth and she meant so much to so many people.* But no answer came to me.

I don't know how long I lay on my pallet; I wasn't aware that I slept but I must have because Old Mag awakened me.

"This will make you feel better, Girl," she said as she pressed a cold, wet cloth over my eyes. "Now I want you to come downstairs and see if you can eat a little bite of food. We'll be going back to Lily's to sit for awhile and Rose will be hurt if you don't go with us."

Trog looked at me with sad eyes when I came down the ladder. Old Mag ladled hot soup into a bowl and set it in front of me.

"Eat as much of that as you can."

I swallowed a little of the hot broth and then pushed the bowl away. Old Mag set a cup of hot tea on the table. "I made you a lavender tea. It will calm your nerves and take away your headache. Drink it up."

The tea was delicious and went down quickly. As I drank, I inhaled the soothing aroma of lavender.

"Do you feel up to going to Lily's, Callie?" asked Trog.

"Not really but I'll go if you want me to."

"I don't want you to do anything you don't want to do. But this will be your last opportunity to see Lily. She'll be buried tomorrow morning and I'm certain you'll want to say goodbye before that happens."

I shot him a surprised look. "Tomorrow morning? Isn't that a little soon?"

"No, that's how it's always done. Friends will call tonight to pay their last respects. Tomorrow morning, Lily will be buried in the little cemetery behind the church. Following that, the ladies of the village will provide a meal for the family and other mourners."

A full moon had risen by the time we left our cottage. I looked to my left and saw the stark silhouette of the furnace, standing tall and lonely in the moonlight. Visibility was excellent and we didn't need a lantern to light our way.

I spied Lily's cottage just before we approached the end of the U. It was ablaze with light. People were everywhere, walking singly, in pairs and in small clusters. All were headed to or from Lily's, all spoke in low voices or in whispers.

My heart pounded against my chest when I entered the door to Lily's. I pressed my trembling lips together and willed myself to be strong. I was not prepared for what I saw. The room was lit entirely by candles, their flickering light cast eerie shadows upon the walls. A circle of straight-backed chairs completely filled the center of the room; most of the seats were occupied. The kitchen table had been moved to one side of the room and on it rested a small, triangular pine coffin.

Rose was seated but stood when we entered. She greeted us with hugs and then led us to the coffin. I squeezed my eyes shut. I couldn't bear to look at Lily.

"Oh, Rose, she looks beautiful," said Old Mag softly.

I opened my eyes and through a veil of tears saw Lily. Her hair was freshly braided and her clothing was spotless. The Christmas doll was cradled in her right arm and in her left hand she held one of her embroidered handkerchiefs. She looked like she was taking a nap.

I took off my cloak and removed the red shawl I had draped around my shoulders. I folded it neatly into a triangle and tucked it across the bottom of Lily's skirt. I leaned over the coffin and kissed the top of her head.

"Goodbye, dear Lily," I whispered.

Then I took a seat in the circle with the other mourners.

## Chapter 38

The entire village turned out for Lily's funeral. Rose insisted I stand next to her at the gravesite. Master Dodd spoke a few words and someone read scripture verses. I heard very little of what was said; I was busy trying not to think about Lily being lowered into the ground to rest forever. We stood there while the earth was shoveled over the pine box. The *thunk* of dirt clods hitting the box filled my ears for days afterward.

Rune walked with me to Rose's after the service. I was grateful for his strong arm around my waist. The women of the village had outdone themselves. Additional tables had been brought into the cottage and they were laden with food and drink. Old Mag and Trog sought me out as did Taw and Vance. I could tell by the expressions on their faces they were concerned about me.

The entire village tried to squeeze into Lily's cottage. All around me people were eating and drinking and laughing. Even Rose wore a smiling face. I forced my lips to curve upward when people greeted me. I smiled on the outside but inwardly I was crying.

I managed to eat a little. I don't know how. The huge lump in my throat let very little slide past. The ache in my chest was so painful I felt hollow. I was glad when Old Mag suggested we go home.

I climbed the ladder to the loft immediately and lay face up on my pallet. The same question kept running through my brain. *Could I have prevented Lily's death?* The scene at the stagecoach stop played over and over in my mind. It was painfully vivid and each time I arrived at the same answer. *No. I tried. I did everything I could.* Eventually I fell asleep and didn't wake until the next morning. I slept so deeply I didn't hear Old Mag and Trog come to bed.

The next few days were a nightmare. I missed Lily terribly. Hard work in the weave house made her loss bearable during the daylight hours. I poured myself into the making of shawls and table runners. I made so many of the latter, Old Mag asked me to slow down a little.

Rune occupied the evening hours. We lengthened our walks and sometimes circled the community more than once on an outing. He encouraged me to talk about Lily and I found that the more I did, the easier it became to do so. During those walks I recalled things about Lily that I had long forgotten, as did Rune.

The nights alone in my pallet were the worst. Visions of Lily lurked behind my closed eyelids and sleep evaded me. I was so tired it was all I could do to drag myself downstairs every morning. My appetite disappeared, too and nothing Old Mag set on the table enticed me. She concocted numerous tonics, some better tasting than others and I drank them down to please her. I knew nothing but time would heal my heart.

One morning after Trog had gone to light the fire in the weave house and Old Mag and I were straightening the cottage before joining him, she said in a quiet voice, "Girl, I know how much Lily meant to you and I think it's fitting for you to grieve. But if you don't eat or sleep, before long you'll be beside her in the cemetery. You can't weep forever. You have to get on with your life. Lily would want that. What is, *is*, and we can't change it." She paused. "Why, if she were to pop in here right now she wouldn't recognize you. So pale and thin. No smile on your face. No twinkle in your eye."

She stroked my hair. "When my beautiful daughter died I wanted to die, too. And someone sat beside me just like I'm sitting beside you and spoke similar words. The pain and heartache will begin to ease. Just give it a chance. Lily will live in your heart forever. And nothing can take away the memories of the wonderful things the two of you shared. Hold on to your memories, Girl, and they will carry you through this difficult time. Trog and I are here for you, too. Don't forget that."

Old Mag's words stayed with me. I thought of them often and knew she was right. Lily was gone and there was nothing I could do to bring her back.

Life went on. The pain in my chest disappeared, as did the lump in my throat. My appetite slowly returned and while I didn't eat with gusto, I ate well enough that Old Mag stopped putting tonics in front of me.

But some things didn't go away. I still expected to see Lily every time the weave house door opened. I found myself looking for her whenever I went out and about on an errand. And I couldn't bear to look at the candy jar in McQuerrie's.

Late one afternoon I met Rose on the path to the basket maker's. I stopped to chat and she asked me to go to the cemetery with her. I hesitated; I hadn't seen the grave since the day Lily was laid to rest but I sensed that Rose wanted a little company and agreed to go. As we walked along arm in arm, she talked about her family and how well they seemed to be adjusting to the loss of Lily.

"And how are you doing, Rose?" I asked.

She paused briefly before replying. "About as well as can be expected I guess. The others occupy a lot of my time but of all my children she was the happiest as well as the busiest. I miss the whirlwind that always seemed to surround her."

*Whirlwind*, I thought. *That word describes Lily to a 'T'.*

We were quiet as we wound our way through the cemetery to Lily's grave. It was raw and barren but I knew in time it would be grass covered like the others. Her name, date of birth and date of death had been carved on the little wooden cross that marked it. Rose knelt and ran her hand across the brown earth. Not knowing what else to do, I knelt beside her.

"I come here, Callie, and tell her what her brothers and sisters are doing. And that I love her and will never forget her. I don't want to come every day but for some reason I can't stay away." She wiped away a few tears. "She isn't here you know. This place is far too quiet for our Lily. She's where the hubbub is." She looked at me with a smile. "Don't you agree?"

I put an arm around her shoulders. "Indeed I do, Rose, indeed I do. And if there is no hubbub, she's doing her best to stir some up." And to my surprise, I laughed joyously at the thought of Lily kicking up a ruckus. Rose joined me.

The visit to the cemetery proved to be a turning point for me. On the way home, I noticed the blue sky for the first time in days and greeted all those I met with a smile as bright as sunshine. There was a little spring in my step, too. I was back in the land of the living.

The moderate weather gave way to one more heavy snowstorm before the end of February. The storm raged for three days and brought with it a blast of frigid air that kept us huddled near the fireplace as much as possible. The winds were icy and relentless. Snow lay in huge drifts. No one ventured out to build snowmen or toss snowballs. The daily trips to the community woodpile were painful. I tucked a fichu around my neck before donning my cloak and wrapped a shawl around my head, pulling it around my face to keep my skin from being exposed to the bitter cold.

Rune did not appear for our evening visits. Nor did I see him during the daylight hours. I found myself worrying about him. *Losing Rune so soon after Lily would be too much to bear,* I told myself. I shared my concern with Old Mag.

"Don't you fret about Rune, Girl. He's crawled into a hole somewhere and is safe. I expect he's as anxious to see you as you are to see him. He'll be along as soon as he can."

257

I knew she was right but visions of him hurt and in need of help haunted me. Every evening I found myself listening for footsteps on the path or a tap on the cottage door. My fears increased with each passing day. I had to force myself to keep my hands occupied with sewing or some other task. Otherwise, I would have wrung them in despair.

A weak winter sun shone on the fourth day. By noon, snow was melting from the rooftops and the shouts of happy children rang through the air. I was standing at the window watching a group of boys engage in a wicked snowball fight when I spied a familiar figure making its way along the snow covered path from the U.

"Rune," I cried to Old Mag and Trog. "I see Rune!"

I threw on my cloak and hurried out the door to meet him. I stumbled as quickly as I could through the snow, calling his name as I went. And then I was in his arms, all my fears forgotten. He kissed me hungrily before he wrapped his arms around my waist and swung me around and around. His touch was intoxicating. My head whirled with desire and I leaned into him for support.

"Oh, Rune, I've been so worried. I thought something had happened to you. I imagined all sorts of horrible things. And now you're here and they all seem so silly."

"Let's get in out of the cold, Callie, and I'll tell you all about it." Arm in arm, we made our way toward the cottage. Trog held the door open for us. Rune shook his hand as we entered.

"Sit down, Rune. Here's hot tea with a slosh," said Old Mag. "Would you like a bite to eat? We have meat and bread left from the noon meal."

"Just tea will be fine, Old Mag. Taw and Vance fed me when I got to their place an hour or so ago." He picked up his cup, took a big swallow, and stood in front of the fireplace. "I'm still trying to warm up. I've had quite an adventure and I hope I don't have to repeat it again any time soon."

Rune drained his cup and Old Mag replenished it with more tea. Trog sat at the table and lit his pipe. The woodsy scent of the tobacco I had given him for Christmas filled the room. I added several logs to the fire and it blazed brightly sending a shower of sparks up the chimney.

Old Mag picked up her needlework and joined Trog at the table. I sat, too, my back to Rune and waited patiently for him to begin his story. He drank the second cup of tea slowly as though gathering his thoughts and then sat beside me. His hand sought mine under the table.

Rune cleared his throat and then began a strange tale. "I was out looking for a good stand of hardwoods for the woodchoppers. Charcoaling will begin soon and the felled trees will be used up pretty quickly. I was deeper into the forest than I thought when the storm blew in. Like a fool, I started back. I wasn't worried because I know most of the forestland as well as I know the back of my hand and was pretty sure I knew the way out. I had walked for several hours when I realized the wind was blowing from every direction and the trunks of the trees were snow covered all the way around. I couldn't tell east from west or north from south. That got my attention."

He paused briefly and then continued. "I had a little food with me and I always carry a blanket so I began looking for a place to hole up. I finally found an open area where the trees had been cut and hauled away. I wanted to locate a hole where the roots of a large tree had been pulled up and out. I figured if I burrowed down into a hole and covered myself up I might be able to stay warm enough. Well, I found a hole all right, a big hole." He laughed.

"I didn't have to look for the hole. It found me. I was shuffling along, bent into the wind when I saw the root ball of a big old tree half buried in the ground. I hoped I could nestle in those roots somehow and I moved in for a closer look. Next thing I know, the snow gave way and I tumbled about four feet down before I managed to stop myself. I waited a few minutes for my eyes to adjust to the darkness under the tree. There wasn't much snow under the root either, just the little bit that fell in with me. I was thinking how lucky I was to have found a spot where I could keep warm when I realized I wasn't alone in that hole."

Rune held up his cup. "If you don't mind, I'd like another bit of tea, Old Mag. My throat is a little dry."

I squealed in protest. "You're stalling for time, Rune. Don't stop now. We want to know who or what else was in the hole."

Old Mag poured the tea. "In good time, my love," said Rune. "In good time. It is not polite to rush a story-teller."

Trog blew several smoke rings toward Rune. "Well you do have us hanging on to the edges of our seats."

Rune sipped from the cup and then continued. "The largest black bear I have seen in these parts was in that hole sleeping like a baby. His odor was so bad I almost gagged. But his body heat was wonderful. I curled up beside him, pulled my blanket up, and took a long nap. I lost track of the time and couldn't tell if it was day or night. But when I poked my head out this morning the storm had passed. I thanked Mr. Bear and crawled out of the hole. In the bright light of morning, I knew where I was and I made a beeline for the medicine house."

"It took me quite a while to work my way home. Those drifts out there are high and I sure didn't want to fall into another hole. Taw and Vance were really glad to see me, too. They were just sitting down to their noon meal. Food looked pretty good to me. I felt like my belly was pushed up against my backbone. Vance was afraid they didn't have enough food to fill me up."

"Lucky for you that bear didn't mind sharing," commented Trog. "I'd like to have seen the two of you snuggled up close. What a sight that must have been."

We all laughed. I kissed Rune lightly on the cheek. "I'm glad you're home, you old bear hugger."

Old Mag invited Rune to stay for supper. She heated leftover rabbit stew. To that we added thick slices of bread with butter. Rune ate three bowls of stew and would have eaten more but there was none. Old Mag opened a jar of applesauce and we had that for dessert.

Shortly after supper, she and Trog retired to the loft. Rune and I had the rest of the evening to spend together.

## Chapter 39

We didn't walk that evening. The snow was too deep; walking any distance was too difficult. Instead, we lay close to each other, in front of the fire. For a long time we did not speak. Nor did we need to. Our kisses said it all.

Rune broke the silence. "I was worried, Callie, lying in that bear's den. I knew you'd be imagining the worst. And I didn't want to do that to you." He raised himself on one elbow and looked at me.

Tears filled my eyes. I stroked his cheek. "I was so afraid, Rune. I envisioned all kinds of horrible things happening to you."

He gently brushed the tears from my eyes. "But you shouldn't have. You know I can take care of myself. Didn't your heart tell you I'd be back in one piece?" He laughed softly.

"It did, it did," I answered. "But my head wouldn't listen. Old Mag knew, though. She said you were probably holed up somewhere. And she was right." I paused. "Weren't you afraid of the bear?"

"No. He wasn't likely to wake up. And if he had he'd be groggy at first and I'd have gotten away."

I snuggled close to him. "I missed you so much, Rune. So much."

He sat up and pulled me to a sitting position. Cupping my chin in his hand he looked me in the eyes as he spoke.

"And I missed you, my darling. Thoughts of you filled my head and my heart. The way you smile, the sparkle in your beautiful eyes, the little swish your clothes make when you walk."

He pulled my face toward his. I stared directly into his eyes as his lips gently touched my nose, my cheeks, my forehead, my chin. His partly open lips came closer and closer. I leaned into his kiss, letting it take me away.

"I love you, Callie, and I want to marry you. Will you take me for your husband?"

I stared at him, speechless, eyes wide, mouth gaping. The question was so unexpected, I was at a loss for something to say.

"You haven't answered my question. Will you marry me?"

I threw my arms around him and kissed him passionately.

"I take that as a *yes*," he finally managed to say.

"Yes, yes, yes," I cried as I struggled to my feet. I danced around the cottage in wild delight. A startled Chance arched his back in fright and then sought shelter behind a crock on a pantry shelf.

"Calm down, calm down. You'll wake Old Mag and Trog," cautioned Rune.

"I don't care. I think I'll wake them anyway and tell them the good news."

"Tomorrow will be soon enough to tell them. We have to make a few plans. They'll have questions to ask and we need to have answers."

"Questions? What kind of questions?" My head was whirling so I couldn't think of a single question that Old Mag or Trog could possibly ask.

His answer was somewhat sobering. "For one, *When do we plan to marry?*" "For another, *Will you still work in the weave house?* And the big one, of course, is *where shall we live?*"

"Those are excellent questions, ones they'll have every right to ask," I said sitting down beside him.

"I think a little cottage near Taw and Vance would be nice," said Rune. "There's lots of space near the medicine house. I don't want a cottage in the U."

"Why not?"

"Those cottages are all too close together. I like space."

"I do too. So, a cottage near the medicine house will be fine with me as long as Vance and Taw don't object."

"They won't. And," Rune continued, "I don't think we should marry before our little cottage is ready. We can't start building it for at least another month."

"Oh, Rune, this is so exciting. Just think. Our own little cottage!"

We huddled together in front of the fireplace for several hours, making plans for our future. Stars glittered brightly in the dark sky when I let Rune out the cottage door. I watched him walk away with joy in my heart. I fairly skipped up the ladder to the loft. Snuggled deep in my blanket, Chance at my side, my thoughts turned to Rune and the life we would share together. Jack and my other life were light years away. They didn't once cross my mind.

Trog was at the table sipping tea when I came down from the loft the next morning. "Good morning, Callie," he greeted me cheerfully. "Did you sleep well last night?"

"Yes, I did. Very well."

Old Mag emerged from the pantry area. "I figured you would. Just before I dozed off I thought I heard you dancing."

I burst into nervous laughter. "I was, sort of."

"What do you mean, sort of?"

"I was dancing around by myself." I poured myself a cup of tea and took a sip before continuing. "Rune asked me to marry him and I accepted."

"Well, goodness gracious," exclaimed Old Mag. She plopped down at the table, mouth open in astonishment.

"Callie, that's wonderful," interjected Trog. "I knew you two were smitten with each other but I didn't realize you were considering matrimony." He gave me a generous hug.

Old Mag's voice was gruff with emotion when she spoke. "I'm happy for both of you, Girl. And I'll help you with the wedding in every way I can." She paused for a moment and her silence was poignant.

"I just want you to do the right thing, that's all," she continued. "Does this mean you aren't planning to go home? You plan to stay in this time plane?"

My heart skipped several beats. "I don't think I want to go back, Old Mag. I want to be with Rune. And with you and Trog. You are my family now. I have no reason to want to return."

"You say that now, Girl, because you're thinking with your heart and not your head. I'm not trying to spoil your happy thoughts. I just want you to make the wisest and best decision. One you won't look back on later and regret." Tears welled into her eyes.

"Old Mag, I think I am making the best decision. Staying is what I want to do. I'm sure of it." I took her hands in mine and looked into her green eyes.

"Then by all means, we'll have us a wedding," she said in a joyful voice as she gave me a hug. "How soon will it be?"

During breakfast the three of us discussed the plans Rune and I had made the night before. He was right. They asked a lot of questions, some of which I couldn't answer. We continued our discussion in the weave house. Neither of us got much work done that day; we were too busy setting up housekeeping in a house yet to be built.

Rune stopped by late in the afternoon. Trog and Old Mag greeted him warmly.

"Congratulations, Rune. You've made a wise choice for a wife," said Trog thumping him soundly on the back.

"That you have, Rune. You'd better treat her right or you'll have me to contend with," cautioned Old Mag. "I love that girl like she's my own."

My heart swelled to near bursting as I listened to the conversation. These people cared about me. They loved me. They were my family.

Rune stayed in the weave house until we stopped working for the day. Old Mag and Trog went to the cottage while Rune and I stayed behind to bank the fire and straighten the work areas. When we stepped outside I was surprised at how quickly the snow was melting.

"This is probably the last big snow of the winter. The weather will start to warm up soon and if it does snow, it won't stay on the ground long," said Rune.

"Let's grab a couple armloads of wood before we go in," I suggested. We made our way to the woodpile and then turned our steps toward the cottage.

Rune deposited his wood beside the fireplace and then gave me a kiss on the tip of my nose. "I'll see you later, after supper."

The next several days passed quickly. Thoughts of the upcoming wedding filled my head and I made more mistakes in my weaving than I had done as a beginner. When I discovered a mistake in a shawl that required me to rip more than half the stitches out, Old Mag admonished me.

"Enough is enough, Girl. You've got to keep your feet on the ground when you're in this weave house. I know you're excited and happy but you've also got work to do. Trog and I are depending on you to do a good job. We can't be double checking all your work."

Her words had a sobering effect. "I'm sorry, Old Mag. And I'm embarrassed, too. I'll do a better job of concentrating from now on. I promise."

"See that you do."

I turned back to my work with renewed concentration on the task at hand. I lost half a day repairing the shawl and decided to let that be a lesson well learned. I wanted no more reprimands from Old Mag.

The snow melted rapidly just as Rune had predicted and in less than a week there was not a trace of white left on the grounds. Rune and I resumed our evening walks and one night, upon our return to the cottage, he asked Trog if I could be away from the weave house the next afternoon.

"I'd like to show Callie an area that's perfect for our cottage."

"Of course Callie may go with you," replied Trog. "I wish I could go, too, but I'm working on a special project for the Iron Master and it must be completed this week. Maybe I'll look at the spot later if you decide you want to build there."

"Thank you, Trog. Taw and Vance are willing to go with us tomorrow. But I definitely want you to see it. I value your opinion."

Early the next afternoon, shortly after the noon meal, Rune and I set out for the medicine house. I was so excited I didn't feel my shoes touch the earth. It was all I could do to walk like a grown woman. I wanted to skip and jump and hop around, shouting with delight. Rune sensed my enthusiasm and gave me a wicked smile; one that dared me to cavort like a colt. I managed to restrain myself as we walked past the houses in the U but as soon as we passed the blacksmith shop and headed toward the forest, I raced ahead on nimble legs. I reached the medicine house door first and looked over my shoulder to give Rune my best "I knew I could out run you" look. We were out of breath and laughing like idiots when Vance opened the door.

# Chapter 40

Rune led the way to the spot he had selected on the outskirts of the forest. It was not far from the medicine house. The flat, grassy area was surrounded by a stand of hardwoods but was open enough to let in sunshine for a garden. It was a private place, tucked out of the way, invisible to the casual eye. Quiet. Peaceful. Serene. It was perfect for a cottage.

"I love it, Rune. It's perfect," I cried excitedly.

"I thought you would," replied Rune. "Thank Taw and Vance, too. They helped me scout around."

I hugged each one in turn before I asked, "Which way should the cottage face?"

They all spoke at once. "You'll want to keep the sun to the south if you put the cottage in the center" said one. Another said, "You need to consider the direction of the prevailing winds if you build the cottage closer to the trees." "Where you put your path might help determine where you build the house," said the third.

"Whoa! Hold on! You're all talking at once," I replied laughing. "I can't understand a word any of you are saying."

"Let's not worry about that now," said Rune, always the peacemaker. "It's enough to know you like this spot."

We all agreed with him. We walked back to the medicine house for a cup of hot tea. The men were full of talk about building. I sat still and quiet and let their conversation wash over me. Let them talk and plan all they wished; I had my own visions of my cottage and when the time was right, I would share them. For now, I was content to listen.

The weave house was especially busy during the next few days. The women in the little community were anxious to replace worn items with new in anticipation of spring. Several women wanted new shawls and I talked to them about colors and designs. One of them was Dusty's wife. I wanted to make her something special because he went out of his way to make sure we always had pies and bread.

She said blue was her favorite color. I showed her yarn in both light and dark blue. The colors complimented each other and looked nice against her fair skin. She fingered the yarns lovingly as I described the weave I planned to use. She spoke softly and I had difficulty hearing everything she said. I found myself nodding my replies and hoped I was giving the correct answers. I must have because she left with a smile on her face.

"Callie, you work well with difficult customers," commented Trog. "Do you realize that is the first time Dusty's wife has actually committed herself to getting one of our shawls?"

I shook my head. "I don't know her very well. I remember how nice she was to the Millers when their cottage burned."

"Oh, she's always pleasant," said Old Mag, "but she can never make up her mind. I've made her a shawl or two but when it came time to take them, she always had an excuse not to. Maybe this time will be different. I hope so, for your sake."

"No matter," I said. "If she doesn't want it, someone will."

February, the shortest month in the calendar year, somehow seemed the longest. I was glad when it finally drew to an end. It had been an emotional month for me. With the death of Lily followed by my decision to marry Rune, I felt like I had been tossed about on the high seas during a heavy storm. Old Mag and Trog had stood by me through it all. They were my anchor lines.

I noticed activity around the furnace during the first week in March. I commented on this to Old Mag and Trog.

"The furnace will be fired soon, I expect," said Trog. "Work usually begins around the middle of March.

Right now, the men are busy making sure everything is in good working order."

"I for one have enjoyed the quiet with that furnace shut down," said Old Mag. "But after the first week, I don't even notice the noise."

Trog turned on his stool and looked at me reflectively. I sensed he had something else to say. I looked at him with steadfast eyes, waiting patiently for him to arrange his thoughts. He fumbled for his pipe, tamped the tobacco in and lit it. He puffed several times and then blew a perfect smoke ring in the air above his head.

"Callie, I'll try to word what I have to say as delicately as possible." He paused. "If there is any doubt in your mind about marrying Rune and remaining in this community, now is the time to voice it. Once that furnace is fired and work resumes, it will be extremely difficult for you to return to your time plane."

He blew another smoke ring. It floated lazily above him before it widened and dissipated. I opened my mouth to speak but he held up his hand for silence.

"It is very likely," he continued, "you will be here for the remainder of the year, unless something unforeseen happens, of course. Mag and I want you to stay. We do not want you to make a hasty and unwise decision, one you'll later regret."

I waited until I was sure he had finished before I answered. "I have thought about my decision. I think about it day and night. I love Rune and I want to marry him. If that means giving up my time plane, so be it. I'm content to stay."

"That's fine with us, Girl. We just want you to be happy. And if your happiness is here, then by all means stay. There will always be a job for you in this weave house."

Nothing more was said but I took their words to heart. That night I lay on my pallet and made myself think about Jack. My heart did not flutter once. I tried to recall his face and to my surprise, I couldn't. I took that as a good sign. My last thoughts before I fell asleep were of Rune.

One evening, shortly after supper, Trog asked me to take a few table runners to the boarding house. He had completed them that day and knew they were anxious to receive them. Rune had not yet stopped by and I decided not to wait for him.

It was already quite dark and I carried a lantern to light my way along the path. I had visited the boarding house several times on errands but always in the daylight. I was glad to see its shadowy bulk looming ahead on the path, light streaming from many of the windows.

Many single men working in the area resided in the boarding house. For a small fee, they received a bed and board. Visitors also stayed at the boarding house. Sometimes they arrived by stagecoach but more often than not, they rode in on horseback. I had never entered the boarding house; I usually knocked on the door and handed what I had for them to whoever opened the door. Tonight was no exception.

I was on my way back to the cottage when a figure stepped onto the path ahead of me, blocking my passage. For a moment or two I was startled and I held the lantern high in hopes of getting a better look.

"Well, hello there, my pretty. Are you out and about alone tonight?"

"Yes," I said, warily watching the approaching shadow. And then the lantern light caught the gleam of teeth. Snoop!

"Callie, isn't it?" he asked. "Do you remember me?"

"Of course I do, Snoop," I replied. "What are you doing here?"

"I live here. At least for a few more nights. I'll soon be going out into the forest to make charcoal for the coming season. I heard you were getting married."

"Yes, soon," I replied. I felt uneasy with him blocking the path. "It was nice seeing you but I must get back. Old Mag has another job for me."

I tried to move past him but he caught my arm. "I doubt that, Callie, my sweet. Every evening you and your soon-to-be stroll around the grounds. I know. I've seen you often enough. Where is he by the way?"

He put pressure on my arm and pulled me off the path.

"Let go of me. You're hurting me," I cried. I dropped the lantern and hit him, a good solid slap that resounded through the still night.

"You want to play rough, do you? I figured you for that kind of girl when I saw you making eyes at me. Well, I'll show you rough." He pulled me up against him hard. I struggled to get out of his grasp but was no match for his strength. He put one hand on the back of my head and pulled my face toward his. The thought of kissing him was repugnant; I tried to hold my head away from his. My efforts proved futile.

"I don't want to kiss you," I cried. In desperation I reached out for the only thing I could reach. I grabbed a handful of his long, red hair and yanked hard. He let out a scream of pain and rage. He threw me to the ground so forcefully I lost my breath.

"You witch," he yelled. "Nobody teases Snoop and gets away with it. I'm going to teach you a lesson you'll never..."

His sentence remained unfinished, suspended forever in the night air. From nowhere a pair of hands reached from the darkness, grabbed Snoop around the shoulders and pulled him away from me. I scooted across the ground to rescue the lantern but it had gone out and I had no way to relight it.

The sounds of fists on flesh and bone made me cringe. Several times there were cries of pain. And then Snoop was on the ground, cowering, begging. "Stop! Stop! I've had enough! Leave me alone!"

Rune's voice, when he spoke, had an icy edge I hadn't heard before and hoped I'd never hear again. "I

272

promise you, Snoop, if you've put one mark on Callie, I'll kill you!"

I trembled all the way back to the cottage. My legs felt like jelly and Rune kept his arms around me to keep me from falling. Old Mag let out a cry of dismay when we stumbled through the cottage door.

Rune's face was cut and bleeding in several places. His bottom lip had a jagged tear near one corner and there was no doubt that in a day or two he would have a very black eye. My cloak was filthy with dirt and small twigs and I had a small scrape on the palm of one hand but other than that I was unharmed. I curled my fingers into my palm. I didn't want Rune to see the scrape.

"What has happened to the two of you?" exclaimed Trog jumping up from the table and hurrying toward us.

"Snoop happened," replied Rune. "I found him on the path to the boarding house, wrestling with Callie. I let him have it but good. I don't think he'll bother either of us again."

"From the looks of you, he got in a few good punches, too. I'd hate to see what he looks like," muttered Old Mag. She poured hot water into a small bowl and brought it to the table. "Sit down, the pair of you."

We did as she asked.

"I'm going to cleanse your wounds, Rune. I may have to hurt you a little."

She took a small rag and began to wash the cuts. When she had finished, she gently rubbed a salve into his wounds. "This has bruisewort in it; your cuts and bruises will heal quickly. If Vance doesn't have any on hand, come back tomorrow and get mine."

Trog fixed us both a splash of rum. "This will calm your nerves," he said as he handed us each a cup. Rune drank his in one swallow and held the cup out for more. I sipped mine slowly, savoring the warm burn in my throat.

I finally felt strong enough to talk about the incident. "He just stepped out on the path in front of me. He was insulting and when I tried to pass, he attacked me. Thank goodness Rune happened along when he did." I shuddered to think what would have happened.

"I didn't happen along," Rune said. His swollen lip altered his speech somewhat. "I stopped by here to take you for a walk and Old Mag told me where you'd gone. I went looking for you thinking we'd just walk for a while before we returned to the cottage. I'm glad I did, too." He stroked my hair gently.

"Had I known there was going to be a problem, Callie, I would have gone myself. I'm so sorry," said Trog.

"It's not your fault, Trog. Who could have guessed something like this was going to happen?" I shook my head in bewilderment.

That night, fear gripped my heart as I lay on my pallet unable to sleep. Rune's words to Snoop scrolled through my brain like a broken record. *I promise you, Snoop, if Callie has one mark on her, I'll kill you.* I had heard the fury in Rune's voice and there was no doubt in my mind, that if provoked, he would.

# Chapter 41

By noon the next day, the weave house was plagued with visitors seeking, as well as sharing, information about the fight between Rune and Snoop. As the day progressed the stories grew wilder and more startling. No matter that I had been a witness to the event. The wounds inflicted grew larger and more critical; I fully expected to hear that one or the other was dead before the day ended.

Rune tried to make light of the injuries he sported but I knew his pride was as wounded as his face. He refused to discuss the incident further and spent the next several days in the forest looking for hardwood trees ready to be felled for charcoal. Vance's remedies worked well and the lacerations and bruises healed quickly. Interest in the fight waned and by the end of the week no one entering the weave house mentioned it.

Activity around the furnace intensified and I knew the furnace would be charged and fired soon. Each morning when I woke, I was surprised not to hear the clack, clack of the bellows. Trog told us the charging ramp was delaying the start-up. It was in need of repair and until it was safe for the mules and charging carts, work could not proceed. The sound of hammers rang throughout the daylight hours.

The bitter winter chill was gone from the air and I enjoyed running errands for Old Mag and Trog. Immediately after the fight, they were reluctant to send me out but eventually they relented and once again I found myself visiting the broom maker, the basket maker and the baker regularly.

I missed Lily on such outings. She had been a fun companion, walking beside me, her warm, little hand tucked safely into mine. Her idle chatter had brightened many a walk and I longed to hear her cheerful voice.

To quell my thoughts of Lily, I began to pay attention to the gardens near the U. The milder weather had brought a renewed interest in them. The women and children toiled in them daily, pulling weeds and turning over the soil to get it ready for planting. Single-family gardens were small and it was difficult to believe enough could be grown in such a tiny area to sustain a family throughout a winter. Sometimes several families put their gardens together. Such plots were larger and the families shared the responsibilities for planting, growing, and harvesting. They also shared the harvest.

I knew nothing about gardening and had no desire to learn. I wondered if I was expected to have a garden when Rune and I set up housekeeping. I certainly hoped not. If I continued to work in the weave house I wouldn't be able to care for a garden.

*I need to ask Old Mag,* I thought. *She'll give me good advice.*

We were well into the second week of March and still no sign of a furnace start-up. Trog brought us news from McQuerrie's.

"The furnace won't be fired for a few more days yet. Something is wrong with the water wheel and work won't commence until it is repaired. McQuerrie did tell me charcoaling has begun. That means Snoop is no longer in the community but is off lighting his pit fires."

"That is good news, Trog," said Old Mag. "I'll breathe a little easier. I've been worried that he and Rune would cross paths again."

"Well," continued Trog, "I've heard all kinds of bad things about Snoop. Seems he creates trouble wherever he goes. He knows charcoaling though, and because of that he's always able to find a job."

I felt better knowing Snoop was no longer around. I didn't want to meet him face-to-face, day or night. I told myself I wasn't afraid of him but deep in my heart I knew I was.

That evening I mentioned Snoop to Rune. "Trog heard that charcoaling has begun and he's left the community for the season."

"I heard that, too, Callie, and I don't mind telling you how happy that makes me. I hated the thought of you having to deal with him again, especially if I wasn't around."

I snuggled into his arms and kissed him. "Rune," I asked cautiously, "will you really kill him if he...?"

I didn't get to ask the complete question. "Of course not, Callie! But I'll give him a whopping hurt. I was very angry when I said I'd kill him. People say lots of things they don't mean when they're angry."

"You sounded like you meant it to me," I persisted.

"I did at the time, Callie. But wouldn't that be a stupid thing for me to do? I don't want to be hung for the likes of Snoop." He looked at me. "Are you satisfied?"

I nodded.

"Good. Let's end this discussion. I have better things to do than to talk about Snoop."

Late the next morning, an errand took me near the blacksmith shop. Smitty and Taw were standing near the anvil, chatting. I joined them. Taw was in the middle of a funny story when a shout went up from near the canal.

We looked in that direction and saw a group of men clustered on the bank near the water wheel, looking into the water, talking excitedly. More men ran to join the group as we watched.

"Let's go see what's going on," said Taw, taking me by the arm and propelling me in the direction of the canal. "Are you coming, too, Smitty?"

"Of course I'm coming. I love excitement on a boring day," laughed Smitty as he followed us down the hill.

We elbowed our way through the crowd to the water's edge. Two men had poles in the water and were prodding something to make it move closer to the bank. As the crowd parted I caught a glimpse of a body, floating face down in the murky water.

277

"Is he dead?" someone asked.

"Indeed he is," came the reply. "He's deader than a doornail."

Two men in front of me moved toward the bank and I got a good look at the body. I gasped and clutched Taw's arm tightly. A sense of dread filled me to the core. Tendrils of bright red hair floated lazily in the cold water.

Two men pulled the body from the canal and turned it over. Snoop's face and hands were blue with cold. His hair fanned out on the ground to frame his head with a red halo. A knife protruded from the left side of his chest, just at heart level.

It was a beautiful knife. An unusual knife. White ivory etched with a tall ship. Rune's knife. The one I had given him for Christmas.

My knees buckled and had it not been for Taw I would have fallen to the ground.

"Callie, we've got to get out of here. Now!" He propelled me through the crowd and up the hill. "You go back to the weave house. Tell Trog and Old Mag what has happened. I'm going to get Vance and the two of us will look for Rune. We have to find him before this crowd figures out that the knife in Snoop is his."

I was hysterical by the time I reached the weave house. I burst through the door crying, "Snoop has been murdered! With Rune's knife!" I fell to the floor sobbing.

Trog reached me first. He lifted me to a chair, then knelt beside me and rubbed my hands. "Callie, Callie, calm down. Calm down."

Old Mag wiped my face with a cool cloth. "Trog, get her a little slosh of spirits. Her face is pale as a ghost. And get me one, too."

The rum felt warm against my tongue and throat. "There, Girl, the color is returning to your face. Breathe deeply. That's it," crooned Old Mag.

"Now, take your time, Callie and tell us what has happened," said Trog.

I slowly related the story. "I knew it was Snoop when I saw the red hair in the water. But the knife, Trog. The knife is Rune's. Taw has gone to look for him now with Vance. Do you think Rune killed Snoop?"

"No, I do not," said Old Mag.

"Nor do I," added Trog. "Rune has great respect for living creatures, even ones who do not deserve it. His threat to Snoop was made in the heat of anger. It was not a threat he intended to keep."

"I heard his voice when he told Snoop he'd kill him, Trog. It was icy and cold. He meant what he said. And now he's done what he promised." I put my face in my hands and wept.

"Girl, no such thing has happened. You're jumping to conclusions. Just because the knife is Rune's doesn't mean he killed him," cautioned Old Mag. "Look at me and tell me you believe he killed Snoop."

I looked into her green eyes and found strength. "I don't think he did, Old Mag."

Trog looked out the window. "A big crowd has gathered at the canal. From the looks of things the discussion is getting very heated. I think we need to close the weave house for the rest of the day. Let's go home. Quickly, ladies."

I spent the remainder of the day pacing the cottage floor like a caged animal. My heart was so heavy with fear I struggled to breathe. Old Mag fixed a light noon meal but I ate nothing. Nor did I eat supper.

Darkness fell and with it, no sign of Rune. Time seemed to stand still, the minutes ticked by slowly and anxiously. *Why doesn't Taw come with news,* I wondered. *He must know I am out of my mind with worry.*

Old Mag, ever the philosopher, tried to cheer me. "No news is good news, Girl. Sit tight."

Trog slipped out after supper in hopes of finding out what was going on. He returned in half an hour or less with grim news. "The sheriff has been sent for. A number of folks think Rune killed Snoop. Just as many don't. Everyone says good riddance. But the law is the law and if a crime has been committed, the criminal must be punished. I'm sorry, Callie, but things don't look very good for Rune."

The evening dragged on. Old Mag and Trog retired to the sleeping loft. I turned all the lamps off but one and kept my vigil in the rocking chair, Chance curled tightly on my lap. The creak, creak of the rocker was soothing and at some point, I dozed off. I was awakened by a soft tapping at the window. *Rune?*

I jumped to my feet, ran to the door and flung it open. To my dismay there was no one on the stoop. My eyes searched the darkness but I saw nothing. *Did I imagine I heard a tapping on the window?* I asked myself.

"Callie. Callie." My name was spoken softly, almost a whisper. It seemed to come from my left. I looked in that direction.

"Turn off the lamp. I don't want to be seen entering the cottage."

I hastened inside to do as I was asked. In the flickering firelight, I watched Rune slip through the doorway. He closed the door behind him. I was in his arms in an instant, his lips pressed tight against mine. We held each other close for several long moments.

"Rune, Rune," I murmured against his ear. "I've been beside myself with fear and worry."

"I know, I know." He pulled me closer to the fire and held me at arms length. His eyes looked into mine with an intensity that made me shiver. "Callie, I did not kill Snoop. You have to believe me."

"But your knife, Rune. Your knife was sticking in his chest."

"I lost that knife a few days ago, Callie. I don't know where. One day I had it in my pocket and the next day it was gone. I didn't tell you because I didn't want you to be upset with me for losing it. You believe me, don't you?"

I looked deep into his eyes and knew he was telling me the truth. "Yes, Rune, I believe you." Tears filled my eyes. "Oh, Rune, what are you going to do? Will you turn yourself in to the sheriff?"

"I can't do that, Callie. Everything points to me as the guilty party. The fight. My knife as the murder weapon. In the eyes of a lot of people, I'm guilty. If I turn myself in, they'll hang me for sure." He paused. "No, I'm going to go away for a while, let the furor die down. Maybe they'll find the real killer."

He pulled me close. "You understand why I have to go, don't you Callie?"

"But if you're innocent..." I began to protest but he put a finger on my lips to silence them.

"I can't prove I'm innocent, my darling. I can't prove it. So this is goodbye for a while."

He kissed me long and hard and then he was gone. Despair washed over me like an incoming tide. I threw another log on the fire and returned to the rocker. In the morning, when Old Mag came down from the sleeping loft, I was staring into the ashes of a long-dead fire.

I tried to weave that morning but my hands were all thumbs. They shook so uncontrollably I had difficulty holding the shuttle. I rewove an area of the same shawl three times before I decided to stop. Thoughts of Rune filled my brain; I could think of nothing else. *Was he hiding? If so, where? Was he alone or were Taw and Vance with him? Had the sheriff arrived? Was he searching the area for Rune? Did he have a posse with him?* The questions ran non-stop through my mind; I couldn't stop them.

Just after the noon meal, my worst fears were realized. The sheriff stepped through the door of the weave house. He didn't look like a sheriff. He was short and rotund, with balding brown hair and a wide moustache. His eyes, however, belied his mild demeanor. They were

281

black and seemed to see into my inner being. I was frightened and it showed.

He tried to put me at ease, said he just had a few questions for me, that he wanted to get the facts regarding the fight straight in his mind. I related the entire story as best I could. I was honest and truthful and tried to hide nothing. When he asked if Rune had threatened to kill Snoop, I nodded.

"But he didn't mean it," I added. "He was just very angry and spoke the first words that came to his mind."

The sheriff asked several more questions, too. He was interested in the knife and whether or not Rune had shown it to Snoop on the night of the incident. And he wanted to know if I knew where Rune was. I couldn't answer his questions. I wasn't privy to the answers.

We didn't get much work done after the sheriff left. I sat, still and stiff, at my loom, while Old Mag and Trog hovered over me. Nothing they said made me feel better. I felt worse knowing they were unable to weave because of me.

I needed to do something but what? The one thing I could do was look for Rune - but where? *Taw and Vance might know,* I told myself. *If they do, they'll tell me.*

I rose from my loom and went to the door, throwing my cloak around my shoulders as I did so. "I'm going to visit Vance. Maybe he and Taw know where Rune is."

Old Mag had a stricken look on her face. I gave her a weak smile. "I just cannot sit here and do nothing. Don't worry, Old Mag. I'll be okay. And I'll be back in time for supper."

I didn't look back but sensed their eyes watching me as I hurried along the path toward the U. I met no one until I passed the blacksmith shop. Smitty was outside working the anvil. He smiled and threw up his hand in greeting. I waved back. Once I passed the blacksmith shop, I ran along the path to the medicine house.

No smoke floated above the chimney. The door opened easily. The room was very cold; there had been no fire in the medicine house the night before. Nothing was disturbed that I could see. Everything was in its place, the pallets were neat and tidy, and no dirty dishes lay about. There were no coats and hats. The pegs where the outer garments usually hung were empty. The silence in the room was deafening. Vance and Taw were gone. I would get no answers from them.

I ran from the medicine house, tears streaming down my cheeks. I wasn't ready to face Old Mag and Trog. I turned my steps toward the clearing Rune and I had chosen for our cottage.

It lay, dappled in brilliant sunlight. I heard birds singing in the nearby forest and the wind made a soughing sound as it passed gently through the treetops. My eyes covered every inch of the area looking for a hidden message from Rune, a message that only I would recognize and understand. I didn't see what I was looking for.

I stood in the center of the clearing, arms outstretched to the sky. R-U-N-E! I shouted at the top of my lungs. There was no answer.

# Chapter 42

I sat in the clearing until the sun sank behind the trees. Only then did I make my way back to the cottage along the darkened path. I met no one and for that I was thankful. I was wrapped in a cloak of misery, one I had no desire to share.

The cottage was warm and cheery when I entered. The lamps were lit and a blazing fire danced in the fireplace. Trog was seated at the table smoking; Old Mag was stirring a stew. They looked up when I entered and when I saw their faces, I realized the cheeriness was a façade. Their expressions mirrored my own.

"Did you find out anything from Taw and Vance?" asked Old Mag as I removed my cloak.

With heavy feet I walked to the table. "They're gone, both of them. I don't know for how long but I'm pretty sure there was no fire in the medicine house last night." I slumped dejectedly beside Trog.

He put an arm around my shoulders. "I was afraid of that, Callie."

"You let me walk all the way out there when you knew they were gone? Why?"

"Because you needed to see for yourself. If I had told you they were gone, would you have believed me?"

I looked at him with eyes as dull and dim as I felt.

"Of course not. See, I was right." He patted my shoulder gently.

"What am I going to do?" I cried, eyes brimming with tears.

"The first thing we're going to do is have a bite to eat. And after that, we're going to think. Think hard," said Old Mag. "A body can't think well on an empty stomach."

"I'm not hungry, Old Mag. I can't eat a thing."

"Yes you are and yes you can." She began to ladle turkey stew onto our plates. She set one in front of me.

284

"You won't be any use to Rune if you don't have the strength of a kitten. Pick up your spoon and eat, Girl."

I did as I was told. To my surprise, I was hungry and the stew went down easily. I ate it all and wiped my plate clean with a thick chunk of bread. Not a word was spoken during the meal nor did we make eye contact with one another. I kept my thoughts private and close to my heart.

I helped Old Mag clear the table and wash the dishes. When everything was put away, she brought out the tea box. Trog spent a few moments selecting the tea of his choice and the leaves were put into a kettle of hot water to steep.

I set out cups while Trog lit his pipe. The tea was dark and fragrant and I detected the faint aroma of chamomile. I held my cup between my hands to warm them while we waited for Old Mag to join us.

Trog puffed gently on his pipe and then blew a smoke ring high into the air above his head. It floated lazily in the candlelight for a few seconds and then began to lose its shape. *My life is like that smoke ring,* I thought. *Two days ago it was perfect and now it's fallen completely apart.*

"Now, Callie, let us all put our heads together to solve this problem." Trog's voice was calm and confident.

No one spoke for a second or two and then Old Mag asked, "Where do you think Taw and Vance went, Trog? Do you think they are with Rune?"

He blew two more smoke rings before he replied. "I think the three of them are together. Most likely in a place where no one can find them until they wish to be found."

"And where is that secret place, Trog? In the swamp? Deep in the forest? I don't like to think of them without food and shelter. After all, it is still winter."

"Those three men will be more than able to survive the swamp or forest in the dead of winter, Girl. They've been out in the cold before. But, I don't think they are hiding in either of those places," said Old Mag with conviction.

"Where then?" I asked.

Old Mag exchanged a look with Trog. *They know something I don't,* I thought. *Why are they keeping it from me?*

Trog blew several more smoke rings. The man was maddening. I bit my tongue to hold back the angry words that wanted to tumble out.

"They are time travelers, Callie. You seem to have forgotten that."

Trog's words brought me up short. My eyes widened in acknowledgement and understanding. *What had Rune said to me just last night? 'I'm going to go away for a while and let the furor die down.'*

I looked at Trog, desperation in my eyes. "Where have they gone? I'll follow them."

Trog shook his head. "Callie, those fellows could be anywhere. They come and go all the time." His eyes were soft with sympathy.

"No, he'll be back for me. I know he will." I was in denial. "We've made plans for a life together. I know he'll be back."

There was nothing more to say. Old Mag and Trog retired soon after our discussion. I stayed up and kept a lonely vigil, warmed only by the crackling fire and Chance. I rocked all night, getting up only to add more logs to the blaze. The hours dragged by slowly, painfully. I waited in vain. There was no tapping on the windows, no knock on the door.

When the first streaks of dawn heralded a new day, I rose from the rocker and walked on stiff legs to the window. The grounds were peaceful and quiet. So was I. The heavy lump I had carried in my chest for the past several days was no longer there. I had made my decision.

I worked diligently in the weave house that day and, late in the afternoon, finished the shawl for Dusty's wife. It was beautiful with a delicate weave that belied a beginner to the craft.

Old Mag was very complimentary. "Girl, you have a real knack for weaving. It will take you far in this life if you choose to become a weaver."

I smiled my thanks. With no intention of beginning a new project, I decided to take the shawl to the bakeshop. Dusty's wife was very pleased with it. She threw it around her shoulders and modeled it proudly for her husband. He smiled and scratched his head with a flour-coated finger.

"How many pies will I need to make to pay for that beautiful thing?" he inquired in jest.

I didn't feel like returning to the weave house when I left the bakeshop. I turned toward the U and followed the path that led in front of the cottages. The sun was ready to drop behind the trees and the gardens were in deep shadow. I pulled my cloak tighter against the late afternoon chill.

I walked without thinking and my footsteps took me past the church and up the path that led to the cemetery. I located Lily's grave and knelt beside it. I had no flowers to place beneath her marker and for that I was sorry. I smoothed several rough clods of earth, then kissed the tips of my fingers and touched her grave.

It was almost dark by the time I reached the cottage. I felt guilty that I had not helped Old Mag with supper but her look of relief when I entered the door assured me she was not angry. The table was set for three and she ladled the vegetable stew while I got out the bread and butter.

I don't remember the conversation or if there was one. I felt hollow inside; like the living part of me had been ripped out and I was a shell of my former self. I sat beside Trog and drank hot tea with a slosh of spirits and then helped Old Mag clean up. When the kitchen was tidy, I took a lamp from the table and climbed the ladder to the sleeping loft.

I was surprised my shorts and tee shirt fit. I had eaten well the past several months and had not exercised regularly. But my clothing slipped on easily. I put on my jewelry, picked up my knapsack, and descended the ladder.

Old Mag and Trog showed no surprise. "So, you've decided to go back," commented Trog.

"Yes. I think it best that I do. Staying here will be too painful."

"I want you to stay, Girl. But I think I understand how you feel. There's no guarantee that Rune will return soon, if ever." Old Mag paused and then continued, "I want you to know that I love you like my own and I'll never forget you." Her bottom lip and chin quivered with emotion.

"Nor I you, Old Mag." I embraced her tightly. "I love you, too. You and Trog have been my family. The best family I've ever had."

Trog looked at me with sad eyes. "There are no words to express what I feel, Callie. I'm going to miss you. There won't be a day go by that I won't think about you." He wrapped his arms around me. I kissed him lightly on the cheek and then stepped back.

I stood awkwardly looking at them, my face wet with tears. I had to go before I changed my mind. "What do I do now, Trog."

"Get out the paper on which you wrote the exact date the day you arrived. You'll need that." I rummaged in the knapsack. "Read it and keep the date in mind. Now, put on your cloak and we'll go down to the furnace. Are you coming, Mag?"

She shook her head.

I tossed my cloak across my shoulders and drew it around me. As I did so my eyes fell on Chance, curled in a little ball in the rocking chair.

"Can animals travel through time unharmed?" I asked.

"I don't see why not?" replied Trog.

"May I take Chance with me?"

"Of course. He's your cat," answered Old Mag.

I swooped up Chance and put him in the knapsack. He had plenty of room and an opening large enough for air but too small for escape. He stirred for a second or two and then settled himself comfortably. I slung the knapsack over one shoulder and stepped out into the night, just behind Trog. He turned toward the furnace and I followed.

I looked back once. Old Mag stood silhouetted in the doorway, one arm raised in farewell. I heard her call softly, "Goodbye, Callie. Godspeed."

A nearly full moon lit our way. We encountered no one and before many minutes passed, the black hulk of the stack loomed large to our right.

"Here we are, Callie. Sit where you sat the day you traveled," said Trog. "Lean back just like you did before, close your eyes and repeat the date you have on that paper over and over in your mind." He paused as if at as loss for words. "Goodbye, dear Callie. I hope our paths cross again."

I did as he asked. He leaned down, gave me one last kiss and then he was gone. The sound of his footsteps faded away. An owl hooted from somewhere deep in the forest; another answered its call. I heard a rustling in nearby bushes and wondered briefly what critter was searching for food.

A myriad of thoughts raced through my mind. I had been happy here and I was reluctant to leave. Old Mag and Trog had been wonderful to me. They had shared their home, their food, their skill, and their love. What more could I have wanted?

"I love you like my own," Old Mag had said, "and I'll never forget you." I repeated her words softly to the night air.

*Callie. Old Mag called me Callie for the very first time.* My eyes filled with tears. I shivered a little and wrapped my cloak tighter around my body.

*This is the moment of truth,* I thought. *I can walk back up the hill to my home and stay or I can go back. Which will it be?* My thoughts turned to Rune. *I love you so much, my darling. I can't bear to stay here without you.*

Chance mewed from the depths of the knapsack. I stuck my hand through the opening and stroked his head. His little body vibrated as he purred with contentment.

*The date,* I thought, *I have to repeat the date.* My head felt fuzzy. I tried to recall the date. The summer of 1810 popped into my mind. Old Mag always visited her daughter in Paris during that time. *I've never been to Paris.* I hummed a few bars of 'I Love Paris.'

*Concentrate on your return date, otherwise you'll find yourself in Paris!*

I settled myself more comfortably against the structure. I stretched my arms up and rubbed the bricks. They felt strangely warm to my touch. My fingertips tingled. I leaned my head back and closed my eyes. I was tired, so tired. A gentle buzzing filled my ears. It reached a soft crescendo and then slowly spiraled away into nothing.

Voices woke me. A mother and daughter passed by. My eyes finally focused. They were dressed in shorts and tee shirts. The mother carried a camera. I smiled at them before they disappeared from view along a trail that led into the forest.

I tried to rise but couldn't. My feet were tangled in my cloak. I snatched it off and stood, stretching, looking up toward the top of the furnace. *That's a sight for sore eyes,* I thought, touching the brick surface. *I've come back to the right spot.* Chance mewed plaintively. I put my hand in the knapsack to soothe him.

*What time is it?* I asked myself. I looked at my watch. It was 4 p.m. on a beautiful sunny day. *I've got to get out of here.*

I rolled the cloak into a ball and tossed it into the bushes that grew beside the canal. Then I picked up the knapsack and started up the hill toward the visitor's center. I followed the corduroy road right to the door of the building and stepped inside. A wave of cool air met me. The interior was dimly lit compared to the bright sunshine outside.

The clerk greeted me with a smile and asked if I had enjoyed my visit. I replied that I had and hoped to return sometime soon. Directly over her shoulder, I saw a calendar. I was back on the right day.

I stopped at the soda machine for a bottle of water. Both Chance and I needed a drink after our long journey. He was probably as hungry as I but we'd have to wait a while longer for a bite to eat.

I stepped outside once again and turned my steps toward the parking lot. I paused long enough to open the bottle of water and take a long swallow. It was delicious. The sounds of late summer enveloped me. Birds twittered and the wind soughed gently through the treetops.

"Chance," I said, "you and I are going to get my things from the condo and head toward the city. How would you like to be a city cat?"

My car was just where I'd left it. I unlocked the door. One turn of the key and the engine roared to life. I opened the windows to let the heat out and then I retrieved my purse and cell phone from the trunk. I found a piece of aluminum foil on the back seat, fashioned it into a saucer and poured Chance a drink of water. I lifted him out of the knapsack and waited while he eagerly lapped. When he was finished, I returned him to the knapsack, placed it on the seat beside me and fastened my seatbelt.

As I turned toward the exit, I saw three men emerge from the forest. They were tall, almost the same height, and lean in a rugged sort of way. They walked together, side by side, with long easy strides. Each was clean-shaven, incredibly handsome, and smiling. The one in the middle caught my eye. His face was framed in blonde-white hair that hung to his shoulders.

As I slowly drove closer, I could see his dimples and cleft chin. His deep blue eyes sparkled. As I stared at him, he waved and called out to me.

"Callie! We've been waiting for you."

My heart gave a sudden lurch. I stopped the car, threw it into *PARK,* and jumped out.

Rune! Oh, Rune!

Tears of joy streamed down my face as I ran to meet him with outstretched arms.

# Ordering Information

To order additional copies of
The Weaver's Girl

- Online at www.lindenhill.net
- By mail: $15 + $4.50 Priority Mail
(Up to two copies)
- Md residents add 5% sales tax

Send check or money order to
Linden Hill Publishing
11923 Somerset Avenue
Princess Anne, MD 21853
Or use PayPal.
Our PayPal account is
lindenhill2@comcast.net

Linden Hill Publishing also has a wide selection of books available that can be ordered online on our secure server. Learn more about these books on the website www.lindenhill.net